THE
SOONER
YOU
FORGET

www.mascotbooks.com

The Sooner You Forget

For more information, please contact:
Subplot Books, an imprint of Amplify Publishing Group
620 Herndon Parkway, Suite 220
Herndon, VA 20170
info@mascotbooks.com

Library of Congress Control Number: 2024911922

CPSIA Code: PRV1024A

ISBN-13: 978-1-63755-960-4

Printed in the United States

To the heroic soldiers who broke an oath of secrecy so that those who died at the hands of the Nazis would never be forgotten. And to my wife, Kelbe, for her unyielding devotion.

THE SOONER YOU FORGET

a novel

CHRISTOPHER BENSINGER

SUBPLOT

Save one, save all.

PROLOGUE

R acing through the tall, crisp cornstalks gripping my glass jar, I head for the creek, my favorite place to catch fireflies. It's dusk, almost the perfect time they come to light. Thunderous vibrations rattle my spine from a crop duster roaring overhead, scanning the landscape, searching for me. I hole up at Mrs. Williams's dilapidated garden shed until I receive the all clear from a tractor driver tilling the fields. He honks, indicating it's safe for me to move out. I bolt from the shed until I reach the creek. But when I do, a blast opens up the earth. Shrapnel sears my leg. I crumble to the ground as the crop duster circles and descends toward me at breakneck speed. I roll into the creek, landing on emaciated bodies swaddled in striped prison garb, their faces contorted in anguish. I don't want to die in this trench. It starts to snow. My blood turns to ice. I pray, "Our Father . . . Our Father . . . who art . . . who . . . ." I can't remember the Lord's Prayer and beg the prisoners to help me recite it, but they no longer can speak; the Jewish Star of David has been singed into their smoldering faces. I touch mine and feel the insignia burning into my skull. I try and climb out, but Dad holds me down under the bodies. "This is a mistake!" I scream. "I'm not Jewish! Tell them, Dad! Tell them I'm not Jewish! Help me out . . . please help me out . . . out . . . ."

A faint voice shutters the despairing cries as I unlock my jaw and gasp for air.

1

"Charles, dear!"

I peek from the trench to glance over the coverlets and catch Sandee's silvery hair glistening from the moonlight shining through our window. The bedsheets cling to my wet skin as I reach down on instinct and grab my leg to quiet the phantom pain shooting into the empty space below my knee—an agonizing ritual I've had for over a half century. I'm slowly awakening from yet another nightmare.

"You're freezing, darling."

Sandee embraces me with her warm body, but I'm unable to tolerate her touch just yet. I ache from the dream still banging at my brittle bones. I release myself and flick on the bedside lamp to grab a clean liner from the side table and stretch it over my stump, then lock my prosthetic into place. The engineers on the last version finally took my suggestion to shorten the pin, allowing for increased range and mobility. That was years ago. I'm due for a replacement but see no reason this one shouldn't walk me to the end.

Sandee squints through her pale blue eyes wreathed in fine wrinkles.

"Do you need help to the bathroom, darling?"

"I can make it. Go back to sleep, Dee."

"Don't stay up. I planned for an early breakfast since Ginger is on East Coast time."

"I'm aware."

I turn off the light and wobble past the bathroom door with the assistance of my well-worn wooden cane. As I make my way down the hallway to the study, I try to shake the past, but Berga still beats like a second heart inside my chest: the ungodly cold, the punishing hunger, the last rattling breaths of my brothers. I've told no one about that place, not Sandee or my son, Ben. I've kept my word to Uncle Sam, keeping it quiet since 1945. *The Nazi slave labor death camp for Jewish soldiers never existed.*

How I yearn for my true liberation as night draws near.

The milky glow from a full moon over Lake Michigan beams through the seventeenth-story windows of our Chicago prewar city apartment, throwing shadows across the burl wood–paneled walls of my study.

Still trembling from the dream, I drop into my desk chair, close my eyes, and pray.

"O God of forgiveness, forgive us, pardon us, grant us atonement. *Avinu Malkeinu*, our Father, our King, we have sinned before You. Avinu Malkeinu, in Your abundant mercy, cleanse us of our guilt before You. Avinu Malkeinu, bring us back to You in perfect repentance."

I open the top drawer and take out the letter I received last week from the Conference on Jewish Material Claims Against Germany, the letter that has reawakened the painful return of my nightmares. But before I'm ready to read it again, I slide open the bottom drawer, push aside my Purple Heart, and retrieve my most treasured keepsake: my high school baseball glove. I wiggle my wrinkled hand into the webbing and stare into the worn crevices of my youth and drift back to a time when the air was sweet, bratwursts sizzled on the grill, and baseballs soared like comets across a barren sky.

PART I

WAUWATOSA, WISCONSIN, 1944

CHAPTER 1

The Citywide High School Baseball Championship was riding on my bat—and so was my future. Either I was going to earn my ticket out of this dead-end pastoral town with one mighty swing or end up withering away like a crisp leaf falling off a dying maple tree in winter. Two baseball scouts strolled the sidelines on a hot June afternoon, studying my every move, evaluating whether I had the stuff to fill in for the professional players who had left for war. They had also come to look at my rival, John "Rails" McNamara, the catcher on the other team. We were the two top prospects from the state of Wisconsin.

I glanced toward the rickety stands, which were spilling over with hyped-up high schoolers, anxious fathers, and mothers holding their collective breath, and found Mom and Ginger, my eleven-year-old sister, sitting in the top row, the two clutched arm in arm. The seat next to them sat empty as usual. I didn't think Dad would fill it—not even today. But I'd held out hope regardless.

I stepped into the batter's box in the bottom of the ninth inning with two outs, down by one run, knowing a deep blast could tie the game. I dug a rut with my cleat, sending dust over home plate. I raised my thirty-four-ounce Louisville Slugger and took a fastball down the middle. Another, I fouled off the barrel for strike two. Two bad pitches hit the dirt before fouling off a stinker that stupidly I should have left alone. I stepped out of the box to slow my heart rate and held my Saint

Christopher pendant dangling off my neck. I took a breath, tucked it back inside my jersey, and stepped back into the batter's box. I could feel the scouts' eyes on me, anticipating something spectacular.

"Fuck you and your sister, Chuck-a-Duck!" barked skinny-as-a-rail "Rails" McNamara. He was crouched behind home plate in the catcher's position. "Swing the bat like the pussy you are," he added, then blew a bubble that exploded over his pockmarked face.

"Watch your mouth, Rails," I said. "Or I'll have to wash it out with soap."

We'd been battling against each other ever since we sprouted from the same hometown outside Milwaukee, called Wauwatosa, which meant "firefly" in the language of the Potawatomi tribe. Fireflies still flicker on hot summer nights.

Rails lived on the right side of the tracks in a limestone two-story home set on a wide, tree-lined street. I was on the other side in a one-story kit home bought from Sears, Roebuck and Co. At least my house had a running creek in front where we could fish for salmon and skate in the winter.

"I'm gonna eat your fucking head off, Upchuck." Rails bit with soft teeth.

"Then you'll have more brains in your stomach than in that empty skull of yours," I countered.

And so it went, each trying to outfox the other.

"Let's play ball, fellas!" barked the umpire with tobacco spilling from his mouth.

Knowing Rails as well as I did, I knew he had a terrible tick of sticking his fingers over home plate to deliver the sign to the pitcher. He did it again, flashing the curve. I winked at my teammate Bob Apgar, who was hitting next. I planted my feet, ready to hit, knowing which pitch was coming. I reared back, and crack! The ball exploded off my bat and shot into the right center-field gap. Washington Park didn't have enough money for a fence, so the ball traveled all the way to the edge of Mrs. Williams's farm. A rip like that had triple written all over it. With slow-footed "Pudge" McGrady playing right field, an inside-the-park home run was possible. As I made a blazing turn around the two-bag, I glanced back to see Pudge tumble over the ball. His chubby hand lobbed the rock toward the frenzied second baseman.

Our third-base coach raised his hands, indicating for me to put on the brakes, but with dust in my wake, I made a run for it—knees churning, cleats burning, arms whirling. Rails hurled his mask aside to set up like a middle linebacker bracing for a colossal collision. I looked back to see Pudge's throw sputter to the second baseman, who spun and threw a burner to the right side of the plate, popping into Rails's mitt. That left me with a life-changing decision: go back to third base; barrel through the loudmouth, hoping he'd drop the ball; or go for the high-risk "hook" slide to tie the game.

Sprinting down the chalked line, I could see Rails's twisted smile salivating for the chance to pound me. Houdini jumped into my body. I disappeared before impact and reappeared on the left side of home plate. Throwing my right leg straight and contorting my left leg underneath, I slid a yard wide of the plate and reached back to hook the edge of the plate with my outstretched hand. Rails's puffed-up mitt swallowed the ball and did a flyby tag that missed my arm. Dirt exploded into the air. I'd done it!

"You're out!" the umpire yelled.

A collective "No!" screamed from stands.

"Are you blind? You missed the call!" yelled Bob Apgar, who ran over to the umpire and bumped into his chest protector. "He was safe!"

The umpire turned and walked away. And that was that.

Rails busted out laughing and gave Bob the finger. Bob had a quick trigger and slugged Rails right smack-dab in the kisser. Before Bob could jump on Rails, I tackled him, hoping to stop a fight before it might escalate into a full-on team brawl. Too late. Both sides came running and started to rumble. Elbows flew, knees buckled, bodies blended into an angry scrum until the police car parked next to the field rang its siren, sending us scattering to our dugouts.

"Rails, you know Charlie was safe!" yelled Bob. "You fucking know it!"

I told Bob to shut his mouth; it was over. I dusted off my jersey and headed back to the dugout, blind with disappointment. I turned sick watching Rails and his teammates jumping all over themselves, reveling in their glory as champions. I tossed my hat and slumped next to Bob on the bench, our heads held low.

"You were fucking safe," cried Bob, tears wetting his apple-red cheeks.

"I appreciate you having my back, but Rails would've pounded you."

"I know." He sniffled, wiping his eyes.

Everyone packed up to leave. The entire dugout of players emptied out and headed for summer trouble without a care, while I couldn't move a muscle. I might have lost my chance to escape this nothing town. I peeked through the fence to see if the scouts were waiting for me, but they'd gone, probably determining I was too much of a hothead to play pro ball.

I gazed out over the field where I'd played baseball since I was six years old. This ballpark was my sanctuary from the chaos at home—and now it was over.

"Your mom and Ginger gone?" Dad finally showed up. "The new tractors at work don't fit in the goddamn crates. Held me up. I kept telling the idiot engineers to change them, but they have their pencils stuck up their asses, fussing over the B28 bomber wing contracts. The war's breaking my back."

His back, my heart.

Dad leaned against the dugout fence to catch his breath. I could smell the bourbon from where I was sitting. He probably bellied up to the bar at Puddler's Tavern after working his shift at AC Machinery.

"Ya couldn't make it to my last game? Leave work early for once?" I shook my head while using my hand to wipe the blood caked on my elbow from the slide at home plate.

"The foreman would've made me work a double. Not William Buckley. And don't be shaking your head. Someone's gotta pay for that filthy uniform."

AC Machinery was named after the founders, Addington and Calhoun, who launched the company in the late 1800s, making tractors, corn pickers, and military tanks. My grandfather Poppi emigrated to Wisconsin as an unskilled, uneducated farmer from the southern coast of Ireland. The locals in Milwaukee called him a potato wop. He found work at the factory pumping out the great Industrial Revolution. Dad followed and hadn't missed a day in twenty years. But lately, he was acting sick. His hunter green overalls had outgrown his body.

Dad was rubbing his stomach. "I made it in time to see the last play. You should've stayed put at third. Cost you the game, lad." He turned and limped across the field to take the shortcut home. "Don't be late for supper. I'm starving."

I threw my bat, cleats, and glove into my bag, then sat back down on the bench and looked up in the sky to find Sirius welcoming in the night. The brightest star in the galaxy was blinking, as if telling me everything was going to be all right. That I'd find another way out of Wauwatosa.

"Tough loss."

Out of nowhere a girl appeared in the dugout while I was searching the sky for my escape. The team had a serious unwritten rule: no girls allowed in the dugout. She bent over to pick a bright yellow dandelion and placed it behind her ear. I took a step forward, thinking I'd move her out of our sacred ground, but she didn't budge. In fact, she took a step forward. I didn't recognize her from school. I would have because she was a doll: auburn hair, blue eyes, dressed in rolled-up jeans and a yellow T-shirt—and her feet were bare.

"You might want to try football," she said with a raspy, sassy voice, "the way you tackled your teammate." She squinted and took a step closer to me. "I'll race you in the hundred-yard dash, and I bet I'll beat you."

"Huh?" I needed a second to catch up with her.

"A race." She paused and moved in even closer. "I sat next to your mom and sister in the stands, told me you live right across the creek from where we just moved in." I went dumb. She was so beautiful, I couldn't breathe. "Your sister, Ginger, is a real pistol. She'll get along well with my sister. They're about the same age."

"What?"

"Your sister?"

"Oh, I call her Gingersnap."

"That's a sweet nickname. I'm Sandee. Sandee Gold." She reached out to shake my hand. I felt an electric jolt shoot up my arm and into my heart. "Was that your father who just left?"

"Uh-huh."

"I bet he thought you were safe."

"He didn't say." I let my bag drop, sending a plume of dust into the air.

"I see." She came closer. "I'm fast." She dusted off my shoulder. "Can we race, Mr. Baseball Man?"

"I-I don't really . . . well, what I mean to say is, I've never raced . . ."

"Someone with curves in all the wrong places?" Her glare halted the breeze between us. "Or the right ones, depending on how you look at them." She spun around and gave a mischievous grin.

"I didn't mean . . ." I was caught on flypaper. "What I mean to say . . . look, you saw me run those bases, right?"

"So?"

"So? I'm fast, so fast I might be running out of this town with one of those pro baseball teams watching me today."

"Is that what you want to be when you grow up? A baseball player?"

"Yeah, or a pilot."

"Hmm. Hope you won't fly like you run. That slide to tie the game, Charlton Barkley . . ." She leaned in almost close enough to kiss. "You could've been hurt."

Her sweet scent tilted my world. I didn't know what to make of this. I sure as all get-out didn't want to lose a footrace to a girl, no way, nohow. Especially not to one who suddenly took all the breath from me that I'd need to beat her.

"I just turned eighteen. You?" she asked and backed up a step.

"Yes. No. Soon. Next month."

She rocked her hips side to side, then began deviously pacing, sizing me up. Her hair tossed in the wind, her smile crooked to one side, her piercing pale blue eyes never leaving my brown ones. It all came in a rush. I was agitated *and* excited, which was unnerving.

"I'm not sure I want to beat a measly seventeen-year-old, do I?" She kept pressing and gave another smile, this one more pensive and alluring.

I wanted to tighten the line to keep her near the boat, but I couldn't fish out any words, except "Uh-huh."

"We'll race on your birthday, Charlton. Do you pray?"

"Huh? Yeah, I go to church."

"Good. You'll need all your prayers to beat me." She came up close. "By the way, from where I was sitting, you were safe all the way. And you did a real nice thing out there too—trying to stop that fight. I wouldn't have come over and introduced myself otherwise."

She took the dandelion from behind her ear and gave it to me, then left me with her smile and dashed off, showing me her smooth gait. I kept my eyes on her bobbing hair as she turned the bend on Jefferson Avenue. She was right. She *was* fast—fast enough to steal my heart without me knowing it. For the moment, I forgot all about the game.

I took a break from studying for my final exam when the phone rang in the front hall. I leaped from my desk and beat Mom to it.

"Charlie Buckley," I answered confidently, praying it had to be one of those baseball scouts at the game.

"Upchuck, you sittin' on your ass? You're not gonna believe it, buddy boy. The Cubs just called. They picked *me*! Can you stand it?"

"Good for you, Rails," I whispered, then bent over from what felt like a gut punch.

"Dad wanted to enroll me at West Point, where he went. Fuck him. Hey, scouts call you yet?"

I went white with disappointment. Rails was going to the show, and I wasn't.

"You gotta learn to hide your signs if you want to last a week up there, Rails. I knew the curve was coming, ya dummy."

"Yeah, yeah, always worrying about nothing, Charlie."

"Be up-and-up with me, Rails. You missed the tag on me, right? I was safe, wasn't I?"

"I'm taking that one to my grave, buddy boy."

"Thanks for nothing, Rails. I got to go study."

"Later, you little nerd."

I sat at the kitchen dinette, dazed at the prospect of being held captive in this house forever. Mom took the dishrag over the counter for a second time, then stopped to look at me with those glossy, distant brown almond eyes that were just like mine. We also shared the same black hair and large nose. I headed for the cookie jar to grab a lemon chip. Her eyes followed me.

"What is it, Mom? Your stare is burning a hole in my back."

"*Thy* will, not *my* will be done, Charlton. Have faith for the right outcome." She came over and kissed my forehead. "And wash that dirty hair of yours."

After studying, I headed out to the garage to pummel the punching bag that Mom had bought for me for Christmas last year. I pounded that bag until my fists bled. She knew what was boiling below the surface: that it would be better for me to leave home as soon as possible, that we suffered in common from the same oppressor: William Buckley.

On my way to the bathroom to wash my bloody knuckles, I glanced at the grandfather clock in the hallway. Twenty minutes before ten. No calls from the scouts. I bypassed the bathroom, went to my bedroom, grabbed the firefly jar off my shelf, and headed outside to catch a few down at the creek. I unscrewed the top and readied myself for one to light up at the water's edge. While waiting, I peered across the creek to Sandee's house, wondering which bedroom was hers. I thought about her creamy white skin, her smile. I couldn't wait to see her again.

The wind kicked up. A sudden cold front from the Great Lakes tore through the weeping willow, crashing into the high temps, causing thunderbolts to crack the sky like an egg. I screwed the top back on the firefly jar and ran toward the house as cold, pearly drops of rain danced on the steamy driveway. I hustled in through the side door and shook my wet hair. Mom was darning Dad's socks in the mudroom while he, no doubt, was still slapping drinks back at Puddler's Tavern. It took me a moment to wrestle out the words.

"Did any of those baseball scouts call for me while I was outside?"

Without raising her chin, she cleared her throat, releasing the trapped air I'd imagined she'd been holding in. "No, Charles. I'm sorry."

There are sadness and hopelessness. This was both. I became instantly untethered, floating through the kitchen—on my way to nowhere. My heart pounded out drumbeats for help. The house was dead calm, Gingersnap sitting at the dinette, deep into one of her summer reading books; the clock ringing the ten chimes; Mom turning off the lights in the front hallway—all this seemingly happening in slow motion. I was in shock.

I headed back to my bedroom, grabbed my mitt, and flung it against the wall. The room spun like the Tilt-A-Whirl at the carnival. All the games flashed through my mind: the awards, the wins, the hits. I took deep breaths and wiped the sweat off my brow. What now?

I paced back and forth, walking off the panic, when Gingersnap crept into my room wearing her horse-dotted pajamas. Her strawberry curlicues bounced in the light streaming in through the window from the streetlamp.

"You hated the book *The Good Earth*, didn't you, Chuck?" Her disingenuous tone gave her away. She knew all too well what was going on.

The effects of vertigo had subsided. I picked up my glove and sat on the bed beside her.

"What do you want, Gingersnap?"

"I need to find examples of exposition."

"I didn't get picked, if that's what you're after. Mom probably told you. No more baseball. Any other questions?"

"You're right. Mom told me. Sorry, Chuck. They're stupid stink bombs." She rolled over and put a pillow inside her pajama top to look like she was pregnant. "Anyway, this book, it's too long. The wife, O-Lan, has a baby by herself and uses a reed or something to cut the baby cord and goes back to working in the fields all day." Gingersnap leaped off the bed and bent over, pretending to work in the fields while carrying her baby. "That's what they do—work-work-work—until they die. What kind of life is that?"

She took the pillow out from her pajama top, walked over to the window, and placed her finger on the glass, tracing the lines of rain pitter-pattering on the pane. "Are you going to leave, Charlie?"

"It's all going to work out, Gingersnap. Just watch yourself. You know what I mean, don't you?"

She wandered over to the shelf and picked up my model airplane and spun it in the air until she pretended to crash it, adding an explosion for a sound effect. "Yeah, yeah, I know. I'm going to bed." She returned the model airplane to the shelf and leaped into my arms, knowing I'd catch her. I swung her in a circle and tossed her on the bed. "Maybe you'll stay," she added.

No, I won't, I thought. Gingersnap bounced off the bed and zoomed out the door. I was ready for sleep but wanted to read the fighter pilot journal I'd checked out at the library to take my mind off imagining Rails in a Cubs' uniform. I picked up where I'd left off.

> Tossed around like never before, I tried to hold the controls in neutral, but the bird rolled and bobbed like a tiny boat at sea. I struggled to stay right side up. I was losing her. The windshield tore away. My goggles fogged up. I pulled them off and got pummeled with oil. The bird dropped out of the loop and glided without power. Down, down, down . . .

I woke from a noise that shook the house. I left my bedroom to find the front door had swung open. There he was, leaning against the doorjamb, soaked from the storm; the dim night light in the front hall revealing his sad, familiar frown. Dad was home.

"What the hell are you looking at, lad?"

Gingersnap ran to me and grabbed my shoulder. "Chuck, can you help me with something in my room?" She was shaking, knowing the wrecking ball was about to tear through the house at any moment.

"Why's the pup still awake?" He wiped his nose with the back of his hand and stumbled. Mom approached him, but retreated back toward the kitchen after seeing him gather himself and come for her with blood in his eyes. "Donna, come back here." She froze. "I asked a question: Why can't you get the pups to bed on time *for once*?" He backed her up against the wall.

It took one final stroke of the match to ignite the spark that set off a blaze that had been contained in me for far too long. Dad swung his fist, which careened off her forehead. She yelped and buckled. I caught her before she hit the ground. It was that desperate look in her eyes calling out for help that ignited the spark.

I ran at him. He threw the first punch. I caught it before it landed and twisted his arm behind his head.

"Stop it!" screamed Gingersnap.

Dad threw his other fist, striking my ear, sending it ringing. I tackled him to the floor, pinned both arms over his head, and straddled his chest. This sad sack of a father never taught me how to fix things, throw a ball, drive a car. And now he was losing his war, his liver shriveled, his God gone.

He had a smear of lipstick on his undershirt and smelled of cheap perfume. His chest heaved in and out as I drove an elbow into his throat. I had him. He whimpered like a dog struck by a car as his eyes swelled with cloudy tears, helplessly searching for redemption.

"Let him go, Charlton," implored Mom.

I've been trying to do that my entire life.

I removed my elbow from his neck and bolted out the front door, leaving Gingersnap and Mom shattered. I ran through a torrent of rain that blurred the landscape. I found my way down to the creek and curled up against the base of the weeping willow tree as thunder rumbled across the sky. With my Saint Christopher pendant chattering between my teeth, I cried myself to sleep.

I woke to the reflection of the half-moon glittering off the creek as flashes of lightning illuminated the horizon. The storm had moved west. I looked over the creek to Sandee's house, and behold, dancing before my eyes—a firefly! I tried to follow it, but it vanished in the dark.

I'll keep searching, though. I won't give up, ever. And like that firefly, I'll disappear, then reappear somewhere else—where he can't find me.

CHAPTER 2

————————

I wasn't hungry and hadn't been for days. I left the house without eating breakfast, void of direction and hope. I walked aimlessly to the creek and lay in the grass by the water's edge. The sunbeams splintered through the giant willow. A brilliant red cardinal landed on a branch, sensing I needed companionship.

"I don't need a friend. I need a job," I called out to the red bird. I let my eyelids fall while listening to the breeze rustling through the branches, lamenting, knowing it was time to ask Dad for a job at the factory. The thought of that killed me.

"I hope you're not dead." My eyes shot open to find Sandee barefoot again at the top of the bridge, holding a large piece of bread.

"You keep catching me off guard."

"What are you doing down there?"

"Daydreaming."

"Of?"

"Well, I-I was running, running faster than ever. As a matter of fact, you were in my dream. We were racing, and I beat you by a mile."

"Hilarious, Charlton Buckley. I'm going to beat you, you'll see."

"You keep calling me Charlton."

"I don't know what else to call you, other than cute." She smiled that smile, and my heart jumped.

"Charlie will do."

I hopped to my feet as she skipped down from the bridge. She broke off a chunk of bread and offered it to me.

"It's still warm from the Jewish bakery on Forty-Eighth. It's challah. We're Jewish—in case you didn't know."

Sandee held my gaze while I took a bite, perhaps appraising whether I liked the bread or worried about her being Jewish. There weren't many around. I knew one: Leo Bloomberg. He was spit on during PE my freshman year. His family moved away before the start of the second semester.

"Tastes good," I said.

"I'm glad you like it. I have to get back to the house to help my sister." I waited for her to leave, but she didn't, which was a relief. I wanted to be with her all day. She rocked back and forth, then asked, "Would you like to come over to my house?"

My stomach flipped. I wanted to, but I had never been inside the home of Jewish people. I didn't want to slip and say the wrong thing in her house, being Catholic and all.

"It might not be a good time," I uttered, backpedaling.

"Nonsense. Mom will, of course, ask you some questions about yourself, so be ready. That way I can learn about you too. We have it all planned out. Questions like, have you ever committed a crime, stolen a car, robbed a bank, been an axe murderer? That sort of thing." Sandee turned and ran up the hill to her front porch. "Come on! And don't worry."

The window frames were freshly painted, the brick on her house newly tuck-pointed, the driveway recently paved. On our way inside, she touched something on the doorjamb, then kissed her hand.

"A mezuzah," she said before I could ask. "It reminds us of our Jewish faith when we're coming and going."

Sunlight flooded her spotless home; nothing was out of place. Sandee offered me a chair in the kitchen that matched the color of the checkered linoleum floor. Everything looked brand new: the green GE fridge, the crisp red drapes, the snow-white stove—the house looked straight out of a home magazine.

I looked down at my dirty hands.

"Glass of milk, Charlie?"

"Sure."

My knee was shaking off the cap.

"Stop worrying. Mom won't bite—but I might." Sandee gave me a crooked smile and handed me a glass of milk.

As I took a big swig, Sandee's mother rolled her sister sitting in a wheel chair into the kitchen. I saw Sandee's features in Mrs. Gold's face, but her hair was wavy and brown. I jumped to my feet.

"Charlie, isn't it?"

"Nice to meet you Mrs. Gold."

Mrs. Gold held my hand, gently shaking it, offering me a kind and nurturing smile.

"Eloise, this is my friend, Charlie. Charlie, meet my sister." Eloise rolled herself over to me. Her eyes bright, hair black with tight curls, cheeks full.

"I'm the smart one," she said and put out her small hand. I took it with care, but she gave me a firm shake. "Cat got your tongue, Charlie? I can't walk, but I can talk." She smiled.

"Nice to meet you, Eloise," I finally responded. She blushed while Mrs. Gold laughed. I had no idea why until Sandee wiped the milk off my chin.

We moved into the den, where Sandee and Mrs. Gold assisted Eloise to the ground to help her with a series of exercises that helped to stretch out her bent spine. Although she winced, she never complained. Afterward, Mrs. Gold made sandwiches while Sandee and I played Eloise's favorite game: hide-and-seek; Eloise wanted to be the one always hiding. As I looked for her for a third time, I took notice of some of the books on the shelves: *What Is a Jew?*, *The History of the Jews*, *Handbook of Jewish Literature from Late Antiquity*. Sitting prominently on the shelf was a photograph of Sandee with her parents at Temple.

"That was taken at my bat mitzvah." She put her hand over her face. "I looked awful at that age."

"You should have seen *me* at thirteen—with my big nose and all. Still is."

Sandee tenderly ran her finger down my forehead, my nose, to my lips.

"I like everything about you, Charlie."

We listened to big bands on the Victor and played cards all afternoon, then went outside to pick the dead dandelions and blew the seeds in the air until the sun set behind the evergreens that bordered the backyard.

"I have Shabbat in a few minutes."

"What's that?"

"Friday at sunset we pray and light candles to remember the people we loved who've died. I'll walk you to the creek."

As we started off, Sandee's father pulled up the drive.

"Hold on there! The sun is still up. That gives me just enough time for this young man to introduce himself since he's obviously taken a shine to my daughter."

"Dad, cut it out."

"I'm sorry. I meant to say my daughter has taken a shine to *you*." He walked over and extended his hand. "I'm her mean father, Dr. Gold." He stood tall, with thinning hair and kind eyes behind his dark-rimmed glasses.

"Charlton Buckley."

"I saw your championship game. You're one hell of a ballplayer, Charlton. You clobbered that ball."

"Thanks."

"Did that catcher tag you? Didn't look like it from where I was sitting. Safe all the way."

"I didn't feel a thing."

"I knew it!" He shook his head. "Life isn't fair." He glanced at Sandee. "Shabbat in ten minutes. Nice meeting you, young man."

Sandee and I stopped on the bridge.

"Your dad seems nice."

"I'm not crazy about his dumb jokes, but yeah, I'm pretty lucky."

"I'm working at AC Machinery over the summer working with

my dad."

"You don't want to be a pro baseball player anymore?"

"I have to save up for college—if I go." I didn't have the stomach to tell her I struck out with the scouts.

"I'm taking summer classes in German. My grandparents came from a small town in Germany after finding an advertising pamphlet on their doorstep from the Wisconsin Commission of Emigration looking for farmers and industrial laborers. They cut off part of their Jewish name—left it on the shores of Hamburg and came over to Milwaukee. My name should really be Sandee Goldenberg."

I took her hand.

"Sandee Goldenberg. How do you say 'I'll see you around' in German?"

"*Bis demnächst.*"

"*Bis demnächst*, Sandee."

"*Bis demnächst*, Charlie. Of course you will. I live just across the creek." She smiled.

As I approached the house, I noticed the shingles on our roof were curled at the edges, the wood frame windows were cracked and rotting, paint was peeling off the siding, the dining room picture window had a crack that went from one corner to the opposite, and the lower part of the front door had black smudges from the sole of Dad's work boot. The house had been taking a beating for years.

Mom's roast was sizzling in the oven. I poured a glass of water from the kitchen sink and sat next to Gingersnap, who was reading her book in the dinette.

"I hate, hate, hate this book!"

"Where's Mom?"

"Sewing my sweater."

"What happened to it?"

"Dad grabbed me and ripped the sleeve, all because I was playing tetherball with the Stevenson brothers during lunch. I won every game, Chuck."

"I bet you did. Let me see your arm." The skin of her underarm had turned eggplant purple. "Be smart, Gingersnap! Don't blab to him about what you're doing. Lie if you have to."

"I didn't say a word! Mom did, thinking he'd be happy that I beat those idiots." Gingersnap went back to gnawing on her pencil. That was her thing, chewing on pencils, straws, fingernails—whatever she could put in her mouth.

"Speaking of . . ." She motioned to the front window. Dad was limping up the drive.

"Good luck with your book," I said.

"Thanks for nothing."

I put my empty glass in the sink and headed for the living room, hoping Dad would go straight to his bedroom and we'd miss each other. I dialed in *The Jack Benny Program* on the Victor and flopped on the couch and opened the *Reader's Digest* to an article I'd been reading from the *New York Herald Tribune* on Hitler's victories. Dad entered the living room and poured himself a drink at the bar located underneath a painting handed down from my grandfather Poppi. "The only stinking thing in the house worth selling," Dad often said. The painting depicted an Irish immigrant tilling the land during a light rain, his face straining from the arduous labor, his muscles attenuated, the oxen's ribs pressing through its hide, mouth agape, frothing with fatigue plowing through the wet sludge. If the painting was worth so much, I'd have sold it years ago and fixed up the house.

Dad collapsed into the mold of his well-worn recliner, glaring at me while jiggling the ice in his glass.

"Ya didn't have the courage to ask me yourself, did ya?"

He took a sloppy gulp of his drink. Not a sip like a normal person.

"Ask you what?"

"My little pup—had to have your mummy do it for ya."

"Do what?" He stared into his glass and watched the ice swirl.

"You'll start work at the factory tomorrow. Can't be lying on the couch all summer."

"I-I would have asked you. Mom just beat me to it, that's all. Look, I-I'm sorry about last night if that's why you're so pissed off at me."

"I don't know what you're mumbling about." He finished off his drink. "Don't I get a thank-you, for Christ's sake?"

"What department will I be working in?"

"Foreman Kelly will meet you tomorrow at eight sharp. Better not be late and make me look like a fool. He'll hand you off to old George in parts. Never liked him. He's always looking for new ways, changing this, changing that."

"Thanks for the job, Dad."

"I wouldn't get too excited. Work is work." He tipped the ice from his glass into his mouth. "Donna, when we gonna eat, for Christ's sake?" he yelled, then spit the ice back into his glass.

Mom brought him the *Late Edition News*.

"The roast will be done in ten minutes, dear." She closed the heavy flowered curtains and took a seat on the couch next to his recliner. "More terrible news overseas, Will. Those poor boys." She picked Dad's glass off the side table and swirled the ice, readying for a sip.

"Get your own drink." Dad grabbed back the glass. "Charlie boy, pour me a jigger of Four Roses, like a good lad."

I picked up the pewter jigger off the bar and poured him his medicine. The jigger was engraved with "The hair of the dog."

"Will ya look at that!" Dad said, reading the paper. "Germany double-crossed its friend, invaded the dirty Russkies—again." He belly laughed, then grabbed his side and threw the paper down on his lap.

I gave him his jigger, which he poured over the melting ice.

"War is for men, not for those who play a kiddie's game. But I guess you're all done with baseball now, Charlie. Coming to work with your old man." He smiled. The booze was setting in. "Donna, bring me my dinner on a tray. I want to listen to the news hour. Turn the dial up, my boy."

"British intelligence tapped into classified radio transmissions describing systematic mass murder in Lithuania, Latvia, and later the Ukraine. News also came from the Soviets. Prime Minister Churchill summarized the news in a broadcast earlier today: 'As Hitler's armies advance, whole districts are being exterminated . . .'"

"He's a madman, that one," spouted Dad.

"Thousands of executions in cold blood are being perpetrated by the German police troops upon the Russian patriots defending their native soil. Famine and pestilence have yet to follow in the bloody ruts of Hitler's tanks. We are in the presence of a crime without a name."

"Took it right up the wee arse. '*Dur omadhaun* Russkies,' my old man would say."

"Enough of that language, William," Mom said and placed the tray on his lap.

"Fooled into thinking they had an ally against those Polacks. And that fat English fart thinks he's some kind of poet. No balls of steel, that's for certain. Jacobins don't hold a candle to the Irish, or the US for that matter. Off you go, you two. I want to eat in peace."

Mom and I joined Gingersnap in the dinette.

"Did your father say who would be supervising you at work, Charlie?"

"I think he said a guy named George?"

"George Underwood? That's a relief. Wonderful man. His wife, Beverly, is in our bridge club. They lost their boy to the war somewhere in the Pacific. Never found him. I can't imagine." She put her hand on mine. "On to a brighter subject. Have you met the girl who moved in across the creek?"

"Sandee." Saying her name flipped my stomach. "She came over to say hi after the game. Wants to race me. Thinks she'll win."

"Ha! What a dingbat." Gingersnap laughed. "She better pray to Jesus for a miracle."

"Not to Jesus. She's Jewish."

The air thinned. Mom slowly rose to put the dishes in the sink.

"I'd be mindful to keep that to yourself, Charlie Buckley. Particularly around your father."

After finishing dinner, I went to my bedroom. Without turning on the light, I walked straight to the window to look at Sandee's house. *"Keep that to yourself."* I shouldn't have said a word.

I went to bed and stared up at the knotty pine ceiling, imagining flying my plane to each of those knots in the planks, as if they were different cities. *As soon as I get enough money, I'll move out, go to flight school, and fly out of this town.* But I'll keep that to myself.

CHAPTER 3

M om woke me up and handed me brand-new overalls, boots, and a work shirt for my first day on the job. As I dressed, I thought back to when I was about ten years old and sneaked down to the factory and hiked up onto a brick wall so I could peek through the broken windows to see the tractors being built on the line. Dad caught me and pulled me down off the wall and brought me inside. The building smelled of fresh latex paint. The enormous tractors seemed to be sent down by Zeus. I was in awe. *I'll work here when I graduate from college,* I'd hoped. That was then.

AC Machinery was a short bike ride down Wisconsin Avenue. A round man was waiting for me at the steel doors and handed me my time card. He grumbled his name, "Foreman Kelly." No handshake was offered. He quickly passed me on to the man Dad mentioned was going to be my supervisor, an older man with crinkled wrinkles circling his sparkling blueberry eyes. His silvery beard matched a full head of hair that was combed straight back.

"Charlie? George Underwood." He firmly shook my hand. "Two rules: keep up, and stay away from the boiler room. Let's go."

George stopped to talk to a mechanic who was half under a tractor. He was patient and chose his words slowly, as if deciding on which fly to use to catch a certain fish. "Mr. O'Leary, a problem with the mix, I presume?" George put his hand on my shoulder and winked. "He's been spinning that gear shaft since the beginning of time. O'Leary, grab Donovan, and the two of you figure out a way to dilute the oil. That way, when the stem slides, the link won't catch."

"Easy for you to say," responded O'Leary. "Who's the kid?"

"This young man is Charlie Buckley, Will's boy." George turned to me. "He's going to learn every part of the King 44, right?"

"Yes, sir. What's that?"

"Our flagship tractor parked right behind you."

The R44 Silver King tractor was the *king* of all the tractors at AC Machinery. I marveled at the slick gray pencil trim that ran along the side of the dark-green shell in the shape of a tank.

"Charlie, it's the first tractor to have four-wheel drive, a three-point hitch, live hydraulics, and a complete hydraulic transmission, not to mention a horn and a headlight. Our bestseller," said George, smiling. "Unfortunately, Uncle Sam is giving us a giant headache. The war department is telling us to make *fewer* tractors to conserve resources for the war effort but make *enough* tractors to keep the farmers feeding the troops. Good golly! President Roosevelt can't have it both ways. But he won't listen to me. Come on, Charlie, let's head over to parts."

Throughout the day engineers came to George with a slew of designs. He'd show them all to me and ask, "Can it work?" As if I knew. I'd say, "Maybe," thinking I'd better say something. We kept walking, he kept talking—all day. My head was spinning like that gear shaft O'Leary had been working on. George sat me down at a desk inside four chain-link-fenced walls called the Cages, constructed to allow the designers to see out to the production line. George handed me a pad of graph paper.

"You recall that brake system I showed you on King 44?"

"Yes, sir."

"Draw it."

It had two round cylinders stuck together. The front one was slightly larger than the other, so I drew it that way.

"You strike me as a pretty smart cookie, kid. Tell me about yourself." He twinkled a smile.

"Um, I play . . . played baseball. We lost in the state championships.

The pro scouts came to watch me but . . ." I shook my head.

George took his time before responding. "Not many kids are lucky enough to be considered. That's impressive, young man. What else are you good at?"

"Physics. I won my senior-year class project. I came up with a way to run a water line from the cafeteria to the science room sinks. Also, I have this model airplane, a Boeing 307, a real beauty with over two hundred parts. Took me three months to finish her."

I wasn't used to talking so much about myself to a man I'd just met listening to me with such genuine interest.

"My wife heard from your mother—said you're some kind of genius. Well, I've got a sticky wicket maybe you can help me figure out. The two-layer cylinder brake system on the R44 is too damn bulky, causing the discs to slip like a bad back. You'll work with the engineers to reconfigure it for a cleaner fit. When you come in tomorrow, be ready to take apart the disc pads and cylinders. That might lead you in the right direction since they depend on one another."

"How about grinding down the edge of the cylinder to—"

"Nope. That would flatten the coping. Take your time. This is your desk now. Welcome to AC Machinery." He patted me on the back.

"Mr. Underwood, my mom . . . she told me . . . about your son . . . I'm—I'm awfully sorry."

"That means a lot, Charlie. We're coworkers now. You call me George."

∽

The July heat inside the steel walls of the factory was stifling. The swamp coolers hanging from the beams were too covered in soot to do any good. There was either some kind of olfactory immunity among the laborers or a ban on using deodorant; the place reeked of body sweat. I toiled for days at my desk, drawing circle after circle to replicate the cylinders, trying to draft a design that would accomplish what George wanted without increased labor cost. After going through five pencils, it occurred to me that we had a more serious problem. Even if we came up with a new concept for the brakes, AC didn't have the tools that could scale its production, which it needed to keep up with the orders and shipment dates.

The day I realized this was the day Frank Calhoun, a descendant of the original founder of AC, put me on the line.

"Come on, little Buckley, I need your help."

I hadn't been trained in any specific skill that would qualify me to get near the line, but I didn't hesitate to learn. Mr. Calhoun welcomed me to AC and patted me on the back with a little too much force, almost sending me to the ground. He placed me in front of one of the tractors on the line as it was moving along.

"I'm going to show you how to screw on the bolts to secure the tires before the shell is dropped on the chassis," he yelled above the noise coming from the soldering and drilling on the line. "I'll screw on the front tire, then you quickly go behind me, and you do the rear tire. Got it?"

Once I finished watching him use the hand tool to tighten the bolts on the large tires, he smirked and walked away, holding the hand tool that I needed. I looked around for anyone who would help me, but I saw a bunch of grimy faces smiling. The line sped up, causing the rear tire to fall off and go whizzing by Foreman Kelly, almost taking out his legs. The mechanics doubled over with laughter. Not the foreman.

"Buckley! Never to step foot near the line again, damn it! Get back to your doodling with Grandpa George!"

"I'm sorry, but Mr. Calhoun was supposed to . . ."

"I see the apple doesn't fall too far from the tree, Buckley. Now get the hell out of here."

I went back to my desk and ate my lunch. George came by and took his lunch with me, giving me a wry smile while I ate my bologna roll. He'd seen the humiliation doled out by Calhoun.

"Let's show them a thing or two, shall we?" George said. "I'm going to put you *to the test*. You'll attempt to assemble by hand the latest model R tractor in under three hours. My boss started this when I was about your age. If you're successful, you'll get a colored patch of the new R series to wear on your work shirt forever." George had earned six patches on one shoulder, five on the other. "The R44 will be a tough nut to crack. Our senior engineers are stealing the military tank designs and throwing them into our tractors."

"Dad won't let me in on this."

"Tell him you'll split the money with him. You get five bucks added to your pay. Charlie, I want you to be ready in four weeks."

"I don't really want to work here," I let out. "I feel trapped."

"I see." George looked at me and smiled into his wrinkles. He put his hand on my shoulder. "Four weeks. That, you can do."

At the end of my shift, I learned why George cautioned me about going into the boiler room. Dad grabbed my arm. "Now that you're going to stick around at AC for a while, it's time you meet *the boilers.*" He used a key to unlock and open the double doors. Cigarette smoke escaped like a five-alarm fire.

"Fellas, as most of you know, this is my boy. One day he'll get his own key to this room."

Not if I have anything to say about it. These guys were worn at the edges: nicotine-stained teeth, bloodshot eyes, nipping from their flasks of liquor. I could barely breathe from the cigarette smoke and showed myself out and clocked out.

A sprinkle of rain was welcomed on my ride home; the heat inside the factory was exhausting. I found Sandee at the bridge, her feet bare again, wearing a yellow rain slicker. My stomach twirled with excitement as I approached. At first, we avoided each other's eyes, staring at the creek, trying to find our way back after not seeing each other since I was invited into her home. The water in the creek was running high from the rain.

"You have a smudge of grease on your jaw, Charlton." Her crooked smile sent me.

"You have one on your cheek," I responded. "At least I can wash mine off." I chuckled.

"That's not a very nice thing to say. It's a birthmark. You won't find another one like it—or someone like *me.*"

I crouched into a runner's starting position, then launched forward and sprinted until I took off at the creek's edge and landed on the other side, just barely making it over the water. Sandee ran over the bridge to brush the wet grass off my shoulders, sending tingles all the way down my legs. I turned to face her, wanting to hold her, to kiss her ruby lips.

"I . . . I use a protractor at work."

"Use a what?" She squinted.

"I tool that helps me draw perfect circles for the R44 brake system cylinders for a redesign." Sandee moved in close. "Tomorrow I'll draw one with you doing a cartwheel inside."

"Bring it home to show me." Sandee's breasts brushed against my chest, then she moved back a step as the wind played with her fine hair. "When's your birthday, *Charlton*?"

"July twenty-eighth, *Sandra*."

"We'll race at the field where you were tagged out."

"I was safe, and you know it."

"I'll meet you after your shift at six o'clock sharp on your birthday."

"It's a date."

"It's not a date, Charlie. It's a race. A date is something entirely different."

Sandee twinkled a sassy smile, then pulled me down to the ground. Pressed shoulder to shoulder, we watched the waterlogged clouds floating across the purple sky.

"Do you miss baseball?" Sandee asked.

"So bad it hurts. It was my first love." Sandee grinned. "What are you smiling about?"

"Knowing I'll be your second."

She leaned her face toward mine, inviting me to make up the difference between us. It only lasted a split second, but the kiss felt eternal. Her lips were soft and warm. She put her hand in mine.

"I guess we're at the time of our young lives when all the parts aren't assembled yet. You're the engineer, Charlie. I'm counting on you to figure this out for us."

I was being yanked in different directions: Sandee was here in

Wauwatosa, while an unstoppable force was pulling me away from Dad and a town becoming smaller by the day. But Sandee was with me now, lying on the thick grass laughing, smelling the dandelions, listening to the sparrows. That was all I knew—or wanted to think about.

"Weil ich habe mich in dich verliebt."

I tried to mimic what she had said, but I spit out slosh, then switched gears and recited math formulas in the voice of an English Shakespearean actor. She rolled around the grass in hysterics and yelled for me to stop because her stomach hurt.

"What was it you said?"

"That's your homework for tonight."

With that, we kissed until the moon broke through the clouds.

⎯⎯

The dining room table had spindled legs that Mom dusted in the afternoon in preparation for Sunday dinner. A lace cloth, handed down by some ancestor, covered the ebony-colored tabletop, which allowed for two extension leaves in case company was invited. The leaves never came out of the front-hall closet; there they sat for as long as I could remember, untouched, gathering dust behind the winter jackets.

Gingersnap ran to the table and took her seat opposite me.

"What's with the towel around your head?" I asked.

"Lice wash. Susan Kirby brought them to school. She's got gobs of them everywhere! They were crawling out of her nose. Yuck!" Mom placed the silverware settings handed down from the last century while Dad took his seat at the head of the table. "Mom was too rough on me with her comb. I don't even have *any* of those wretched parasites in my hair."

"The eggs were ready to hatch," Mom responded. "Thank the Lord, we extracted them before they burst into those *wretched parasites*."

Dad was freshly shaven, drowning in Barbasol to mask the bourbon on his breath. He raised his hand, indicating we had best change the subject. Gingersnap took her fork and dove into the peeled potatoes steaming in a bowl.

"Don't fill up on those, pup," Dad grumbled.

"When do you race your new *girlfriend*?" asked Gingersnap. "I saw you two lovebirds by the bridge."

"Mind your own business, Virginia," Mom interjected. "Now eat your carrots."

"She's not my girlfriend," I snapped.

"Well, I saw you two kissing . . . "

"Damn it, Gingersnap, I'm gonna pound you into next week!"

Dad slammed his fist on the table. He took a sip of water and shifted in his chair. My gut tightened.

"This new family across the creek, what's their surname, Charlie?"

I glared at Gingersnap for bringing up the subject.

"Gold, isn't it?" Dad continued. "Her father's a fancy doctor on Milwaukee Avenue. I read the write-up on him in the neighborhood directory. Goes to Temple. Big shot, Dr. Gold. A Jew kike is what he is. No doubt overcharging the sick."

Mom dropped her fork. "William!"

"He's a what?" asked Gingersnap.

"All they do is cheat ya, grind you down on pricing. I hear it from our salespeople who are on the phone with them Jews all the time. They'll tell ya."

I clenched my fists under the table.

"Best not go around with that girl, lad. The Jewish will stick on you."

"I'll do what I want!" I shot back. "I'll be eighteen next week, so that's that. Save my plate for later, Mom." I made to leave, but Dad jumped from his chair.

"Who do you think is hanging around that neck of yours? Saint Christopher, that's who. There's no blimey mixing. If you want to go about with a Jewess, you better start looking to find another place to live. Until then, sit back down."

Mom wiped her eyes. Gingersnap shrank like a parched flower. He'd done it again. The man who had no friends except the slime bags at work, the man who terrified his wife and children, the man who lived drunk was the same man who hated Jews. Why would I ever listen to a damn word he had to say about anything?

He downed two more drinks while we suffered in silence.

After finally escaping the table, I flopped down on my bed and looked up at the knotty pine ceiling like I'd done countless times growing up after he'd imprisoned me in my room for doing nothing. I grabbed one of my fighter pilot journals from under the bed and read about the first American aircraft to fly in WWI: the Nieuport 28s. They were issued to four American squadrons in 1918, becoming the first aircraft to see operational service with an American fighter squadron. I read deep into the night, fantasizing about flying one of those birds right out of Wauwatosa and into the Second World War.

CHAPTER 4

M y shoulders felt larger than the day before, my head more determined. I turned eighteen and was flying through my push-ups in the living room. On push-up number forty, the Victor suddenly went quiet before an emergency news bulletin broke in.

"On this day, July 28, 1944, there has been some success. Seven weeks after D-Day, it appears the First Army's Operation Cobra has finally secured victory in the Normandy campaign, while the German forces have launched a massive tank offensive near Kursk in the Soviet Union."

"Krauts!" yelled Dad as he limped into the living room, holding his side. "Should've blown them off the face of the earth when we had the chance. At least they're corralling them Jews into those ghettos."

"What are you talking about?"

"Never you mind, lad. Just be lucky your little Jewess lives in the good ol' US of A."

"You hate the Krauts, *but* you like them for hating the Jews? Which is it?"

"Get to work, lad. I called in sick, so off you go."

He'd forgotten my birthday—again.

It was over ninety degrees at the park while I waited for Sandee. I was beat from work all week; the clogged-up swamp coolers had turned the factory into a furnace, and I would have much preferred kissing Sandee instead of racing her.

"You're a man now, I presume?" And there she was.

"You doth presume correctly, my lady," I said, throwing my head to one side, flipping the hair off my forehead.

"Still look like a little boy to me." She was already in the race, trying to get into my head. "I'm ready for you." She peeled off her sweater to reveal a red halter top that matched her red short shorts. I took a gander at her breasts. "They're not big enough to stare at, Charlie."

She bent over and stretched her hamstrings, easily touching the ground. My legs were turning into Jell-O. *Better get this race on before I drop.*

"Who's gonna say *go?*"

"I'm older. I'll say it."

She paced off one hundred yards and put a stick in the grass to mark the finish line.

"You'll be racing the fastest guy in Wauwatosa, you know."

"On your mark."

"Wait!" We toed the line shoulder to shoulder. "The loser treats the winner to a cream soda at the Jip-Joint right after?" I suggested.

"Agreed. Get set." She readied herself to take off.

"And a burger. They're running a special: ya get both for sixty cents."

"Go!" she screamed.

Sandee Gold took off in a flash. I followed, but my pistons weren't firing yet. Her gait opened up, grabbing the lead. I caught up and bumped her shoulder. We were running step for step for step until I pushed one stride ahead of her, but she wouldn't give in. My chest burned. My legs began quitting on me. Five yards from the stick, we crashed into each other and lunged for the finish line, landing in a tangled heap.

"I won!" Sandee let out from her bright pink cheeks.

"No, no way!" I said, gasping for air.

"I'll agree to a tie. Only because it's your birthday, Charlie."

We kept our legs intertwined and waited for enough air to kiss long and deep.

"I love your chest," she said, placing her hand there. "And your heart. Now—you owe me dinner."

I could smell the burgers and fries coming from the old brick building of the Jip-Joint. We took our seat in the red booth by the window that faced Main Street. I took my spoon and spun it in a circle on the table.

"When I was young, Gingersnap and I would sit at those round seats at the counter and spin around, making ourselves dizzy. I'd order the same thing every week: two cheeseburgers, fries, and a thick strawberry milkshake. After sharing a banana split, Mom would give us each a penny to buy a gumball to chew on our way home."

"What was your favorite color?"

"Blue. Gingersnap couldn't stand getting any other color than a pink one. I'd pray I'd get one just to see her turn purple. It was nice for Mom to get out of the house, beyond the yard, away from Dad." I let that slip. Sandee reached for my hand.

"What will the two of you have?" asked Pauline. She'd been waitressing at the Jip-Joint since I was in diapers.

"A grilled cheese sandwich, thank you," Sandee ordered.

"A cheeseburger for me."

"Just one, Charlie?" Pauline raised an eyebrow and smiled at Sandee. "Are you new to the neighborhood, dear?"

"A few months."

"Didn't take you long to find the finest young man in Milwaukee County."

"I can't imagine *anyone* finer," responded Sandee. Pauline winked at me. "And we'll split a strawberry milkshake—extra thick. It's Charlie's birthday."

"Not only extra thick, but it won't be on the bill. Happy birthday, Charlton. I'll be right back with that shake."

I focused on Sandee's crimson lips while she talked, revealing a tiny chip off the corner of her front tooth. Sandee watched me watching her and smiled.

"The Cardinals beat the Cubs last night," she said. "Dad loves the Redbirds. He kept talking about what a great ballplayer you are, Charlie. Says you're a real hot dog."

"My dad wouldn't know." I took another spin of the spoon. "He missed every game this year. Couldn't care if we won or lost . . . did you just say your dad's a Redbird fan? What a loser. The Cubs are a way better team."

My mind went white. I wanted to throw a net around the words that had just tumbled from my stupid mouth and haul them back in.

"My dad is *not* a loser. You are—for saying *he* is," Sandee shot back. The air at the Jip-Joint seemed to collapse into a black hole. I felt as if everyone turned to stare me down. My spoon stopped spinning and came to rest.

"I-I don't know why I said that." I felt I was going to cry. We sat in silence for a bit while I bit my lip. "I wasn't picked up by a baseball team. Rails made it in, the lucky stiff. I don't know what I'm going to do. I feel like I'm trapped in this town."

I reached for the spoon, but Sandee beat me to it. She moved it over to one side and took my hand.

"I don't ever want you to hide your disappointments from me, do you hear? I don't care about baseball. I care about you."

My entire being had been defined by how fast I could run, how far I hit the ball. Sandee changed all that with *I care about you.*

After paying the $1.10 bill from the money I'd been saving, we walked hand in hand down the gravel alleyway behind the Jip-Joint. I stopped and turned to face Sandee.

"I'm sorry for what I said back there about your father. *My* dad's the *real* loser."

"That makes me sad for you, Charlie." Sandee nuzzled her nose against mine and licked her lips. Her tongue explored my mouth. I couldn't help myself and pressed my groin against her, then eased back, afraid she'd noticed. "It's okay." She panted and grabbed my hips, pulling them back in. "It feels nice being close to you like this. Let's go to my house."

"Where's your family?"

"Mom is at her bridge club, and Dad took Eloise to her clinic. Let's hurry before Shabbat."

Lying pressed against each other on the couch, I cupped Sandee's breast as she rubbed over my hardness. Quick pulses of air blew across my ear. Her scent, her moan, her soft tongue—it was all intoxicating. I was lost in her embrace until the kitchen door slammed. I sat up and snatched the crocheted throw pillow and placed it over my lap as Mrs. Gold entered the living room.

"Oh hello, Charles. What a nice surprise."

"Hey, Mrs. Gold."

She raised her chin, glanced at Sandee, then headed back to the kitchen. I gave Sandee an *I'm-in-big-trouble* face. She mischievously put her hand under the pillow and squeezed.

"Shabbat in a few minutes," Mrs. Gold called from the kitchen. "Eloise and your father are home." Sandee slid her hand back just as her father entered from the back door with Eloise.

"It's about time you joined us for Shabbat, Charlie—if you're comfortable."

I nodded and smiled at Eloise.

"Charlie and Sandee up in a tree," Eloise sang. "K-i-s-s-i-n-g . . ."

Mr. Gold put his hand on my shoulder and guided me into the dining room. I looked at my flushed face in the mirror hanging above the oak buffet where the candles rested in silver-plated holders and saw Dad's ugly face reflecting back at me, saying, *"The Jewish will stick on you."*

Mr. Gold struck a long match and lit one of the candles and prayed.

"Baruch ata, Adonai, Sloheinu Melech ha-olam, asher Kidshanu b'mitzvotav vitzivanu l'hadlik ner shel Shabbat. We remember our grandparents, Harold Goldberg, Mazel Rosenstein, and Aunt Marie Stone."

Sandee lit another match and handed it to Eloise, who triumphantly recited a prayer. *"Baruch atah, Adonai Eloheinu, Melech haolam, asher kid'shanu b'mitzvotav, v'tzivanu l'hadlik ner shel Shabbat."*

"Charlie," said Mr. Gold, "the prayer says, 'Blessed are you, Adonai, our God, sovereign of all, who hallows us with mitzvot, commanding us to kindle the light of Shabbat.'"

I recalled my eighth birthday, when Grandpa Poppi and I went down to the creek after dinner. He was carrying my firefly jar with his large brown-spotted hand. We had to go back early because he said he wasn't feeling well and died the next day.

Eloise handed me the lit match and smiled, encouraging me to add a name.

"My grandpa Poppi."

Watching the burning candle and praying with the Golds, remembering loved ones, captured my affection. I thanked them, and Sandee walked me to the bridge.

"Charlie," Sandee said, holding my hand. "Lighting the candles also reminds us that each flicker of light represents God's soul. We reflect His light, no matter what happens to us."

We kissed good night. And as I walked up the drive, it was clear to me that Dad had it all wrong.

Mom made Dad's breakfast the way he ordered it every Sunday morning: eggs over easy, bacon burned to a crisp, the coffee black. He rolled out of his hole to the smell of grease cooking on the skillet.

"Good morning, William. The choir is singing, so I thought we'd all go to church and then eat lunch at the Jip-Joint. The little ones are joining in to sing—"

"Oh, rejoice, rejoice!" Dad bellowed in a mocking singing voice. "No heaven on earth for me, Donna. Done my time. Not going back."

"I have a solo part—"

"Damn . . . thought I was hungry." Dad grabbed at his side.

He rose and shoved his chair aside and went back to bed.

"I'll help you clean up, Mom," I offered.

"Me too," added Gingersnap.

"No! I need to do it."

As we left the kitchen, Gingersnap shook her head. "I'm never, *ever* getting married. You gonna with Sandee?"

"Don't ask dumb questions."

"Well, are ya?"

I gave her a stern look and headed into the living room to settle on the couch. Mom came in after a while and sat at the window, staring into the gray sky as if praying for someone to whisk her away from her troubles. I went back to a section in the *Reader's Digest* on the upcoming third anniversary of Pearl Harbor.

> War came on, quiet as a whisper, over the dark green Pacific. Wind was out of the west. The horizon split the world in half. A minesweeper patrols the waters two miles outside the harbor as the boys on the base sleep comfortably after a long night of jitterbugging, fortified with a spiked Hawaiian libation. Something out of the ordinary is bobbing at the surface forty-five yards out from the bow—a dark gray pipe. Uninvited company.
>
> Time: 7:45 a.m. A shadow appears on the radar board—a new tool used for air defense. Fifty aircraft are bearing down.
>
> The ground shakes. The aircraft carrier runway lifts into the air like a flying carpet and cracks into a thousand pieces. Air activity roars overhead. A navy commander glances up on the starboard side of his massive warship and spots a low-flying plane. A reckless hot dog, he thinks, infuriating him. He contemplates punishment until he notices the rising sun insignia on the bird that is now soaring down on his ship. He grips the railing. His fingers turn white. Two flaps under the bird spring open. A rotund object drops from its belly.

Mom interrupted my reading and turned on the Victor to catch the news.

"Your local recruiting office beginning today. Don't delay. Eighteen-year-olds from Milwaukee County are now eligible to enlist under Selective Service for the US Army, Navy, and Air Force. Interviews are at Marshall Junior High School. We hope you'll serve your country, young men. There's no better cause than the fight for freedom. Apply today."

"The air force," I let out and dropped my *Reader's Digest* and rose off the couch. My life flipped over like a record on a phonograph, ready for the second side to be played.

Mom cut off the Victor.

"Looks like the Nips and Krauts are bleeding our soldiers dry," Dad said while limping past me toward his recliner, the smell of liquor in his wake. "They're sending the pups to war after all."

"They can't do that, William. No, no, Charlie. William, tell him, for God's sake."

"He's a man now."

"I'm going for the interview." I dashed to the hallway and phoned Sandee to meet me at the bridge. Mom hovered behind me as I felt the ground shift. She tried to stop me, but I was already out the door.

Sandee was waiting at the top of the bridge, engulfed in one of her father's old sweaters.

"Eighteen-year-olds are eligible to enlist," I said. "I'll get my pilot's license on the government's dime—"

Sandee put her hand to my mouth and pulled me in tight.

"I'm not letting you go, Charlton. To the army, yes, but not from me. Do you understand?"

"I'll be back with my wings and take you up higher than you've ever been."

"Kissing you does that for me, Charlie. Kiss me."

CHAPTER 5

The gymnasium at Marshall Junior High School was teeming with adrenaline-spiked eighteen-year-olds from all over Milwaukee County lining up to apply for the Selective Service. My childhood screams echoed through the rafters and across the varnished wood floors where I'd avoided incoming dodgeballs and raced behind enemy lines to capture the flag. Long tables were set in place of volleyball nets. Men in uniform were sitting on one side, hopeful applicants on the other. I drew a number and took a seat against the padded brick wall underneath the basketball hoop to wait my turn. A guy I knew from junior high summer league was sitting next to me. We barely said hello. Oddly, competition was swirling in the air like a twister, even though we were all on the same side.

My number crackled over the loudspeaker. I hustled over to the table and sat opposite a steely-eyed recruiter and handed him my application.

"What's so interesting about your shoes?"

"I'm sorry?" I asked.

"When you talk, eyes up. Understood?"

"Yes, sir."

James T. McGraw was on his glistening silver nameplate. I took in quiet, deep breaths while he went over my paperwork.

"You want to fly in the air force, Buckle?"

"It's Buckley, sir. Yes."

"What's with the knee?"

"It shakes when I get nervous, that's all."

"Hmm. Your grades in the sciences are high. Summer job?"

"I work at AC Machinery, designing tools for building the R44 King tractor. I'm trying to come up with ways they can build them faster."

"Hmm. What are your hobbies?"

"I used to build model airplanes and played baseball. I almost made it to the pros."

"Any allergies? Phobias?"

"No, sir."

"Are your parents patriotic?" My stomach recoiled. "Do they love what this country stands for?"

"Yes. Dad says he hates the Krauts and Nips."

He paused. "What about you?"

"What Germany is doing to the Jewish people and taking over other countries has to be stopped."

"Have you ever been convicted of a crime?"

"No, sir."

"Have you ever held a position in your school student government?"

"No." The interview was moving fast. I wiped the sweat off my forehead.

"Do you have a problem with student government?"

"No. I . . . I played baseball all the time, like I told you."

"Do you have a problem with the US government?"

"No, sir."

"Religion?"

"Catholic, sir."

"Last question, Buckle. Give me an example of when you exhibited extreme bravery."

I scanned the flat landscape of my life in search of heroism. At eleven years old, I returned a pack of Lik-M-Aid I'd stolen from the five-and-dime and apologized to the store manager. I was the only kid in my PE class who was able to touch the gymnasium ceiling by climbing the rope. I took Dad down after he belted Mom. How small my world was, I thought.

"Today, sir," I responded. "And my last name is B-U-C-K-L-E-Y."

"Today?"

"Yes." I pointed to my Selective Service application.

"True, Charlton *Buckley*. Quite true. We could use young men like you." Finally, he smiled and rose to shake my hand.

⌒

On a brisk, star-filled night in September, Sandee and I kicked up crisp autumn leaves piled on front yards as we skipped down our street. She stopped and pressed her warm body against mine under the glow of the streetlamp that cast our long shadow down the sidewalk.

"Time to celebrate," she said and kissed me.

"What are we celebrating, San . . ." She kissed me again. "Dee? Dee. Hey, I like that. Kiss me again, *Dee*."

"Two months ago I beat you in our race."

"As I recall, we agreed to a tie."

She slid out two tickets from her bra, giving me a peek at her breasts. "They're both my treat." She winked.

We dashed down Washington Avenue, where bloodcurdling screams pierced the night. The carnival was in town. I pointed toward the entrance, where an army air force recruiting depot had stationed a large blue contraption. It had a B-17 bomber decal attached on its side. Recruiting booths had popped up at banks, grocery stores, and local events, making it feel like World War II was heading to Wauwatosa. I'd never seen anything like this machine before.

"Hold on a minute, Dee." I approached the recruiter. "Sir, why is there a B-17 logo on this?"

"By the looks of your baby face, I'd say you are years away from being able to fly. It's a simulator."

"He just turned eighteen," Sandee interjected.

I looked at Sandee, then stole a peek inside the simulator. "Holy moly! It's really the cockpit of the Flying Fortress B-17."

"I don't think you'll last thirty seconds in the 'Blue Box,' but go ahead," he sneered.

"Don't fly too far, Charlton." Sandee pushed me forward.

I stepped into the small enclosure, shut the door, and took a seat in the dark cockpit. When I placed my hands on the cool levers, the panel lit up. Numbers flashed on the viewing screen at eye level, giving the view out the front window of the cockpit: 3, 2, 1. The Blue Box vibrated and roared its engines. The screen showed a dirt runway with tents sprinkled out in the fields. I pushed the throttle forward. The B-17 sped ahead and lifted off. I was flying! I held the wings level on the altimeter as the bomber burst through the clouds. Two enemy fighters flashed on both sides of the screen. I bobbed and weaved to avoid incoming bullets. I circled around and watched one of the enemy bombers explode and fall from the sky. I kept oscillating the wings to avoid getting hit. After dodging three more enemy fighters, my right wing was hit. The simulator screen went black. Thirty seconds, my foot.

With sweat dripping off my nose, I begged for another round. Sandee grabbed me by the arm and dragged me away.

"How long was I in there?" I yelled back to the recruiter.

"Seven minutes. Come get your wings when you're done riding bicycles, whippersnapper."

The low rumble of the Blue Box was still vibrating inside my chest as we entered the park. I wanted more and prayed I'd be accepted into Selective Service and then on to the air force.

"Let's go inside the haunted house," Sandee suggested.

We kissed while being serenaded by a howling cyclops that was gored with a hook through its midsection. It was too much, so we rode the Ferris wheel. At its apex, I located the AC factory and felt a grip in my gut. I didn't want to spend one more day near those damn boilers or my dad. Wauwatosa looked so small from up high.

As we milled around the grounds looking for a secluded place to kiss, my attention diverted to the shooting gallery. I picked off enough rabbits to win a goldfish, which Sandee named Fin. As we passed the kiddie train, a large automated lever attached to a hitch and boom shifted the track without manpower.

"Hold on a second." I moved closer. "Look at that."

"It's a train track, Charlie. I've seen one before."

"No, no. Look there, on the side of the track. See how that piece of steel moves on its own to switch the gear shaft over the boom? We need something that doesn't use laborers to set the tractor shell on top of our engines to speed up production. And maybe even help automatically move other components."

"I'd like some cotton candy, please."

"Dee, if we can make molds for the next generation of tools, we can add more lines. We'll definitely need more space. There's at least twenty acres behind the factory. Holy mackerel. That's the solution to George's problem. In order to keep up, we automate the tools that we use to assemble!"

Sandee leaned in to kiss me, hoping to take my attention away from tractors.

"I need to write all this stuff down that's rolling around in my brain."

"Pink."

"Huh?"

"*Dee* would like pink cotton candy, please."

I balanced my attention between Sandee and tool automation as she picked away at her pink cotton candy. We hopped on each ride until the park closed. As the strobing carnival lights began to flicker out, Sandee kissed me and ran her fingers though my hair, tugging my ducktail. We walked home with Fin bobbing in her glass bowl.

⌁

Kindling wood snapped in the living room fireplace on a cold November evening. Staring at the painting above the bar, Dad raised his glass to toast the Irish immigrant and took a slug of bourbon, arrogantly defying his doctor's orders. He looked down at the gold cross around his neck.

"Here's to ol' Jesus Christ. May He rise again," he said, wheezing. He was good and saucy. "There'll be no baseball cards and bubble gum in your pack where you're going, lad. Nor will your airplanes be plastic. Bomb the fuck outa them bloody Krauts."

He finished off his drink and set his glass on the bar.

"I'm heading over to Sandee's to help her with her sister."

"What's wrong with her sister?" I'd told him about Eloise more than once, but his mind was mush.

"She's handicapped. Born with a bad spine, remember?" Dad's skin and eyes were yellow again, his stomach distended. His legs shook as he tried to walk. "Let me help you to your chair, Dad."

"Looks like I'm handicapped too." His head drifted to one side after I set him down.

I went to the kitchen to find Mom reading a home magazine at the dinette. I stood in the doorway—half there, half at Sandee's.

"Dad's carburetor on his truck needs replacing. I'll get to it in the morning." I felt guilty for leaving.

"Go. Sandee's waiting." Mom gave me a hug. "Careful not to wake your dad when you come home."

I felt tussled up while walking over the bridge, spinning in a time capsule—my past moving away, my future out of focus. What was clear was my love for Sandee and the possibility that I might be leaving her soon.

We sat in the living room, Sandee's parents on the couch facing us, while Eloise hung on my arm. Dr. Gold was in a chatty mood, asking about the R45 tractor and what components would be different from the R44.

"We're putting off building the prototype for the R45. All our steel has been spoken for by the US Army."

"It's brave of you to apply for war, Charlie," said Mrs. Gold. "My daughter isn't happy about it, which makes me quite unhappy about it."

"Yeah, it's a bad idea to make your girlfriend unhappy," said Eloise. "She may find another beau if you go."

"Shush up, El."

The somber talk about the war quieted the room until Dr. Gold offered a prayer.

"May it be Your will, my God, that You lead this young man, and all young men who have gone to war, toward peace. Rescue them from the hand of any enemy or ambush. Send them blessings, favor, generosity, and mercy in Your eyes and on all eyes who see them. Give them courage and passion to fight for the sacred treasure You have granted them: life."

Finally, after a quick game of cards, Eloise gave me a hug good night as Mr. and Mrs. Gold went off to bed. Finally!

Sandee and I made our way to the basement. I laid my jacket on the concrete floor to use as a makeshift cushion. We'd become skilled at keeping our clothes half on in case anyone came knocking. Our frantic hunger for each other's embrace came from a sense that our time together was limited. My hand slid down her soft cream-colored thighs, stopping between her legs. We stroked each other with a sense of longing and desperation, holding on while we could—until we let go.

Sandee rested her head on my chest for a time, then looked up at me.

"Come to Temple with us Wednesday night," she whispered. "It's Yom Kippur, our most holy holiday." I felt my gut tighten. "I think you'll find it moving, Charlie."

"I'll have to come up with some excuse, tell Dad we're going out to dinner or something."

"My dad will want you to let your parents know." She paused. "It would also mean a lot to me if you fasted."

"Fasted?"

"Do you think you can go without food for twenty-four hours?"

"Not a scrap?"

"Not a scrap," Sandee said, pinching her lips.

I nodded. "Since the day we met, you've always been a step ahead of me. Do you know that?"

"I do."

I'd stayed out of the kitchen, feigning the chills to justify why I wasn't eating. Knowing I couldn't eat made me all the more ravenous. I distracted myself by looking up the basics on Yom Kippur in the *Harmsworth's Universal Encyclopaedia* and read, "Once one atones for personal sins, their fate is sealed for the coming year."

When it was time, I dressed in a suit, and headed for the front door.

"I'm off to Temple with Sandee and her family," I shouted. Dad leaped from his recliner and intercepted me in the hallway.

"You step foot inside that Jew place, you'll not step foot back in this house!" He put his chest against mine. His foul breath smelled of bourbon. Mom rushed over to intercede.

"If he's old enough to go to war, William, he's old enough to go wherever he pleases." Mom was holding a dish she'd prepared for me to take to the Passover meal. I don't know how, but mothers seem to know everything. "I looked it up to make sure it was appropriate for this holiday. I bet you're hungry." She smiled.

"I don't approve!" Dad was gasping for air as I moved past him. "Come back here at once! I'll lock ya out of this house, goddammit!"

"Tomorrow you won't remember what you're saying!" I yelled back.

I raced over to the Golds' house, empowered by my own will. He couldn't stop me. I was my own man now, with nothing to fear.

The car was running as we piled into the Golds' family car.

"Charlie, I'll slide Eloise in the back seat," said Dr. Gold. "Sit by her and hold her up, if you would."

Sandee jumped in from the other side, while her mom sat in the front seat. I put my arm around Eloise to steady her as we pulled away from the house.

"I can be your girlfriend while we ride over," she said.

I turned and saw Dad standing in the driveway. I prayed the Golds didn't see him.

"Just a warning, Charlie," said Dr. Gold. "The last Catholic boy who attended our synagogue was burned at the stake."

"Dad!" yelled Sandee. "Enough of your dumb jokes."

"We're glad you're coming," he added.

The temple was surprisingly simple in decor: dark wood pews, beige carpet, hanging globe light fixtures. No bleeding bodies wearing loincloths hanging from crosses. No saints, no sinners depicted in paintings. Just a floor-to-ceiling cabinet opened by two old men to display the only elaborate item in the synagogue.

"That's the Torah," said Eloise, pinching my arm.

Mrs. Gold rolled Eloise inside the synagogue. Sandee took a black silk yarmulke from the bowl and told me to kiss it and place it on my head, then she kissed me right in front of her father. He never gave a second look and went on hugging his friends. Women came over to kiss Eloise. Men, women, and children were embracing as the rabbi raised his hands, stepped forward, and began singing in rich tenor tones, after which he began his sermon.

"Many synagogues are burning in Poland as we sit here tonight." He paused. "Jews are being moved from the ghettos by German soldiers. To where, God knows. It is within our capacity as Jews, in the midst of great torture and oppression, replete with judgment, to garner our strength as a people, to be transformed even beyond the laws of nature. When days and nights are filled with darkness, let the light of courage find its place. Cleanse and renew within me the calm spirit of trust and peace through atonement."

He kissed his hand and touched the Torah behind him, then returned to the podium.

"We pray, *Ba-ruch a-tah A-do-nai, ro-feh ha-cho-lim*. We praise You, Eternal God of all generations. We welcome this festival of Yom Kippur with open hearts. We assemble together as You redeem our ancestors who were enslaved in Egypt. We are certain You will be our redeemer once again and protect us; watch over us as we seal our fate for the coming year. We are ever mindful of those dwelling in oppression among the oppressors. May all our people who hunger for freedom and justice be satisfied, and may all people live in harmony."

After the service, families gathered around large tables and broke the fast with foods that were new to me: lox and bagels. It took me a few bites to get used to it. I offered Mom's plate of tuna casserole. Sandee smiled and squeezed my knee under the table. Wine was poured generously and often. Sandee and I shared a glass. I admired Eloise's grace as she laughed at the children standing on chairs reciting poems and singing songs, chiming in when she knew the words. The utter lightness and joy in the air seemed foreign in a place of worship: *admission, repentance, forgiveness, acceptance*—all words I'd heard in church but not like this. The words landed softly, with compassion and joy, not forewarning or punitive.

The rabbi finished with the neilah.

"Look at this wonderful mess we've made. Some of you are snoring, others ready for more wine. That's life. We accept it and move forward, knowing our fate is sealed throughout the year. What actions we have taken are in the past as we grab hold of the future with a sense of liberation and freedom. Hear, O Israel, the Lord our God, the Lord is one."

Everyone recited the prayer three times. "Blessed be the name of the glory of His kingdom forever and ever."

As it was time to go, Sandee grabbed my hand.

"Follow me."

Out in the hallway, she handed me a tiny box.

"*Baruch Hashem*, Charlie."

She waited for me to respond in kind.

"*Baruch Hashem*. Did I say it right?"

"Perfectly."

I stripped off the brown paper wrapping. Inside was a bright gold pendant.

"The Star of David. When you miss me, or when you're flying, or falling asleep, hold it and dream of me."

"You didn't have to buy me this."

"I did, Charlton. I don't think I can wait much longer to make love with you. We both know what has to happen before that."

I about fell under weak knees. I placed Sandee's gift inside the pocket of my blazer.

"Hey," I whispered as loudly as I could in the presence of people hugging and kissing both cheeks. "Did you just propose to me?"

"Don't worry," she whispered. "You'll catch up."

CHAPTER 6

On a day that hinted an early winter was coming, a letter arrived, resting on the cherrywood table in the front hall. I carried my fate that was tucked inside this cream-colored envelope to my room. As I walked by Gingersnap's bedroom, I let her know I received a letter from the president of the United States. She jumped up and followed me into my room. I couldn't take any more rejection. I threw the envelope on my bed and began to pace. I went to the window and looked out over Meyer Creek. I blew on the glass and quickly played tic-tac-toe before the steam evaporated. I blew again and wrote Sandee's name—only to see it fade away. Then my own name disappeared. As I looked around my room, the artifacts of my childhood began to fade as well: baseball cards, Little League trophies, my teddy bear, the June Lang pinup, *The Hobbit*, *The Story of Ferdinand*, and my favorite book series, Bomba, the Jungle Boy, about a thirteen-year-old who fights off jaguars, vultures, pumas, vampire bats, and the most terrifying characters of all: the Sleeping Souls, who were the ghostly devils of the jungle. I'd force Gingersnap to playact *Jungle Boy* with me, jumping from bed to bed, wearing a washrag as my loincloth, wielding a fake sword, terrorizing her with my screams while warding off the Sleeping Souls. How brave I was. Certainly, more than I felt opening the letter.

"Let me open it, Charlie. Please!" She picked it up and carefully opened it and read it out loud.

The Office of
THE PRESIDENT OF THE UNITED STATES

September 30, 1944
Charlton Antonio Buckley
Order no. 2317

Having submitted yourself to a local board, composed of your neighbors, for the purposes of determining your availability for training and service in the UNITED STATES ARMED FORCES, you are hereby ordered to report for the Selective Service, US Army Air Corps Training Command at Chanute Field, Rantoul, Illinois. Transportation will pick you up at your home on October 11, 1944, at 0500 hours. Provided you pass the physical and academic exams, you will report to orientation.

From there you will enter basic and technical training and receive your general education degree. Given your specific work experience and high school aptitude in the sciences, you are classified as an officer-in-training candidate and will be evaluated for placement based on your strengths and the needs of the military. Failure to report will result in fines and imprisonment. The local board will furnish you with transportation. Bring this letter with you. If you fail your exam, you will be returned to your local board. Bring sufficient clothing for three days.

Corporal James T. McGraw

Gingersnap threw the letter on the bed and stormed out. I picked it up and went back to the window to look at Sandee's house. Everything was about to change.

On my final shift at AC Machinery, George put me to his final test. After disassembling and reassembling different sections of the R44 for weeks, it was time to go for the patch and build the King in less than three hours. All the machines powered down, ending the night shift. The air went still. No new engineers had succeeded in making the time the last two years because the designers and tech guys had added hydraulic technology to keep up with the Fordson tractors sold in Detroit.

The truckers ran their own game, laying bets on whether I'd make it. I watched Dad walk over to one of the boilers and give him some money. Dad stole a glance at me, hoping I didn't see him betting against me, no doubt.

George twinkled those blueberry eyes.

"Since this is it, kid, let's show them what you're made of."

I circled all the parts lying on the ground, ready to be pieced together like a puzzle. A total of 104 moves would complete the build. I went through each sequence, visualizing every turn until the horn went off, indicating it was time for the regular shift to begin their work and for me to start assembling. A symphony of clings and clangs, knocks and bangs, and machine-gun-style hand drills echoed off the steel walls. I put my head down and dug in. Time slowed. Each section flowed seamlessly to the next: the fuel pump, oil pressure switch, hydraulic oil drain plug, and lower-drive transmission gears with the shaft and bearings came together according to plan. An R44 Silver King was being born in my hands.

"Go away. You're making me nervous," I said to Dad when he came over.

"Ya smarter than I ever was," he said and retreated back to the loading area.

I lifted my head deep into the build to wipe the sweat off my brow and looked for George. I found him nodding encouragement. I took the extension telescoping rod with the small loop at the top and slipped it into the lower steering shaft to lock in the column. As I came to the last component, the hydraulic brake system, something looked terribly wrong. The way the disc pads were normally constructed was to rest one cylinder onto the other to displace the fluid when under pressure, but the second cylinder was covered with a clear, slippery coating. If I installed it as is, there'd be no traction. The damn disc pads wouldn't hold with all this crap over it. Someone had monkeyed with a cylinder. I took a cloth to wipe the disc, but it only made it worse. I held the cylinder, praying either the coating would magically disappear or I would. The sweat dripped off my nose. I wanted to ask George for help, but that would have disqualified me. I kept twirling the disc pad, getting more anxious.

With twelve minutes left, my stomach flipped. I remembered a time when Rails and I dug grooves with a knife into our bikes' brake pads to increase the traction so we could screech to a halt and pop wheelies. If I gouged grooves into the single master cylinder and chucked the violated second cylinder, it could work. It also might make the tractor a tad lighter, which would save the owner money on gas. And getting rid of one cylinder would save the company about ten greenbacks per tractor. My hands moved with precision. With the pointed edge of a diamond-head screwdriver, I dug ruts on the side of the cylinder that made contact with the pad. As I dropped it in place, secured the wheels, and drilled on the shell, I fell to my knees. I looked around for Dad to tell him I'd finished. But he was nowhere to be seen.

"I'm done!" I yelled.

The mechanics whistled with approval.

"You rascal, you did it with three minutes to spare," said George.

Everyone who worked at AC gathered around Foreman Kelly while he inspected my build. After a lengthy discussion between the foreman and his two senior engineers, he gave my brake system a thumbs-up and told me to mount the tractor. George sported a wide grin. I turned over the ignition and lined up on the far side of the factory.

"Call out the speed when you hit its maximum!" yelled Foreman Kelly.

He hit the horn, and off I went. "Five!" I prayed the brakes would hold at the end. "Six!" The designers had the R44 max out at 7 mph.

I pushed the pedal to the metal and closed in on the finish line precisely ten feet from the steel wall. I blinked to peek at the speedometer. "Eight! Eight miles per hour!" I screamed while hitting the brakes. The R44 dug in. The pad grabbed the grooves on the cylinder and came to an abrupt halt. The workers blew the factory roof off with cheers. The engineers threw up their arms and shook their heads in disbelief. George rushed over, his eyes misty, beaming with pride, and presented me with the patch.

O'Leary demanded to know how I'd made the R44 fly.

"One of the brake cylinders was covered with a slick coating. It probably came from the supplier like that. So I cut grooves into the good cylinder and tossed the other one aside. That was that."

"Have your mom sew that patch on your shoulder," said George. "If you decide to come back to work at AC after the war, wear it with pride. Heck, you might even end up taking my job one day." He gave me a wink, burrowing those deep-set wrinkles. "I have a confession to make, Charlie. I knew you could put that forty-four together in time. I put the goop on the cylinder to see how you'd think on your feet. You're ready for whatever comes at you, young man. Don't let anyone tell you otherwise."

"It was you?" I never heard George laugh so hard.

I rode my bike back home brimming with confidence, zipping along an old railroad that was once used to bring coal in for the winter. I caught sight of a white owl that whooshed into the pine trees. I hit the skids and watched the owl take its majestic position. I pulled out my R44 patch and let it unfold in my palm.

"I'm taking this with me to Chanute Field as a good luck charm and pass all those damn tests and become a pilot," I yelled to the owl.

I came inside the house through the side door. Mom had drifted despondently into the shadows since the day I'd received my orders to report, so it was nice to see her sporting a wide grin.

"I heard from Beverly. Congratulations on your patch, Charlie. What a wonderful way to finish your time at AC. I'm sure George will miss you." She moved to the stove. "I'll make you two strip steaks, and you tell me all about it."

"George tried to sabotage the entire brake system as a test, but I figured it out."

"That's wonderful."

"Dad left the factory, didn't see me get my patch."

"He's in bed. Having stomach pain again. Don't say I said so."

I slammed my hand against the wall. "Why can't you see it for what it is, Mom? He can't stand to see me do something he can't."

She looked down at her gardening shoes. "I don't think you believe that's true, Charlton."

I let it go. I wasn't at war with her. It was with him.

"Heard you're a big man now, winning that patch," sang Gingersnap as she entered the kitchen. "And now—you're leaving." She shook my firefly jar and opened the lid. "I'll keep this while you're gone."

"Catch a bunch for me, and keep beating those Stevenson boys," I said and gave her a hug.

"They're too easy." She began to cry, which was rare. I held her until she pushed me away. "Go kiss your girlfriend. I'll be fine. Just don't get dead."

"I'll remember that."

⌇

The grandfather clock struck five. It was still dark outside. Rain dropped syncopated beats on the gutters all night as I lay staring at the pine ceiling, wondering what lay ahead until I saw the headlights of the army van crawling up in the driveway. The letter from the office of the president and three days of clothing were neatly folded into my green duffel bag. I went into Gingersnap's room to kiss her goodbye. She barely stirred. The bruises on her arm had faded.

I made my way to the front door, where Dad was waiting, freshly shaven, wearing his Sunday best. His suit had outgrown him, as had I. He reached out his quivering hand for me to shake, but I put my arms around him instead. After a short moment of embrace, he pulled away, unable to tolerate the intimacy.

"Make me proud" was all he could mumble.

Mom looked pale, her eyes fluttering. She forced a smile to ease my nerves, but that only made it worse. "Put this fruitcake in your bag. I don't want you going hungry."

Dad and Mom stayed inside as I walked outside to find Sandee standing under the porch light. She swallowed a helping of panic. Her eyes swelled with tears.

"You're gonna pass, Charlton Buckley. I'll write as soon as you send me your . . ."

The driver honked, drowning out her last words. I kissed her too quickly. Within a blink of an eye, I was with her—and then, I wasn't.

A hard shower pelted the van as we banked the creek. None of the guys were talking, perhaps too nervous like I was. I tried my best to not look back but couldn't help myself. My house disappeared as we rounded the bend.

Before exiting the neighborhood, I caught sight of an older man holding an umbrella under the glow of the kerosene streetlamp, the light flickering on his wrinkled face. It was the King of Kings, George Underwood, sending me off—waving an American flag.

CHAPTER 7

—————————

Chanute Field was soaked with puddles that looked like abstract mirrors reflecting the gray sky across the airfield. After filing out of the van, we splashed our way over to a two-story brick building. Inside, the linoleum corridors teemed with cadets scrambling from one room to the next. I found my name card on the registration table. *Charlton A. Buckley, Hangar 1, Tent C, Cot Forty-One.*

Chanute Field erected five enormous tents inside hangar 1 to accommodate the onslaught of hopeful, fresh-faced eighteen-year-olds from the central Midwest, all wandering around looking for their cots as the rain came in rushes, battering the steel roof of the hangar. I was happy to see a bag lunch waiting for me on mine. I downed a jar of baked beans and ham, two pieces of white bread, and a chocolate bar for dessert. Afterward, I went to look over the planes that were parked under hangar 2. A mechanic was working on a model I'd never seen or read about in my pilot journals. The guy looked to be replacing a hydraulic fuel line, but I wasn't sure.

"Do you mind telling me the type of bird you're working on?" I asked.

"A-20 Havoc," he answered, keeping his eye on his mark. "You'll see a lot of her—if the air corps is what you're after."

"It is."

He offered a genuine smile. "Good luck to you, pal."

I hung around the hangar the rest of the day, watching surgeons with grease on their hands operate on one bird after another until it was time for me to meet our staff sergeant back at the main field.

I looked up at the cloudy slate sky stretching over us like a wrinkled bedsheet. A light drizzle spit over a hundred pairs of wide eyes. Some stood tall and still, while others rocked back and forth, looking at their boots. A short-legged sergeant with a barrel chest marched toward the front, as if holding a magazine between his butt cheeks. His black shoes were gleaming. Commendation stripes were lined from his elbow to his shoulder. He made his way to the center and examined his new recruits. He remained quiet until his thin voice broke the silent air.

"Attention," he said, then went quiet. I wondered if he had forgotten the script or was just relishing in his own aura. Finally, he continued, "Good afternoon, boys. I'm Staff Sergeant James Rockwell. Did you notice I just called you *boys*, not gentlemen? Why? Because you're a bunch of snotty-nosed, shitty little boys that don't deserve to be called gentlemen. A hundred pussy-know-nothings. Am I correct?"

"Yes, sir," we stuttered in bemusement.

"Am I *correct*?"

"Yes, sir!"

He closed his eyes, and after a silent meditation, he continued, gaining authority with each word.

"You've been coddled your entire short life, turned flaccid by your mommies and daddies, impotent from the great Industrial Revolution— turning your gut to goop. You're as soft as piglets sucking on their sow."

He turned skyward. "This may be impossible for you to comprehend. You're going to die. Some of you soon, some down the line. What will you be thinking before you take your last breath—if there's time? That I never escaped, even for a moment, my little world, what I wanted, what I needed? I-I-I . . . that *I* finally achieved the American Dream by selling more insurance than was necessary to collect higher commissions to buy useless gadgets destined for the garbage dump located across the highway from a graveyard filled with the bones of men who sacrificed nothing?"

Sergeant Rockwell was fulminating, swinging both arms, punctuating the end of every sentence with a violent nod.

"Men are dying as I speak. Do you understand this? A young man is *dying* on the battlefield to defend the liberties you've enjoyed as little shits. The air you breathe, the food you eat, the life you live, you owe to the men who died for you. It's high time you pay it back with your service, and maybe your life, to defend the freedom you and your family and the citizens of the United States of America have had the privilege to enjoy."

I'd had tough coaches in my life, but I'd never felt more pressure to do as I was told. It was only three months ago that baseball ended for me, but I missed that authoritative intensity, being pushed to win at all costs. I couldn't wait to crush the tests and begin my training and fly a bomber into war.

"If some of you are too ignorant to absorb what I'm saying, let me make this easier for you to understand: Look to your left. Now look to your right. You hold their lives in your hands. If you give your heart and soul to the US Army, by God, I promise you, the US Army will never let you down. Who wants to become a real *gentleman*?"

We roared, "I do, sir!"

Sergeant James Rockwell raised his chin and returned to his thin voice.

"The physical examinations, aptitude test, and lastly, the endurance run will commence tomorrow, 0600 hours. Don't eat. Nobody wants to clean up your mess when you vomit after the run. If you score more than 60 out of 75 points, you will be placed in one of our training camps around the country. You may not request where to be stationed. Once you enlist, you're the property of the US Army. If you fail your tests, transportation will take you home—to suck on your sow."

I went back to hangar 2 and stayed there until lights out; I wanted to be near those planes. I placed my hand on the belly of one of the brawny bombers and felt the vibration of my future.

I woke in the middle of the night, startled by the thunder. I looked up at the rows and rows of cots filled with guys who'd be defending freedom roughly four thousand miles away. *Who will fail the tests among this group? Will I make it through and be sent to war after my training, pull a trigger, drop a bomb? I'll make Sandee proud. An army man I'll be, don a uniform, come back having served my country. Where will I be stationed? Will Sandee be able to leave her family to come visit me on the base? What would it be like if bombs rained down on the hangar right now—like at Pearl Harbor?* My mind was racing. I took from my pocket the R44 patch that George had awarded me and squeezed it with my shaking fist as it hit me: I feared getting killed at war and yearned for home, for Sandee. I wasn't alone. Others were stirring in their cots, perhaps missing *their* gals or mothers and fathers, dogs, or pals. I even missed Rails. I fell back to sleep to the sound of rain.

The rising sun beamed though the windows into the linoleum corridors of the main building crowded with frantic recruits trying to find where the tests were being administered. We all wanted in—a hundred young cubs ready to become kings of the jungle. You could feel the collective energy bouncing off the walls from a pack of restless eighteen-year-olds hoping to become "gentlemen." All eyes were searching, no one talking, everyone in their own uncertain world.

I found my exam room, where the auditor handed me a blue booklet and recorded my start time. I sat next to guys already scratching away. The questions on the exam ranged from math fractions to identifying public leaders and poets. There was a quote I knew that I'd studied during my senior year, and luckily, I remembered who wrote the quotation: "If she'd but turn her head, you'd know the folly of being comforted." William Butler Yeats. The last question asked: Who is the current secretary of state? Cordell Hull. As I closed the booklet, I heard a familiar voice.

"Buckley, I'm blanking here," whispered Buddy Davis, a fellow classmate from my high school. I didn't know him well but knew that he was a decorated track-and-field athlete. "What's the capital of New York?"

"Albany. Great to see a familiar face."

"We're gonna be real soldiers, Buckley. What tent are you in?"

"C. My cot is in the far north corner."

"Shut up over there, kike!" said a fella, staring at me from behind Buddy.

"Do you know why the fuck we're fighting this war?" Buddy shot back. "Because of assholes like you."

The auditor put her finger to her lips.

"Forget him," Buddy whispered. "I'm hoping to get into the air force."

"Me too. Let's both make it in. I'll see you at the endurance run."

"Deal."

"See you at the race, Jew nose," said the asshole as I walked by him.

"If you're lucky enough to pass the tests, pray that Jesus keeps you out of my infantry," I shot back. "And I'm not even—"

"Shush!" the auditor hissed. "Or I'll throw out your tests."

I didn't even know there was such a thing as a Jew nose.

We waited hours in line to see the eye doctor. Nobody said much; most of the guys looked at their shoes. I wasn't worried, though. I could see a baseball coming at seventy-five miles per hour and tell if it was a curve, slider, or fastball by how the stitches were spinning. Finally, it was my turn to go in.

"I'm Doc Olsen." He wore thick glasses. Rails would have made some bad joke on that one. "Let's see how your peepers are doing. Call out the letters of the smallest line you're able to read on that board over there."

I rubbed my eyes and read the bottom line. "A-E-C-F-O-T-N."

"Well, okay then. We're done here. Head over to see the physician in room 73A."

The physical exam took place in a science lab; black-topped islands, stainless steel sinks, and natural gas spouts to heat up the beakers filled the room. White bedsheets covered the windows for privacy. The thin-lipped doctor with a flattop pointed me toward the scale. "Strip down to your boxers," he ordered. "Height and weight." He never mentioned his name, never shook my hand. I wouldn't have wanted this guy at my bedside with his manner. "Five feet ten, one hundred seventy pounds," he mumbled.

"I grew two inches in a year?" I asked, in disbelief. He didn't seem to care as he peppered me with questions.

"Any ailments, chronic conditions, sexually transmitted diseases?"

"No, sir."

"Voices in your head, delusions?"

He was jotting down my responses without facing me.

"No, sir. I'm not crazy if that's what you mean."

"Uh-huh. Pull down your drawers." He took hold of my nuts. "Cough. Now open your mouth and say *ahh*. Okay, lie down." He felt my abdomen. "Okay, let me look at your feet. We're done."

I nodded and headed out for the final test: the two-mile endurance run. I wriggled into a pair of shorts and a T-shirt and laced up a floppy pair of sneakers provided by the army. The track was sloppy from the rain. I checked out the other guys to see which runners had the longest legs, wanting to determine who might pose the greatest challenge. I found Buddy stretching his hamstrings and sidled up next to him. The good nerves were back; the buzz of competition was flowing throughout my body. How I missed this feeling.

I followed Buddy to the starting line. I figured I'd put in a good enough time if I stayed close with him to the end. The lieutenant yelled for everyone to toe the line. Buddy gave me a wink as the gun went off. I exploded into a full-on sprint, then kicked it back to an easy stride, taking the early lead. The pack of runners who trailed my tail at the half-mile mark had dwindled down to just three. Buddy was leading them. The headwind was strong as we turned into the second mile just as my left sneaker slipped off. I kicked off the other one to balance my stride and was now running barefoot. *Sandee would be proud.*

I could hear Buddy's steady breath closing in on me. My burning feet skipped along the wet track. I picked up the pace, shortened my stride, and kept my elbows in tight. Buddy burned the turn and met my eyes as we made for the final bend. I opened up my stride out of the curve and turned it on down the stretch, compartmentalizing the pain from blisters forming on my feet. Buddy moved ahead of me. Then I pulled ahead of him, using all the energy I had left in the tank. Buddy's legs were too long and edged me at the finish line.

Buddy showed real class by retrieving my sneakers, then keeled over and threw up his breakfast.

"Mom calls me Pepto-miserable 'cause I always do that after my races."

His kindness took away the sting from losing to him. As did knowing we put in a great time.

"Nice kick, Buddy," I huffed. "I thought I had you."

"You would've if you hadn't run out of your sneakers." Buddy grinned, showing off his million-dollar smile. "Let's show them that us guys from a small town like Wauwatosa can earn their wings with the best of them. What do you say, Buckley?"

"I say, I'm all in."

The next morning, one hundred of us sat on folding chairs under two large maple trees fronting the officers' building. We waited one by one for our names to be called. Buddy was biting his nails. A panic was building inside my chest, so I focused on the scent of freshly cut, wet grass to calm the nerves.

"Good luck to you, Mathew," the staff sergeant said. Mathew, looking forlorn, was sent packing. "Charlton Antonio Buckley." My heart jumped.

He led me into his office lined with photos of military depots, dignitaries, and declaration certificates. A golf-ball-sized lump formed in my throat. The sergeant took a seat behind his desk and flipped through the test results and application form. I gripped my legs with both hands to steady my knees.

"Relax, Buckley. You scored near the top." He continued fingering through the paperwork. "However . . ." He paused. "During your initial interview, our recruiting officer had some concern about your homelife. In particular, you mentioned your father hating 'Nips and Krauts.'" *Dad was going to ruin this for me.* "We don't use those terms from army men representing the United States of America. We fight, we win, we don't disparage. We call them our *enemy*, not Nips or Krauts. Understood?"

"I've never used that language, sir."

"You want to join the air force?"

"Yes, sir. More than anything."

"Attention, Private Buckley." I stood up. "Private Charlton Antonio Buckley, you've been accepted into the United States Army Air Force flight program at Myrtle Beach Army Airfield located in Horry, South Carolina." He handed me an envelope. "Honor your country. And if you enter the theater, finish this damn war. Take the letter out and read it aloud, and if you accept the order, sign it."

"Yes, sir!"

"Private Charlton Antonio Buckley, number 4243486, mindful of the secret trust about to be placed in me by my commander in chief, the president of the United States, by whose direction I have been chosen, and mindful of the fact that I am to become guardian of one of my country's most priceless military assets, do here, in the presence of Almighty God, swear by the pilot code of honor to keep inviolate the secrecy of any and all confidential information revealed to me, and further to uphold the honor and integrity of the army air forces, if need be, with my life itself."

"Any and all information that's revealed to you under the pilot code of honor is confidential," added the sergeant. "Do you understand?"

"Yes, sir!"

I signed the letter and thrust my fist into the air and saluted.

On my way out, I saw Buddy Davis sporting a shit-eating grin. I didn't need to ask to know we had both made it into the air force. The question was: Where would we be training?

"On three," I said. "One, two, three!"

"South Carolina!" We shouted and slapped each other on the shoulder and ran over to the cutters' tent, where we, *snotty-nosed, shitty little boys*, would make our first sacrifice to our country.

After the clipper cruised my cranium, leaving my black hair on the floor, I found a phone booth and jammed two nickels in the slot and dialed Sandee's number. On the third ring, Mrs. Gold answered. She was so excited I was calling she went on and on about the late heat wave and running into Mom at the butcher and how she knew Dad preferred extra marble in his strip steak. I only had a minute left on my nickels and asked for Sandee again.

"Charlie?"

"They cut off all my hair, Dee." She was breathing heavy. I wanted to jump through the phone and kiss her.

"I never had any doubts you'd make it in," she whispered, with trepidation.

"They're sending me to South Carolina." The next caller banged on the double-hinged doors. "My nickel's about worn out. I . . . I love you," I said. The line went dead. I said it again, just in case she could hear me.

CHAPTER 8

I was assigned a room in what had been an old wooden slave owner's home converted to a dorm that had been named after the Confederate Civil War general Stonewall Jackson. The dorm was part of the Myrtle Beach Army Airfield in the town of Horry, South Carolina. My roommate was listening to Frank Sinatra on his transistor radio when I walked in. He jumped to his feet and saluted me as if I were a general.

"Calvin Wiggins. Call me 'Wigs.' You got to be Charlton," he said.

Calvin had already settled in and chose his bed next to the window. He was built strong from the ground up, standing over six feet tall, with blue eyes, blond curly hair, and Hollywood good looks. He grabbed my duffel bag and threw it clear across the room, landing on my bunk.

"Yowee, my head feels naked," he continued. "This here's my first clip since I had to go on the lam a few years back on account of my dang brother. The fool stole a car, and shoot me stupid, I was with him. Damn it all if Mac didn't get me in trouble at least once a week. The cops netted him like a fish while he was fucking his gal in the shed. But when the cops approached the house, I skedaddled out my window into the woods. I knew every branch and rock out there, but it still gave me the willies at night. Ended up under a bridge until Mammy, my grandma, paid off one of the sheriffs so I could go home. She hugged me for a week."

I went to unpack my bag, thinking this guy could talk.

"One of the poor suckers I was hiding with under a bridge had a talent for cutting hair, Charlton. He clipped mine like my man Jingo Jones, the best clipper in Opelika, Alabama. That's home."

I could hardly understand a word he was saying with his thick southern accent, but I liked him from the get-go.

"Call me Charlie. Pleased to meet you, Wigs."

"Now, Charlie, I'm the navigation officer, and you're the lead dog. Got it? The buck stops with you. In fact, I'm calling you Buck! That's short for Buckley." He laughed and slapped his knee. "And you're gonna eat them greens and get eight hours of shut-eye."

I opened the window because the heat was oppressive. I looked out and took in the rising moon over a lagoon.

"This heat here ain't nothing, Buck," Wigs said. "Work a farm for a day during the summer in Opelika and you'll know real heat. Tilling dry land for peas under the fucking sun ain't no picnic. Go take a dip in that lagoon out back. I did after I got here. That'll cool ya off."

"No, thank you. We don't have alligators in Wisconsin."

Wigs turned the transistor dial to Glenn Miller while I finished unpacking and spread out on my bed. The music was interrupted with an emergency news report.

"Governments of the United States, Britain, and the Soviet Union have just issued a joint declaration. German authorities, not content with denying persons of the Jewish race the most elementary human rights, are now carrying into effect Hitler's oft-repeated intention to exterminate the Jewish people of Europe . . ."

"Jesus fucking Christ. I'll change the dial—"

"No, Wigs! Keep it there."

"Poland has been made the principal Nazi slaughterhouse. The ghettos established by the German invaders are being systematically emptied of all Jews, except a few highly skilled workers required for war industries. None taken away have been heard from again. The victims are innocent men, women, and children in the hundreds of thousands in mass executions. The able-bodied are slowly worked to death in labor camps."

"It's all coming out now," said Wigs. "Hitler's a fucking mushroom. My oldest brother, Brig, he called anything he thought would kill ya a 'fucking mushroom.' Poison, a piece of rotten meat. Hey, why don't I buy us a couple of soda pops? Be right back."

"Before you go, can you spare a couple sheets of paper? I want to write my mom."

"They sell these fucking Christian notepads of Jesus walking on water at the little drugstore next to the commissary. Somehow it found its way into my pocket." He laughed and threw one over to me.

"You better lose that habit, or you'll be back living under a bridge." I picked up my pencil and started writing.

> Dear Mom,
>
> Thank God, they clipped my hair. It's a burner down here. They said they were going to move the running drills to sunrise to avoid the afternoon heat. Most of the classes are gonna be tough: formation, engagement, simulation, enemy-bird identification. No time off for Christmas. Seems the war isn't about to lose its flame anytime soon.
>
> I received a "sugar report" from Sandee my first day—a love letter in military jargon. Give Gingersnap a hug, and tell Mrs. Underwood to say hi to George for me. I miss him.
>
> I wish I was home to catch the last of the firefly season.
>
> Yours, Charlie

After two weeks of classes, flight simulation, and two air training flights with our instructor, Wigs and I were ready to make our first solo in an A-20 Havoc.

"Follow the manifest plan!" our instructor shouted. "And remember, you only fly your first flight once, so enjoy it!"

I unfolded the flight plan.

Formation/10,000 feet
Cap/eight-mile radial circumference in formation
Return to base

"Did you wear your diapers, Buckley?" yelled Buddy Davis.
"Hope not to need 'em, wise guy. Good luck on your first wheels-up."
"You too."
The Havoc's pilot seat was positioned high in the nose with the copilot sitting right behind. Wigs had to scrunch his long legs to fit.
"Let's go over the ground checks," I said. "Fuel switches?"
"Check."
"Tires, cells, fuselage leaks?"
"Check. Dry as a bone, Buck."
"How about the nose pin?"
"Nose pin. Where's that?" he asked.
"Not funny, Wigs."
"Locked. We're all set, Private Buckley."
The A-20 Havoc bomber resembled a portly schoolgirl wearing thick glasses. It was a wonder she was able to get off the ground. The flight manifesto indicated she had below-average thrust and lacked agility, born to carry enormous bombs, not complete daredevil maneuvers. We plodded our way down the dirt runway, slowly gaining speed.
"What a fatso!" Wigs yelled.
"Patience. Ninety-four . . . ninety-seven . . . ninety-nine . . ." The simulator had us separate at precisely ninety-nine miles per hour, but here we were at one hundred. My knee shook. *Up we go, please.*
Finally, her nose lifted, and we divinely separated from Mother Earth. The ground shrank below as I guided her into the sky.
"Gears up."
"Check."
"Cross-feed off?"
"Check. We're doing it, Buck!"

The perspective high above ground seemed to relax every nerve in my body; my senses were keenly receptive to the hydraulic system, fuel injection, and turbulence friction. Each vibration in my hands was filled with information. I was hooked.

We circled the base with two other Havocs on our wings in accordance with the flight plan, then made our approach. At the last few feet of altitude, a nasty gust of wind tipped the right wing. I overcompensated and dropped her too quickly, causing three violent bounces.

"Wheels down, Buck. And whatever you hit, you killed."

"Very funny, funny man. I like giving a little love tap before I lay my gal down," I boasted to cover my embarrassment. I was shaking mad at myself.

"Like a dame with two big titties, thumpedy-thump. I knew a gal with legs up to her chest. One bucking filly, I'll tell you. She cracked me in half." We taxied back to the hangar and parked. "Let's get some grub," he added. "I'm starving."

"What else is new? You go ahead. I'm heading to the simulator to work on my damn landings."

Buddy hung out with me in my dorm room, getting some rest before our night class, while Wigs was lifting weights at the gym for the second time that day.

"Want to know how the *Reader's Digest* began?" I asked.

"Nope. Sleeping here," responded Buddy, sacked out on the couch.

"The guy who started it was in the war. His leg got messed up from shrapnel."

"Still sleeping."

"He started writing a bunch of one-page articles on stupid stuff you could read fast. Get a bite and move on."

"I'm gonna take a bite out of you if you don't shut up and let me rest."

Wigs rushed in, soaking wet from the rain.

"Something's up, guys. While I was lifting, Sergeant Willis came in. Wants to see us in his office, pronto, Buck."

My knee started shaking. *I'm being held back because of my landings. Or let go. Maybe Mom is sick or Gingersnap drowned in the creek.* Good thoughts never came easy. The bad ones always seemed to cut the line. I threw on my sneakers and headed out.

Wigs and I waggled off the rain and walked down the long corridor adorned with military photos. One was of soldiers at the end of World War I giving themselves a champagne shower. That was what I wanted, instead of being sent to the sergeant's office for who knows what. A couple of lieutenants walked by us. I tried to read them for clues but got no-look flybys. We rounded the corner and heard shouting coming from Sergeant Willis's office. Bad mood. Not good. He was on the phone and waved us in.

"I don't give a piss about the Girl Scouts of America. And don't tell me it's not patriotic. That's horseshit! We're not moving our drills because you'd rather line your pocket with charity money for their annual what the fuck . . . unless *we* get some of that charity money for some new simulators, you're shit outa luck." Sergeant Willis smiled at us. "What's that? Well . . . truly, it would break my heart to say no to those darling Girlie Scouts. We'll move the drills over to Lang Field so you can set up your booths. Love to Marge and the kids." He put down the receiver with a smirk.

"Gentlemen, keep working hard because we're going to push you to get your wings faster than any air force school in the country. Tonight, I'm giving you leave to go into town and enjoy yourselves because you won't see another single day off going forward. Curfew is at midnight. Dismissed."

Halfway back to the dorm, we realized we were so excited we'd forgotten to salute Sergeant Willis on our way out.

～

Wigs, Buddy, and I hit the Cock-N-Bull after dinner. The bar was located on a seedy side street in downtown Horry. We made our way through the smoke-filled, low-lit room, which was jumping, and settled into a leather booth. Ladies of the night were stationed at the far end of the grimy bar. Hard drinks were served one after another by two colored fellas without much expression.

Wigs popped a dime in the slot and punched the Delta Rhythm Boys on the spiffy Wurlitzer jukebox. I'd never seen women in public dancing like they were having sex, grinding their hips and all. The drink I ordered packed a punch. I looked at one of the ladies at the bar. She caught my eye and smiled. I wasn't used to drinking and had downed a second one before Buddy spun another song in the juke. The lady who smiled at me came over, grabbed my arm, pulled me onto the dance floor, and went into some of her gyrations. I could feel her sweat on my cheek. She pushed her groin against me. I pulled back, but she kept holding on. I thought she was hoping for a little more than a dance, so when the song ended, I escaped her clutches and went back to our booth.

I slammed my fist down on the table and made an announcement to the fellas.

"I'm telling you guys a secret 'cause you're my best friends," I shouted, louder than necessary. "Here it is: I'm in love with Sandee. I really, really love her!"

"We know," said Wigs.

"You don't understand. Sandee, she's the real McCoy. When things got bad at home, she was there, right there for me, right smacking there. My dad . . . he's pretty much an SOB. He's sad all the time . . . he hates himself, takes it out on us. He practically pulled off Gingersnap's arm before I left. Sandee understands when I get upset." I was letting it all out. "But, oh, what a day. Guys! I'm going to become a pilot! Sandee loves me—a lot. I'm dead serious."

"You're dead drunk," Buddy said.

"I *really*, really love her. You know . . . she beat me in a footrace when we first met . . . her skin is so soft . . . well, we tied. She . . . she thinks she beat me . . . oh . . . I love her. I just do . . ."

A different lady, or I thought it was a different one, brought me back on the dance floor, but I couldn't see straight. I couldn't tell if I was dancing with one or four of those girls. I shook my hips and spun in circles until my stomach rebelled.

While Wigs and Buddy closed down the bar, I was throwing up in the men's room. Afterward, they walked me back to the dorm and deposited me in my bed.

～

The pace of training was out of control. Buddy would yell at the instructors for skipping sections in the manuals and ignoring case studies. Even the officers seemed frustrated. We put together our own study groups and tried to cover as much material to fill in the blanks, while Wigs and I flew as many air hours as they could give us. At one of our study group sessions during breakfast, Buddy shared news from overseas. He was always on the minute with the latest developments.

"Hell of a battle going on near Aachen, Germany, and the Hürtgen Forest. Our boys are locked in dragon's teeth. Fucking heroes." Then Buddy displayed the October issue of *Life* magazine he'd picked up at the commissary. On page three was a photo displaying three American soldiers lying dead on the shoreline with maggots crawling out of their mouths; half their bodies were submerged under water on Normandy Beach from the battle back in June. I hated to think of Sandee and Mom seeing this.

"The squeeze is on, fellas," said Buddy. "Get ready to strap in. We're sure to be part of it soon."

"Let's avoid that beach, Buck. Lordy Jesus, if my mama sees this, she'll die from worry."

Buddy read the caption.

"Why show three dead American boys washed up on foreign soil? Why succumb to the War Department's request for wanting the American people to face not with words but with pictures of their own dead that will be seared into our minds? The answer is chiseled into monuments erected in town squares all across our brave country."

"Malarkey!" Wigs shouted with tears in his eyes. "They printed that photo to sell their fucking magazines on the backs of our dead soldiers."

Wigs grabbed the magazine and slammed it down and stormed out. He might have been worried sick about his mama seeing that photo, but in reality, he saw himself lying there on that beach—his head blown to bits. He wasn't the only one rattled. I went back to the dorm to put on my running sneakers to shake the image of those guys dead and rotting on that beach and hit the trail out back that went deep into the woods.

Running over the red dirt cleared my mind. The woods brought me back to the forest preserve behind our house. I pushed as fast as I could go, sprinting toward the war. After a while I stopped to catch my breath and looked through the tree branches toward the sun. *Was I ready?* I'd passed all my series-level-five exams in preparation to fly in the theater. The next-generation C-47 was the bird I'd hoped to be flying while dropping bombs or paratroopers. I'd studied every inch of her. She was a beast. Her wings spread out 95.3 feet, weighed 65,500 pounds, and flew at 35,600 feet at a speed of 155 miles per hour with a 1,600-mile range. I couldn't wait to get her up in the air to help end this war.

CHAPTER 9

I was locked on our target as vibrations rumbled into every part of my body. At ten thousand feet, I engaged the final mission that would earn our wings if executed successfully. After blazing through the curriculum and flying the Havoc every two days for nine weeks, we were to drop two dummy bombs on a train track running along abandoned farmland.

"Three minutes, Wigs. Turn off the cross-feeds."

"Check."

Thick clouds bounced us around as we descended on a dormant cotton field with dilapidated structures dotting an old plantation.

"Are those cross-feeds off?"

"Check!" yelled Wigs.

"They don't like feel it. I'm pulling to one side."

"They're off, but you're right, Bucko. Hate to stall out before we make the drop."

"We're not going to stall out because we're not banking. We're sitting at 130 degrees." I was trying to convince myself we were okay, but I wasn't certain. "Are the cowl flaps completely closed?"

"Check!"

"Are you sure? I don't like this, Wigs. I'm holding."

I was breathing heavy, my heart pounding against my ribs. I'd wanted to be a pilot since the fourth grade and was so close, but was in a panic. I closed my eyes and felt George Underwood divinely enter my mind right when I needed him most—the vision of him under the lamppost on that misty morning, sending me off, waving the American flag calmed my nerves.

We leveled off.

"Wigs, I-I see the track at one o'clock. Are you on it?"

"Check. Let's blow it up."

"I'll ease her down. That's it. Steady . . . steady, my queen. Good. Right there. Okay, going lower." I dipped her nose. We floated without a tremor, gliding on the wings of God. I loosened my grip to feel her gentle movements. I was flying free, wings open, like a bird in the wind. "Okay, Wigs, I need five-feet intervals."

"Check. One seventy . . . sixty-five . . . sixty . . . fifty-five . . . fifty."

"Open the cross-cowl flaps."

"Check. You're doing good, Buckster."

My left arm trembled as I gripped the wheel while counter-pressing against a crosswind. I used my right hand to engage the drop lever. The train track went over a bridge that was about one hundred yards east of the intended drop zone.

"I got a crazy idea, Wigs. You ready?" I yelled.

"Heck yeah."

"We're gonna kill two birds with *two* stones by taking out the track and the bridge. It'll prevent enemy advancements if that bridge is out."

"Check. Love that idea, Buck. So will our instructors."

"On my count. Here we go. Five, four, three, two, one . . . bombs away, number one."

"Number one, out!" yelled Wigs.

"Bombs away, number two."

"Number two, out . . . what the fuck?"

"What?"

"A couple of boys just ran out from under that bridge."

"You gotta be kidding! Close the flaps and let's get back up. Should've spotted that, Wigs."

"Check. Heck, they must have been hiding when the area was cleared for the drop."

We circled back to confirm the bridge and the track had been hit.

"Buckeroo, look at that mess. Those train engineers are gonna shit like a horse when they see what we done. And look at them boys running for their lives, covered like snowmen head to toe! Direct hits to the track from fifteen-hundred-pound sacks of flour exploding all over those poor boys. Oh my, I can't stop laughing. Had to scare the piss out of them. Buck . . . I can't, I just can't stop laughing . . ."

I felt a wave of nausea.

"Stop it, Wigs. Next time those bombs will be real, and there'll be body parts splattered across the track instead of flour."

Wigs went quiet. We were dead silent all the way back to the base, humbled by the carnage that could be inflicted.

That night, three days before the third anniversary of the Pearl Harbor bombing, there was a pounding on our door long after lights out.

"Private Buckley? Lieutenant James."

He handed me a telegram.

Come home. Father in hospital. —Mom

"Corporal Buckley, we've made arrangements for you to take leave. We have readied your papers for your mission." The officer opened a folder and removed a document. I was scrambling to catch up with the moment. "On December 8, you and Corporal Calvin Wiggins will be shipping out to Liverpool, England, with the 101st Army Air Force and the 106th Army Infantry. Your mission will be to drop paratroopers on the Belgium front line near the Ardennes Forest. There's a hot spot that needs support. Congratulations, Corporals Buckley and Wiggins." He saluted and added, "Corporal Buckley, the United States Army Air Force wishes to extend our prayers for your father. Go home, Corporal. Good night and Godspeed."

The soap dispenser released rough granules in my hands. I ran the hot water and scrubbed off the twenty-seven hours of bus rides from Horry to Wauwatosa. I sprinkled in some hair tonic and looked at myself in the opaque mirror; a man with dark stubble, broad shoulders, and an army uniform filled out with muscles was looking back: Corporal Charlton Buckley.

The hour was late. I came out of the hospital bathroom and walked down the long hallway toward a wobbly gurney being pushed my way by a tall attendant. The sound of the squeaking wheels echoed off the ceramic walls. On the gurney lay an old woman with wispy white hair. I asked the attendant where the nurses' station was. He pointed me down to the end of the hall. The old woman fixated her jade-colored eyes on me as she passed. With a raspy voice, she chanted, "It's sinful, sinful . . . sinful."

Arriving at the nurses' station with my army full pack slung over my shoulder, I caught sight of the name *William Buckley* on the chalkboard. My stomach lurched. Behind the desk, a plump, no-neck nurse popped her head out from her shoulders like a turtle.

"It's after midnight, young man," she snapped. "Visiting hours are long over." She took notice of my uniform and stood up. "Oh, I'm sorry, soldier. Who are you here to visit?"

"My dad, William Buckley."

"Of course. Room 127, right down the hallway on your left. God be with you and your father."

I paused outside Dad's door and felt that same sharp rock rolling around in my stomach when I was growing up, garnering enough courage to enter his bedroom, not knowing what condition or mood I'd find him in.

Push the door open, Charlie. You can do it.

The carbolic air in his hospital room failed to mask the foul scent of infirmity. The room was dark, except for a stream of light coming through the window from the streetlamp illuminating the hand towel draped over the edge of a washbasin that sat on the table near his bedside. An oak chair was perched at a desk on the opposite wall. Acoustic drop-ceiling tiles closed in on the man I hardly recognized as my father. My gut tightened. One side of his face grimaced; the other fell sideways. His frown burrowed, his lips pinched, the corner of his mouth was crusted with dried saliva. And his chest rumbled like stones tumbling along a rocky riverbed. *He wasn't coming back from this one.*

"Dad?"

His cheek twitched. I blinked away tears and took his mangled hand that had been abused from years of labor and placed it in mine. It felt foreign, from a faraway place or a time I'd forgotten or had never known.

"I received my orders. I'm off to England." I used the towel to wipe his cheek. "I think we have. . . the Krauts right where we want them. We'll shut them down for good this time, Dad, don't you worry." His grimace, like a gruesome villain in a horror movie, made it hard for me to look at him. *He was inches from six feet under.*

I needed air and went to crack open the window. The treetops were dusted with fresh snow. I closed back the window and sat in the chair and listened to his slow, gurgling breath and shut my eyes.

In the dark early morning, I woke to Sandee's sweet lips kissing me with tender solace. Her smell was home. I flicked on the lamp to see her pale blue eyes filled with tears.

"It's you," she said, then glanced over at Dad and covered her mouth.

"We tried to stop him, Dee," I cried. "But he wouldn't. Even when his belly bled, he drank."

"Charlie, I'm so sorry."

"I don't want to leave, Dee." I wiped away my tears and took her in my arms.

We held on, saying little to each other for an hour, maybe two, until dawn peeked through the window when Mom arrived with Gingersnap gripping her Daisy Doll, whom she hadn't held in years. Gingersnap jumped into my arms with her head turned away from Dad.

"Sandee, dear," whispered Mom.

"Mrs. Buckley, in Temple we call out the names of those who need our prayers. I'd like to call out your husband's name, if you'll allow me."

"That's thoughtful of you, dear. Of course."

"Charlton," cried Mom. It pained me to feel her trembling body as I hugged her. "The snowstorm covered him like a blanket, Charlie. It was so cold."

"What are you saying?"

"Your father . . . he had his coffee . . . went outside to fetch the paper. I . . . I found him face down in the snow, Charlie. The medic kept striking his chest, trying to beat the life back into him."

Mom went to be near Dad. His shallow breath portended the finality of darkness that had loomed over our home for a lifetime. Gingersnap curled herself up in the corner with her pencil and drawing pad. I took a look over her shoulder. The picture depicted a horse running through a burning forest, trying to escape the onrushing flames. As Gingersnap kept drawing, Mom was incessantly cleaning Dad's grizzled face with the hand towel, as if trying to wipe away the devil that was taking him.

I picked up the *Milwaukee Journal* from Mom's bag and read the headline.

"'United States defense contracts with Milwaukee manufacturing companies tops one billion in revenue.' I'll bet AC Machinery received a large portion of those contracts." I started pacing. My skin was itching. "I wonder if George was moved into the armored tank division. I bet we see a bunch of our tanks overseas, Dad."

"When?" Mom asked, as if reaching for a life preserver.

"Tomorrow morning. Ship leaves the day after."

As if it were just another day, she took a fruitcake from Dad's suitcase. "Would anyone like some?"

"I hate fruitcake. You must know that by now."

"I hate it too!" Gingersnap added.

And so did Mom, who laughed and admitted she didn't care for it either.

"Share the fruitcake with your pilot friends," said Mom.

I went to the window to look out beyond the forest preserve where the town of Wauwatosa ended. I had to escape this room, this hospital, this town. I felt the heat of panic rush to my chest.

"Sandee and I are going for a walk."

"Can I come?" Gingersnap cried.

"You'll stay where you are with me," snapped Mom.

A marmalade-colored glow stretched across the horizon as the wind howled through the pines. Sandee and I ambled our way down toward the forest preserve hand in hand.

"The ground is turning soft," I said. "I don't know where I am."

"You're here with me in this moment."

"I don't want to leave you."

Sandee stopped and kissed me. "You need to go back and be with your family, Charlie. Come over tomorrow morning. The house will be empty. I'll have a surprise waiting for us."

I reluctantly let go of her hand and headed back.

In the short time I'd been with Sandee, Dad's face had become more concave; his coloring was a patchwork of brown and yellow. Mom was pale. Gingersnap was sleeping with her Daisy Doll.

"I never knew you didn't like my fruitcake, Charlie." She smiled. "What *else* have I missed because of your father?"

"You're going to need help if he makes it home."

"I want him to die." She covered her mouth and broke down. He'd finally cracked open her protective shell enough for her to finally admit it. "I did love him."

"I know." I held her as if she were my own child as she called out the Lord's Prayer.

"Our Father, who art in heaven, hallowed be thy name. Thy kingdom come . . ."

∽

Sandee opened her front door wearing her winter coat. Her feet were bare.

"If we're going for a walk in the snow, you might want to put on your galoshes."

"How about we go to my bedroom instead?"

"Is that where my surprise is?"

"Nope. It's here."

She pulled me inside the house, closed the door, and opened the coat to reveal her naked porcelain skin.

"To my boudoir, soldier."

"Your family?"

"At Grandpa's in Madison. Mom left me her car so I can take you to your bus. Follow me."

"Haven't I always?"

"Be careful with Floppy."

Her favorite stuffed rabbit was sitting on her pillow with a suspicious look in her eyes. I moved Floppy over to the desk next to Fin, who was begging for a sprinkle of food in her glass bowl. I turned away from the onlookers, dropped my green duffel bag, and wrangled out of my fatigues. Sandee crooked that smile and let her jacket drop. I kissed her while sliding my hands down her backside. She let out a sigh as I went to my knees to kiss between her legs, then gently moved her back onto the bed. I moved in between her legs to a position that was familiar but not bare to the bone.

"I just finished my cycle," Sandee panted.

With her help, I was in. She flinched. "It's okay," she whispered in my ear.

It came in a rush. I shuddered and let go. Sandee's legs quivered while she dug her nails into my back. We held on with desperation, knowing the first time might be our last.

Once the pulsating aftershocks subsided, Sandee nuzzled her nose against the nape of my neck, and we fell into a short, blissful sleep.

The sunrise had melted the frost off the kitchen window. With a towel around her wet hair, Sandee prepared cheese sandwiches at the kitchen table.

"I'm bringing the Star of David with me."

"Take this too," she said, handing me a photo taken of herself—*topless*. "That's private, Private. Show this to anyone, you won't have to worry about the enemy. Clear?"

"Fast, Dee. I'm a corporal now."

"I've never been bedded by a corporal before." With that, we left the sandwiches and went back to the bedroom.

∽

With my R44 patch, Sandee's Star of David, and her spicy picture tucked away in my duffel, Sandee drove me to the bus station and parked. A couple of other guys in their full fatigues were stepping onto the bus.

"It's strange to think I'll be eating lunch out of a can when you're waking up." I took a book from my pack and handed it to Sandee. "Bomba, the Jungle Boy, the ultimate survivor. I plan on being just like him."

Sandee held the book against her chest. "I'll be waiting right here. I'm not leaving this spot until you come home, Charlton."

"I . . . I don't have a ring, but I'll get you one as soon as I come home. Until I do, when I *do* come home . . . to you . . ." I looked at this sassy girl who picked that yellow dandelion and put it behind her ear when we first met in the baseball dugout. She playfully tried to cover my mouth. She put her hands on my cheeks to wipe my tears. "Will you marry me, Sandee?"

"I will."

I kissed her with all my heart—then headed to war.

CHAPTER 10

....

Twenty hours later, on a cold and windy December 8, 1944, at 1800 hours, the bus let us off at the water's edge of the New York Harbor, where the enormous troopship *Aquitania* was surrounded by a convoy of support boats. The shuffling boots from the 101st Airborne Division and 106th Army Infantry underscored a symphony of nervous chatter. Over three thousand soldiers carried hundred-pound full packs jammed with essentials: a bedroll, a rifle, and a steel helmet. Like inchworms, we gradually made our way toward the ramp. Even through a light snow, I was sweating inside my army jacket. The collective weight of the regiments was crushing my sternum. There was no moving this green glacier of men any faster. I shifted and jostled to find air. Foul language and flying elbows were hurled from all angles as we funneled into a logjam like the last stage of a birth before finally being delivered at the top of the ramp. The newborns had arrived.

"Name and company?" asked the quartermaster.

"Charlton Buckley . . . sir, 101st Air Force," I breathlessly responded. "Has Calvin Wiggins checked in?"

"Negative. You two will be bunking with Corporal Bartholomew Davis in the hull down in section six. The C-47 wings and propellers have been disassembled for transport and will be strapped on the hull in your section. Your orders are to keep them secure. Welcome aboard." I was relieved to know I was making the journey bunking with Wigs and Buddy.

Although still tethered to land, I had to grab hold of the mahogany railing on the third level. The rough edge underneath my palm revealed names engraved into the wood: *Billy Williams, Brian Kendel, John McCaffrey*. Some of the guys already had their knives out carving their own names into the railings. Standing tall on this massive transport ship, I appreciated the enormity underfoot, the magnificence of its authority. I pulled out my knife and found a clean space to carve my name: *Charlie Buckley*.

The choppy, slate-colored water blended into the darkening horizon, preparing to do battle with advancing cumulous clouds. The Statue of Liberty glistened off the Atlantic as her gold torch flickered from the last rays of the shimmering sun. I traced my finger over my carved name, knowing I was part of something big. It was up to us to cripple the German forces and finally finish them off. Not Dad, not George. This was *my* time in history. My generation's burden—and privilege.

I scuttled down the hatches and companionways to find engine room six, deep in the bowels of the ship. The hull smelled of fresh latex paint. The portholes peeked just above the waterline. Egg-sized lights were set twenty feet apart that circled the hull, throwing a dim light. The slightest sound was magnified tenfold down in this steel chamber, creating plenty of noise with two hundred of us settling into the belly of our iron whale. Meshed hammocks, three high, lined the hull. I was assigned the top hammock near a hot water pipe. Buddy was right below me, with Wigs's spot empty beneath him.

"How about we make this fast?" said Buddy. "End the war and get the hell over to the Eiffel Tower." He stood up and bear-hugged me. "Good to see you, pal."

"Paris sounds like a fine plan to me," I responded.

Our assigned hammocks hung a few feet from the C-47 propellers. I stashed away Sandee's letters, along with my essentials, then sat on my trunk. I felt so far from the girl I'd just proposed to less than a day ago. I took out her picture and kissed it.

My heart jumped as the troopship's giant propellers turned over, sending propulsive vibrations through the hull.

Where in the hell was Wigs? The southern bumpkin must be lost in the Big Apple.

Buddy and I raced to the top deck to take in the famous New York City skyline and watch the well-wishers waving from shore. Every inch of the troopship was taken. Buddy and I climbed up the netting attached to the main mast and found a great spot to take in the view. A winter gust gave me goose bumps. We waved to whoever was saying goodbye from ashore while Buddy sang "God Bless America."

"From the mountains to the prairies, to the oceans, white with foam. God bless America, my home, sweet home. God bless America, my home, sweet home."

I finally spotted the Alabama boy I'd left back in South Carolina. He was tromping through the infantries without a care.

"Wigs!"

"Is that you hanging from that net, Buck? Heck yeah, that's you. Stay where you are."

Wigs crawled over a bunch of guys who weren't keen on being stepped on and let him know it.

"I thought you'd gone AWOL, Wigs," Buddy said and reached down to give the big lug a lift up. Wigs grabbed some netting beside us.

"I can't get outa this here city fast enough. It took me three dang subways to get here. Some poor runaways were pissing down on the tracks with the rats. I should've just walked! Got to Harlem before realizing I was on the red line instead of the Q—I think. To tell ya the truth, I'm not sure what line I was on."

"You guys want a hunk of Mom's fruitcake?"

"Nah, had a lip-smacking wiener dog on the street," said Wigs. "Only thing in this stinkin' city worth a spit."

"I'll pass," responded Buddy. "Can't stand fruitcake."

"Hope the food's edible on this rig," Wigs added. He slapped my shoulder. "Golly, oh, golly, we're off to war."

The *Aquitania* churned across the boundless sea to a foreign land. We perched ourselves against the netting and watched the last pearl-white seagull peel off the wake to head back for land scraps. Some fellas played cards, while others showed off their muscles and challenged each other to push-up contests. We were a mash-up of nineteen- and twenty-year-old Polish, Italian, Arab, Hispanic, Armenian, Irish, and German American young men living in one neighborhood now, communicating with uncertain glances, seemingly holding our composure while our insides churned up like the water in our wake. I chewed on the fruitcake until it was soft enough to swallow. I turned back and glanced at the city skyline in its glory as the propellers picked up speed, pushing us across the Atlantic toward the war.

⌇

The *Aquitania* hardly cut a wake heading toward the west coast of England after seven days at sea. I searched for Sirius through one of the portholes, but it had started to snow. My knees had turned purple from washing hundreds of miles of decking using only a hand scrubber while thinking about Sandee the entire passage. Buddy bugged me nightly to show him the topless photo I'd kept hidden. I decided to reveal the picture to him from the neck up, but as we readied for lights out on our last night, the siren rang, followed by orders being blasted from the hull speakers.

"Evasive action initiated. Brace, brace."

There was trouble in the water. The ship keeled, plunging the portholes below the surface. Wigs yelled that he was going to be sick and crawled off his hammock and sprinted into the head. We keeled hard to the other side, tossing us from our hammocks. Everyone held on to crossbars, hatches, beams—anything that was soldered to the steel hull.

"We ain't even landed yet, and we're at war!" Wigs yelled through the bathroom door. Then a cataclysmic explosion sent concussive sound waves into my skull. I fell to one knee and grabbed my head.

"Fucking Krauts! They set water bombs!" said Buddy, gripping his hammock. "We must be getting close to land."

The ship swung to the starboard side, slamming my trunk into my ribs. We zigzagged around explosives set by Hitler's U-boats holding us captive to the horrifying prospect that this might be the end, that we might go down at any moment; the hull would tear open, sinking us to the murky bottom. This was no simulation. Death was real. I was paralyzed with fear for what seemed like hours.

Finally, Wigs came out of the head, after the "all clear" was announced, his face covered in sweat. We secured our contents and inspected the C-47 propellers. Afterward, we rolled onto our hammocks as the hull lights flickered back on.

"We'll make 'em pay!" Buddy yelled.

My head throbbed as we made lazy swings toward land. I yearned for Sandee's consoling voice, her delicate hands, her soft lips.

You're going to be all right, Charlie. Breathe, my love. My open arms await you.

I missed her sassy way, the birthmark underneath her left eye, the tiny gap between her front teeth, her lazy eyelids, the peach fuzz under her sweet, soft earlobes.

Side to side, the pendulum swung, lulling me to sleep.

Drift off, my darling. You're safe . . .

At 0300 hours, we were ready to take land. Over three thousand strong dressed in full fatigues were ready to disembark. We knew the mangled port of Liverpool had been relentlessly attacked throughout the war and could still see sparks spewing into the darkness. How arresting the devastation looked from the water. My heart raced. No stars lit the sky; the air was ungodly cold.

We anchored and were transferred to smaller vessels, which brought us to shore. My pack seemed heavier than when we first came aboard. My knees shook. Wigs nudged me.

"This ain't no joke, Buck." The wind and snow battered our faces as we stepped on land. "Stay close."

"I'm not going anywhere without you, Wigs."

I could barely hold my balance; a half foot under snow, the ground bobbed like the ocean. We plowed through the thick powder behind our division leader until we arrived at a holding area. Wigs, Buddy, and I stayed close to the commanding officer communicating positioning coordinates to the dispatcher. This was no war game. This was as real as the blood pumping through my veins. Then I remembered what our drill sergeant had said.

"Men are dying as I speak to you, boys . . . dying to defend the liberties you have enjoyed as little shits. Time to grow up."

We meandered through the snow alongside neighborhoods burned to the ground; only chimneys were left standing. I was awake to my mortality and its terrifying proximity, shaking in fight-or-flight mode, ready to take cover if shelled or fired upon.

Through the snow and ice, our convoy moved supplies, food, gear, and the C-47 bombers that would be reassembled at the base. We were inextricably woven together, marching forward, our helmets frosted with fresh snow.

"Mangy dogs," Buddy said. "Krauts chewing everything up and spitting it out."

"Had to have dropped two-thousand-pound eggs on these poor civilians, Buck!"

"Keep your mind straight, Wigs. Go through our flight checks, emergency protocols, and stay focused because they're not gonna waste a minute getting us up in the air, no matter the weather."

Teams of Allied infantry with pink faces puffing steam from their mouths chugged the opposite direction toward the front.

"Replacements," said Wigs.

"'Replacements,'" added Buddy. "A rather fucking antiseptic term for backfilling the dead and wounded."

The snow whipped sideways like the storms off Lake Michigan in February. I worried about how the C-47 would handle this weather. *Hoses might freeze; the wings might accumulate ice, bringing us down. Will I be able to handle her? Flying in this weather won't be anything like in South Carolina. Will I see Sandee again? How long until we get to the base?* One worry to the next as I kicked my feet through the snow.

At roughly 0800 hours, we stopped and huddled against a barn that protected us from fierce gusts while we chowed down turkey meal, hard bread, and a piece of chocolate. Packs of Lucky Strike cigarettes were rationed out. Hearing Dad wheeze as he sucked in the tar was sickening. I wanted none of it, but a fella said I'd better take a pack to use as trade bait for an item I'd want in someone's care package.

It wasn't too long after our break that we arrived at the base looking like snowmen. Ten-foot-high snowbanks flanked two runways. I'd never seen so many aircraft line up three deep, ready to sprinkle paratroopers across the front line like fairy dust. Engineers, soldiers, and officers dashed in all directions. Wigs, Buddy, and I went directly to the C-47 simulators, where we spent three hours in training, then wolfed down two cheese sandwiches with the new pilots camped inside a large warming tent and waited.

After an hour or so, the 101st Army Air Force unit was called to the operations desk. Wigs and I were handed our flight manifesto with *Training Mission* stamped in red across the top. The mission was to fly to a specific set of coordinates, open the cargo doors, close them up, then land back at the base. An hour later, Wigs and I went to fly.

The cubic space inside the C-47 cockpit was five-star compared with the poky Havoc. I thought back to the Blue Box at the carnival, and here I was, readying to fly the real McCoy into the war. I passed my hands over the instruments like a pianist preparing for a recital. The panel flickered with multifunctional indicators. One row of switches was singularly dedicated to the hydraulic systems. The white sky was waiting for me to puncture it.

At 1100 hours we rolled into position, my ass buzzing from the fourteen-hundred-horsepower twin wasp engines. I went through our prechecks before being given the "Go fly" from flight control. I pressed down on the lever, and like a grizzly bear, the C-47 raised her chest and roared. The powerful thrust threw my head back. "One hundred, Wigs . . . one-thirty . . . one-sixty . . . lifting off!"

I smiled at him to calm his nerves—and mine—then took our bird through the swirling winds, bobbing and weaving, up to nineteen thousand feet. I ordered Wigs to open and close the cargo doors per the training protocol and turned back to the base to look for a clear runway to land on. At the second level of descent, two other C-47s lifted off on their training mission from the base. Another after that, then two more, heading toward us.

"They're sending birds out too fast for us to get down there, Buck! Should we circle?"

"Negative. Prepare to land." At a thousand feet, I cut the speed.

"Fuck! It's gonna be tight, Buck."

As if dodging the enemy, we zigzagged until runway number two cleared. Twenty seconds later we landed nice and soft. I smiled and shook Wigs's hand.

I was ready for a real mission.

Wigs and I were called to the general's tent and stood at attention in front of the square-jawed, three-star general. After one training mission, we were called to war. He saluted and promptly promoted us to second lieutenants, then pinned us. Wigs sported a shit-eating grin and threw back his shoulders with his chin extended forward, nose in the air, just like conceit of the officers we saw at Myrtle Beach. It was a wise strategy by the general, lifting our spirits before sending us into harm's way. Without further formalities, the general opened the map.

"Drop the 106th paratroopers here." He circled a point twenty-five miles inside Belgium on the edge of the Ardennes Forest, near Bastogne. "A breach needs plugging along that fifty-mile line. If it breaks open, we're fucked. It'll threaten a major railroad junction we must control near Saint Vith. Yesterday, we shut down air support due to the storm. As a result, fucking panzers plowed through the trees and forced back our line of defense. Our contact from Saint Vith said they lost complete radio communication with the 106th and 590th battalions. You'll drop troops that will shore up the front and push those fuckers back so our guys can hook up new radio wire to the transponder, so we can reengage communication with the commanders on the ground."

"Yes, sir," I said.

The general flipped over a more detailed map and pointed to a small meadow on the edge of the Ardennes Forest.

"This damn storm is a real shame, set to be the worst on record, gentlemen. We were about to end this shit war, and now this."

I glanced at Wigs, who was still grinning like a little boy. The war was still burning, and we were going to catch the last of its hot embers before snuffing it out.

"Drop as many jumpers as you can carry and dump 'em out on *that* spot." He jabbed the map as if he wanted to put his finger through it. "Now get to the hangar, Lieutenants, and send the next pilots in. Godspeed. Dismissed."

Our time was upon us. After collecting our gear, we grabbed bag lunches off the mess hall table and rushed out to our C-47. The air swirled as we climbed into the cockpit.

"How we gonna fly in this soup, Buck?"

"Elevate with advance thrust, drop hard through the slop, pick up our target, and let the paratroopers fly. Then, we get our asses back to the base and pick up some more."

Wigs stored our bag lunches, gear, pistols, and ammunition behind our seats. I strapped in. My mind went quiet, unburdened from worry. The butterflies in my gut were gone. Even my knee wasn't shaking. I glanced at Wigs, sitting less than a foot to my right, and gave him a thumbs-up. He was staring out at the snowstorm.

"You with me, pal?" I asked.

"My dinger's already frozen."

"Cal, let's do this."

At 1500 hours, we went through the prechecks, deiced the wings, and called for the fuselage cargo door to be opened for the jumpers who were on their way. The brutal snowstorm shook our enormous plane like a sparrow quivering in the wind. The transport truck arrived with twenty-nine jumpers also battling the wind as they hopped out and headed up into the belly of the C-47. I scanned the group. It was *their* first day at war too.

"These puppies look wide-eyed and bushy-tailed," said Wigs with a laugh.

Runway one was shoveled and ready for takeoff.

"Throttle up," I called out, then pushed down the knob for some juice. Our C-47 roared down the runway and lifted off with world-class thrust. We hit a pocket at seven hundred feet, so I increased our speed. The twin wasp engines growled. Her response was immediate and dynamic as we climbed to twenty-two thousand feet. We bounced abruptly before being swallowed by a capricious wind shear, dropping us five hundred feet in seconds.

"Holy moly, I just swallowed my nuts, Buckster. Get us the hell out of this."

"I'll punch through the shear and level her out. Hold on."

I raised the nose, finally popping out of the turbulence over the English Channel. The brittle air felt like needles tearing at my throat.

"Twelve minutes to the drop, Wigs."

The erratic wind had our bird tipping side to side. I turned to see the stoic expressions on the faces of the jumpers. The hum of the engines seemed to have them in a trance as we made our way toward the intended drop zone. We were closing in on German airspace.

I pushed down on the wheel to get out of the soup and located the meadow next to the majestic Ardennes Forest that bordered Germany and Belgium. I circled while closing the upper cowl flaps. We rolled and banked as we came to our mark.

"Green light," I commanded. The paratroopers unstrapped and prepared to jump into the wild air. Violent gusts forced me to circle again. We were tipping and leveling as I called for the fuselage cargo doors to be opened at five hundred feet.

"All go!" I yelled. Within a minute the belly of our C-47 was empty. I smiled at Wigs and let out a long sigh. "We're true pilots now, Lieutenant Cal Wiggins. Mission one accomplished. Let's get back to the base and pick up more guys."

"Check, Lieutenant Charlton Buckley."

Just before ascending into the clouds, I heard what sounded like a Coke bottle exploding in the rear.

"I think we just splattered a hawk, Buck."

"Unstrap and check the cargo area."

But before Wigs was out of his seat, I calmly rescinded the order.

"Strap back in, Wigs. I'm not able to get lift."

"Piss!"

The ground looked like it was coming at us through a telephoto lens in zoom mode. The hydraulic lights were blinking off the board.

"Buck, we're in the sights of an eighty-eight flak gun from the ground. I can see it at five o'clock . . ."

My head slammed against the side of the cockpit, causing speckles of light to flash in my eyes. The acrid smell of burning steel and smoke engulfed the cabin. I shook my head to fight off losing consciousness as crash-landing protocols rattled around in my scrambled brain. We were flopping around like a duck plugged with buckshot after being hit again.

"Charlie! The trees, twelve o'clock! Pull right, pull right!"

Snowflakes and sparks flew through the fuselage as I pulled our bird to one side. My eyes swarmed over the blurry gauges. I spotted a clearing behind a row of tall pines and throttled down as the belly of our bird scraped the frosted treetops.

"The cowl flaps aren't responding, Wigs. The hydraulics are out . . . brace, brace . . ."

CHAPTER 11

S nowflakes danced wildly above as I opened my eyes, not knowing where I was. Nearby, burned-out artillery trucks were scattered like discarded, broken toys. Sparks spit into the sky as our C-47 hissed to her death a hundred yards away. The mordant taste of metal marked my tongue as I wiggled my toes and stared at my fingers like an infant fascinated by their own appendages. And then I looked to my right.

"Wigs." I reached out and held his hand. "I owe you."

"You owe me nothing, brother." Wigs had miraculously grabbed our packs, Colt .45 pistols, and ammunition and pulled me out before the fire engulfed the cockpit. We lay there holding hands in the middle of a snowy war zone. "This may not be the best time for the truth sayer," he added, his jaw chattering. "But you're plain terrible at landings." He laughed with blood on his teeth. "We fucking survived a crash, Charlie. I guess that means we're stuck together like two lucky peas in a pod." We went through a cursory physical exam on each other, and besides looking like we'd been in a prize fight, we were okay. A lump had formed on the side of my head. My left rib felt broken. Wigs had blood dripping from his mouth. "Where's the line, Buck?"

I had no idea where the battlefront was and was worried the crash might have drawn attention. Wigs blocked the wind while I pulled out the map. It revealed we were close to the edge of the Ardennes Forest, just due west from the Belgium border where the line could have been breached.

We made our way toward the tree line with pistols drawn, chugging through uneven terrain a foot deep in snow. Every muscle shook as I sucked in the frigid air. The visibility in the storm was fifty yards at most. We followed the map's direction toward the forest with nerves on high alert, tracking whatever moved, enemy or foe. Other than the wind and the crunching of our boots, it was dead silent. The adrenaline tempered the pain jabbing at my ribs.

After a few hundred yards, I halted.

"Two o'clock, Wigs. Take off your safety."

With the air so thick with snow, we nearly walked over three dead German soldiers and two civilians lying next to an empty, snow-filled chicken coop. Behind the coop was a cottage puffing smoke from its chimney. Wigs turned and ran back a few yards. He was shaking his head.

"Lord. Dear Lord . . . I've never seen anyone dead other than my brother. Open casket. Promise we won't end up like them." We weren't trained for combat with our boots on the ground, and I worried Wigs was already showing signs of cracking. "Promise me, Buck!"

"You and me, brother, we're gonna make it. Canvass the front. I'll go around back."

I peered through a window and found a pair of bloodshot eyes staring back at me.

"*Êtes-vous des Américains?*" he asked. The boy looked to be about ten years old. A yellowish bruise marked one side of his face.

"Wigs. Get over here!"

"Holy shit," Wigs said, arriving out of breath.

"Quiet! There may be others inside." When I turned back, the boy had vanished.

We made our way through the back door and proceeded into a ransacked living room strewn with patchwork quilts, broken pottery, drawers tossed helter-skelter, and chess pieces sprinkled across the floor. We searched for food, but the Germans had taken most of it, save for a few stale nuts in a jar.

We found the boy down in the musty cellar huddled under a blanket, chewing radishes. He pointed me to a barrel of water. I filled my canteen and offered him half a sandwich from my pack.

"Wigs, General Billings had the 106th hold the German front on the other side of the Ardennes, but it looks like they pushed our forces back into Belgium from a panzer blitz. If we dropped the 106th to the west to hold the line from breaching into Saint Vith, then we're either *behind* the line, or we shoved them back into the forest."

"I'm betting we shoved 'em back in, Buck. If we head into the woods, we'll find the 106th."

"You think?"

"Yep, I do."

"I should've seen the ground fire coming before we took that flak, Wigs. I should've spotted them when we hit the clearing."

Wigs rolled his tongue and spit out some blood.

"No way we avoid those rounds with all the training in the world." He took a bite of his sandwich. "Shit, you got us on the ground punch drunk. You're a superhero in my book."

"Dad would say, 'You don't get medals for being shot down.'"

"Fuck him. He ain't sitting where we are."

We left the kid, hoping to end the war for him. Outside, the blizzard raged on as we plodded our way one slow foot after the other. As the sky darkened, a growl sounding like a pack of ogres on the hunt came from inside the forest where we hoped the 106th had pushed back the Krauts into the teeth of the Ardennes. A blast shook the ground, taking us down on all fours. We crawled a few hundred yards until we came upon utter carnage. The terrifying Sleeping Souls had been here. How else to explain soldiers rent from explosives, opened chest cavities, decapitations, and warm intestines steaming in the cold? I nearly lost my nerve and ran back to that kid in the cottage, but we had to keep moving forward, or we'd be cooked out here in the open. I grabbed onto Wigs, and we hightailed it toward the trees.

The spiteful wind burned my eyes, turning the Ardennes into an impressionistic version of itself. Fueled by fear, we persisted through the hardening snow until we reached the edge of the forest, creating twenty paces between us so that two birds wouldn't be killed by one stone. Step by careful step, we marked our way through the giant ancient spruce trees. I whistled every few seconds to keep in close contact with Wigs.

Darkness heaved upon us as we crept deep into the ungodly cruel forest. Mangled steel and dismembered body parts that had been jettisoned from explosives were hanging from tree branches, seemingly dropped from a venomous sky. My brain vibrated from the horror of seeing and smelling charred flesh shredded from V-2 rockets and MG 42 machine guns. We trudged onward with our eyes wide shut in search of our infantry until we came upon an army medic holding his helmet, kneeling next to a casualty.

"Second Lieutenants Buckley and Wiggins, 101st Air Corps," I offered. "Our plane was shot down in a meadow a few miles back. We're looking for the 106th."

"Medic Tony Avenado, 106th. You mean what's left of it. We're in the shit, boys."

His eyebrow above his right eye was gashed, dried blood on his jaw, eyes set back, cheeks sunken. He was jacked up on fear.

"We . . . we lost communication, can't get air support in this soup. Communication lines torn up from fucking panzers, rolled over 'em—cut 'em." He put on his helmet and placed a small cross on the soldier's chest. "The 106th and 590th battalions were on the line for a week without incident, all quiet on the front. Then . . . the earth opened up.

"It wasn't supposed to be like this. 'Hold, hold, hold till they surrender'—that was the order. We thought we'd won the fucking war. They're dancing in Paris while we're getting shelled. Before sunrise, it was fucking dark and cold in the forest—up through the air, fire pellets rained on us. Panzers bared their teeth like wild fuckin' animals busting through the trees, King Tigers, panzer, panzer, panzer . . . I could use your help, but you better report to General Hawkins first. He'll give—"

Droning shells whistled above our heads. All I could think of was to run. Wigs, Avenado, and I sprinted until we dove into an icy trench. Under the horrific annihilation around us, in my convulse of terror, this trench was everything to me. A handful of soldiers in the trench were engaged in counterfire. As I returned a few rounds toward the area where the shots were coming from, I lost my footing and fell against another soldier who was crouched down, holding his rifle. I reloaded my pistol while I yelled for him to get up and fire his weapon. I finally had to pull him up, but his head fell over, oozing brain matter from his earhole.

"They didn't train us for this shit," said Avenado. "They knew it too. Eight weeks, and we're supposed to know how to fight—in this?"

"Where's the command coming from?" I asked.

"The infantry is due north, three hundred yards, in a shitstorm taking a royal beating. Without radio communication, we're fucked." He grabbed his rifle. "We should back out of this shit and retreat to Saint Vith."

"No, you're coming with us. Let's go."

We had no time to waste processing the crash, the unrelenting cold, the otherworldly landscape, the dead and dying. The sharp cold air ripped the back of my throat as I sprinted over jagged limbs, downed trees, giant boulders, and angular chasms. After a hundred yards or so, I looked behind me to find Wigs on the ground rolled up in a ball, crying.

"Get up and move!" I yelled.

"Can't we wait, Buck? Can't we just . . . stay here till sunup? Please, Charlie? We can. Yes . . ." He grabbed my arm. "We dig a hole right here and throw dirt over us like a warm blanket. We're gonna get shot up if we don't hide . . . gonna get all shot up."

"Listen to me, Wigs! The help we need is over that hill, do you hear me? Over that hill."

I pulled him up, and we ran to the top of the crest and peered down over a vast plateau burned from the battle. Smoke lay sallow over the torched landscape. Hundreds down, others scrambling for cover. We rolled down the hillside into the shell-shocked 106th Infantry.

"Where's the general?" I yelled to a group sitting on a Sherman tank parked at the base of a shredded spruce tree, the soldiers seemingly mute from fear.

"We gotta get the word out to drop some big eggs on this blitz!" offered Avenado.

"Second Lieutenant Charles Buckley of the 101st. Does anyone here know where we can find the general?"

"Hawkins?" The gunner finally answered. "You're looking for General William J. Hawkins? The one from a backwater town just south of Lafayette, Louisiana?" His words had a sardonic nip to them. "His wife is Nancy? Four-year-old twin girls? If you're asking where he's at, Second Lieutenant, you'll find him in a body bag. You bring us any good news, soldier?" he continued, biting on the end of his cigarette. "'Cause we're not getting a lick here. No radio connection."

"Well, damn it, run new communication wire!" barked Wigs. "Where's the post?"

The gunner tossed his cigarette and pointed us forward. Wigs, Avenado, and I left them, and I traversed down a steep snowbank to where the communication's post was set up in a deep trench. The groaning operator had a tourniquet wrapped around his thigh. A spool of wire lay next to a dead field tech.

"We got flushed out," he said, wincing. "The radio post . . . five hundred yards due east of here. Take the wire and tie the end into their transponder." He looked down at his wounded leg. "I can't make it."

"I'll stay and treat his leg," said Avenado.

"I'll set the wire off the ground, weave it through the tree branches to keep from getting cut again, Lieutenant."

"Buck runs like a jackrabbit. He'll get it there."

My personal battles at home and on the ball field, the fear, the intense pressure to succeed despite what I had to overcome, the inexplicable will to win had placed me here at this moment, prepared to lay it all on the line.

With frozen fingers, I managed to loop the communication line through the branches, repeating every thirty feet, until I reached the radio dispatcher hunkered down in a snow-filled trench. It had become so dark that I was only able to identify him by the whites of his eyes fluttering behind his wire-rimmed glasses. Wigs caught up and climbed in.

"Section Leader Jacob Goldmann, 106th. You must have flown here on the wings of Hermes, transgressing boundaries unnoticed. Hand me the end of the wire, my brother." He was wearing the pendant of the

Star of David around his neck, much larger than the one Sandee had gifted me.

More dirt from the scarred earth rained down from an explosion a few feet away, sending a splintered tree branch hurling through the air while dull surges of machine guns clattered all around us.

"Fourth of July in December in this fucking forest," wailed Wigs.

"Second Lieutenant Charlie Buckley, 101st Army Air Force. This is my copilot, Lieutenant Cal Wiggins. Where's the platoon leader?"

"Bled out this morning," he answered, shaking like a cold, wet dog. "Where'd you guys come from?"

"We dropped a load of paratroopers before taking flak," I responded. "Had to ditch the plane."

"Lucky you made it, I pray," said Goldmann.

As Jacob Goldmann transmitted the SOS, the ground rumbled as flames slashed the sky. Squealing shells pounded the earth, forming a wall. We dropped flat. A second shell landed and plastered us with tree splinters, lumps of flesh, and dirt. In the light of momentary flashes, I saw the horror in Wigs's eyes. Soldiers were catapulted from their dugouts, the flowering of their young lives cut short at the roots.

German panzers blasted through a blanket of spruce trees to our left, opening the way for massive numbers of German soldiers pointing their rifles. *"Aufgeben!"*

A dozen panzers circled our regiment, breaking the fourth wall, giving us no way out. In that moment of truth, as pristine snowflakes fell on our ashen shoulders, we lost the battle. We were without leadership, empty on munitions, and half buried in body parts, dirt, and snow. We had no more options but to put down our weapons. I expected to feel the power of a bullet enter my body at any moment. As if I were looking through a kaleidoscope, the stars in the black sky moved in slow circles. I searched beyond the treetops for divine salvation. Up there, beyond all this was heavenly peace. Down here, the devil had emerged from the ravaged earth.

I was a prisoner of war only hours after taking off from Liverpool. I vowed to myself I would not let the Sleeping Souls win, that I would hold on to my humanity in the midst of this horror for as long as I could breathe and make it back to Sandee.

Flanked by an army of German soldiers, the SS officer yelled, "*Raus, raus!*" Wigs and I rolled out of the trench. Goldmann refused to budge.

"Come outa there, fella," implored Wigs. "Or they'll shoot you."

Goldmann held his Star of David pendant. "What does it matter? I'm as good as dead, my brothers." Wigs grabbed his shoulders and hoisted him from the trench.

Leaving our dead and dying fellow Americans in the frozen Ardennes was against human law. But with a gun at our backs, we were ordered to only load the wounded or dead Germans onto their half-tracks and wagons. If the soldiers weren't calling out for their mothers, it was difficult to discern which bodies were from which side; body parts were separated from their blood-soaked uniforms. Only scattered contents of the dismembered gave us clues.

As we loaded one German soldier after another, my body convulsed from the shock of it all, while the officers celebrated by goose-stepping and singing, "Panzerlied."

"This may be a blessing, Buck. I mean, you'd rather end up in a prison camp than freezing to death with bullets in your gut, right? Right? Isn't that right, Buck? Better to be a prisoner than end up—"

"*Sei still!*" yelled a middle-aged guard missing his front row of teeth. He struck Wigs with the butt of his rifle. Wigs apologized to the guard and raised his hands.

With eyes on our boots, fingers interlocked behind our helmets, we trudged forward through tangled terrain until we caught up with the hundreds of other captured soldiers from the US Army 590th Battalion and the 99th Infantry. Together, we marched over felled trees, frozen creeks, and crooked caverns. My ribs burned. My feet were numb. Yet I kept on with the hope that this would end soon, that we would hear our C-47s roar, filling the sky with paratroopers.

The SS and its guards halted and set us down for the night under the pines of the Ardennes. We lay in faith, listening for our bombers to arrive, while the snow kept coming and covered us like a blanket. The SOS Goldmann had sent out signaled our location. We hadn't traveled that far. But silence stole our hope for liberation as the sky went quiet throughout the night; only the sound of gunshots popped the air. Escaping wasn't an option with bullets flying.

The wind whipped through the forest, mimicking the sound of ghosts howling in grief from the devil's deeds. Grunts from giant warthogs joined the clucking of nighthawks in the distance behind us feeding on the dead. No one slept. The brittle air kept us shaking. We were a thousand men puffing steam from our mouths, huddling to keep warm.

I was relieved to have survived, never imagining only hours ago that I'd be looking forward to the warmth of a prison camp.

Dawn spread a golden hue across the edge of a snow-covered farm as we left the theater of war and the Ardennes behind. It wasn't long before slate gray clouds swallowed the sun, dropping the temperature even further. We headed west down a slippery, frozen road with the wind in our face, hands held behind our helmets, fingers numb, lips tight, toes frozen, hearts broken.

One flatbed loaded with dead German soldiers slid off the ice-patched road into a ditch, tipping the frozen corpses into the snow. I grabbed my chest and looked skyward.

This nightmare has to end soon. Our guys will come. Maybe minutes, maybe hours, but they'll come.

The SS ordered to reload the corpses and push the flatbed back onto the roadway.

"No fucking way," said one of our guys. "We're prisoners . . . not supposed to do that shit for you."

The SS officer approached the soldier and grabbed his dog tags and choked him. "*Dieser ist verükt.* 'H.' You're a Hebrew. Bang, bang, Jew gangster."

Then he calmly put a bullet into the prisoner's groin. Wigs grabbed my arm as we watched the wounded soldier writhe like a bug on fire.

"Fuck you!" he cried in agony. Another bullet was fired into his back. His fingers clawed the road, dragging his limp legs along the snow, leaving a trail of tears.

"Fucking Jew." The Nazi shoved the pistol in the soldier's face and blew the back of his skull off, sending it skidding like a saucer across the frozen road, spinning to a stop a few feet from me.

Every bone in my body vibrated. Wigs hunched over and threw up. The air fell silent. Nobody breathed. It hardly seemed possible—out in the open like that, the murder of an American soldier who had surrendered. But on the frozen tundra, in the middle of nowhere with no food nor water, no judge nor jury, the Nazi army did as it pleased—it was evil without measure. The SS officer kicked the dead soldier into the ditch.

With rifles at our back, hundreds of us entered a blown-out cathedral and crammed into the pews for the night. Dispatcher Goldmann was on my left, Wigs on my right, Medic Avenado behind me.

"Look up, guys," said Wigs. "At least we have our protector watching over us."

A life-size replica of Jesus hung from the rafters. One of the wires had been cut loose from the shelling, sending the cross swinging.

"I'm studying to become a rabbi," Jacob Goldmann announced.

"Holy Jesus." Wigs laughed. "Of all the places to hitch our horses to for the night. Fucking Jesus, spinning out of control above our heads."

"When days and nights are filled with darkness, let the light of courage find its place. Help me endure the suffering and dissolve the fear. *Ba-ruch a-tah A-donai, ro-feh ha-cho-lim.* We praise You, God. My brothers, my faith travels with me wherever I end up. We need it now, more than ever."

"My fiancée is Jewish, Jacob," I said.

"Your children will be too." He smiled.

"I didn't know that."

"Jewish law says it so."

I closed my eyes to search for sleep, but the demonic flashes of the day bombarded my mind. I fought the horror by fantasizing I was back at the base under the tent sipping hot soup. The war was over. We were going back home on a troopship. I had my wings and would see Sandee in a week.

Wigs placed his head on my shoulder. I looked up at Jesus and tried to pray in this destroyed vestibule where Communion might have taken place hours before the carnage destroyed this citadel. I imagined the priest giving a young boy a wafer and whispering, "The body of Christ," and the innocent boy's tongue extended with full trust that God would nourish his soul.

I turned around to view hundreds of muddy faces, many with their eyes closed. One of them was Medic Avenado. I whispered for him to stay with us. He nodded and closed his eyes. I joined him and closed mine—until we were awakened from the guards to get us moving.

In an endless line of soldiers snaking the landscape, Wigs, Avenado, Goldmann, and I trudged through the brutally cold, windswept dawn. I felt sick to my stomach from the shock of surrendering to the enemy. My ribs throbbed; Wigs's jaw had turned purple. I took out the other half of my sandwich and split it with Wigs. He was too nauseous and passed it along to Avenado, who passed it to Goldmann. Goldmann gave it back to me because it wasn't kosher. I put it away for later.

As we approached the border, we passed a large regiment of German soldiers traveling the opposite direction to the front. From the look of this raggedy army, it seemed the war was limping to its end. Sickly horses with steam puffing from their nostrils pulled their broken-down vehicles. The enemy dragged their boots, looking dead eyed, malnourished—out of gas. This was a great relief.

I'll be home by Christmas.

We left the Belgian border into Germany through a series of checkpoints without so much as a glance from the German guards at the gates. However, once we entered our first town, villagers swaddled in blankets rushed from their homes and hurled rocks at us.

"Mörder, *schmutzige Schweine.* Fuck . . . fuck . . . fuck America. Die, bullshit Chicago gangsters."

I didn't dare respond, or I'd lose the back of *my* skull; that much was clear.

We walked on through a constant light snow until we arrived at the

Gerolstein train station at dark, having had only a cup of water and some black bread. A children's choir could be heard singing Christmas carols sung in German from a church perched high on a hill that overlooked the rail yard. I listened to the melody of "Silent Night" carried by the wind and wept.

"Stille Nacht, heilige . . . alles ist ruhig, alles ist hell . . ."

Mom would have put up the Christmas lights and trimmed the tree. I imagined seeing her peering through the window in the parlor, praying for me to walk up the drive. Instead, I was far away, ordered with all the other prisoners to clean out horse manure from the boxcars and scrub every square inch of the splintered plank flooring before being shoved in one of them with about seventy other prisoners. The options of what lay ahead spun round and round in my mind: I would suffocate in this boxcar, escape when the chance presented itself, or be liberated . . . die, escape, liberated, die, escape . . .

An SS officer approached, waving his rifle. "Move back," he ordered, then slammed shut the heavy door and hitched the iron bolt. Slivers of light shone through the cracks of the rickety wooden slats that had warped over time.

"I'm going to be sick," said Wigs.

"Let's get him to the waste hole," said Avenado.

A hole was cut through the floor in the corner of the boxcar no larger than the diameter of a dinner plate. Wigs had to hold on and wait his turn.

"This cattle treatment is criminal," Jacob cried out. "We are not beasts!"

"Private Stan Loeb, 590th Artillery Battalion." Stan Loeb was tall and lanky; his eyelids fluttered about while trying to force them open as if he had dust caught in his eyes. "You know what the fuck is going on, don't you?" He squeezed between Jacob and Wigs. "Death camps. Taking us Jews, killin' us off as if we're carrying a disease that will spark the next Spanish flu." Stan's tragic look gave me pause. "We went through Compiègne, France," he continued. "Liberated a detention center after the Nazis scattered. Told us the Nazis were putting Jews on

120

the trains and sending them to a place called Auschwitz, an industrial killing compound. That's what we heard from the Frogs."

"*Die endgültige lösung für das jüdische problem!*" a Russian allied soldier called out.

"You haven't heard? *Die Endlösung des Judenproblems*—Hitler announced on the radio the *final solution to the Jewish problem*. Been secretly murdering Jews for months."

The door was suddenly unlatched and slung back open.

"Make room!" the guard ordered and shoved a weary-looking man in a tattered Nazi guard uniform into our boxcar. The door slammed behind him. The unkept man was positioned with his back against mine. Everyone jostled to find a comfortable stance for what I hoped would be a short transport ride. The guard leaning on my back gave no order for me to give him space; rather, he turned and leaned his head against the siding and took something from his pocket that looked like a child's wooden toy top and kissed it.

"I smell rotten," he whimpered, with a German accent. "I'm sorry." He used his hand to wipe his tears.

"I don't smell you," I responded. "It's too cold to smell anything." I knew better than to engage with the enemy, but his deflated countenance gave me the gumption to press on. "Do you know where we're going?"

"You'll find out soon enough."

"Why are you traveling with *us*?" asked Jacob.

The guard looked at Jacob.

"I see you have an H on your tags. Once we get moving, you best throw them in the shithole. Or you'll be separated from the rest. And that won't be good for you."

Wigs, Jacob Goldmann, and Medic Avenado looked bemused.

"I'm not going to do that," Jacob responded. "They can steal my life, not my faith."

"We're fucking American soldiers," responded Avenado. "Jewish or not!"

"Who the hell are you anyway?" asked Wigs. "Some kind of two-faced Nazi traitor? We're in this fucking shitbag boxcar listening to *a*

Nazi? We should jump you and tear you from limb to limb."

"I'm a *funktionshäftling*."

"A what?" asked Jacob Goldmann.

"A prisoner like yourself, except with specific . . . obligations." He turned his head. "No more questions."

We waited for hours until the train came to life, lurching forward, unspooling into the cold night, moving quicky along the rails. After traveling a good distance, I convinced Jacob to throw away his tags.

Jacob lowered his head.

"A prayer from the siddur: I forgive all those who may hurt or aggravate me physically or emotionally, whether unknowingly or willfully, whether in speech or in action." Jacob tossed his tags into the hole. We all agreed to join Jacob and let our tags go.

I thought of when I'd engraved my name on the wood railing of the *Aquitania* before we left New York Harbor, my only identification left to prove I was in the war.

I had questions for the German pressed against me: why he spoke English and what his "obligations" were. But I was more focused on the relentless spikes of pain shooting into my ribs, spurring on back spasms. I wanted so desperately to lie down, to sleep, to leave this reality, but my head kept bumping the siding of the boxcar. I reached inside my pocket for Sandee's Star of David. *If they find this, I'll be separated as a Jew, so said the funktionshäftling.* I ripped open the lining of my jacket and slipped it inside.

∽

As the train rattled through the night, the thumping ache in my chest competed with the knot in my gut. Without being led by a commanding officer, there was no leadership to assure us we were going to be safe. Our group was composed of one medic, a rabbi-in-training, a Nazi guard, two pilots, and a bunch of infantrymen, some injured, all stricken with hunger and fear every minute of every hour. I slept for a few precious seconds, but the train kept bumping side to side, jerking me back to the hell of being a POW.

Late into the night, I felt new vibrations climb my legs. I grabbed Wigs. "Do you feel that?"

Then I heard the subtle drone of twin wasp engines. The train coasted into a rickety depot and stopped. A single light casting a yellow beam onto the platform was trembling.

"Holy moly! Birds up! Eggs on the way!"

Boeing engines roared in the distance while we beat on the doors, calling out for the guards to let us free. First a few of us, then by the hundreds, we pounded the walls, trying our best to bust our way out. The powerful engines smothered our cries. My knees buckled against the German man who showed no force or fear. Suddenly, dirt blasted against our boxcar made from what felt like a thousand-pound bomb. I prayed this was a tactical diversion by our air force to open up a corridor for ground enforcements and we'd be freed. More and more birds thundered in the sky. One of the guys in the boxcar went hysterical and climbed on top of bodies and tried pulling down the rim of a square vent in the ceiling.

"Fucking SS are setting us up for our own guys to wipe us out. I'm not waiting like sitting ducks ready to be blown to bits. If I don't make it, fellas, I'm Sergeant James Nathan, Presque Isle, Maine."

The vent was frozen shut. His hand stuck to the icy metal as he tried to push it open. He tore his hand away, leaving a chunk of his palm on the rim, then swung his leg up and kicked out the vent and contorted his body through the opening. Two more soldiers climbed on top of us to join James Nathan during the apocalyptic barrage. We held our collective breath as the bombs bore into the earth; each blast sending a jolt of electrical current into my heart. I leaned my head against the siding between explosions, terrified that James Nathan was right. We were going to be sacrificed.

Smoke filled our boxcar from the torched earth. The acrid taste of metal came from the disintegrating bombs. But just as they came, it went. The air went quiet, giving room for the nightingales to sing their mating calls. It was over; our boxcar had mythically been spared. I placed my hand on Avenado's shoulder to stop his hands from banging the wall and looked between the cracks. Snow-covered soldiers, the same who climbed through the vent, were piled under a light post that was half bent from the bombings; the bodies lying in a pool of blood, the light still flickering on their dead gray faces.

We waited most of the night to leave the station until the dead were buried, the destroyed boxcars were removed, and the track was repaired. Once on our way, I tried to sleep, but Lucifer was growling in my gut like it had every second of every day. Waves of panic kept coming. I grabbed hold of my fragile mind as best I could by reciting the Lord's Prayer. I was certain I was going to be shot by the Nazis; they would murder us on this train, in some field, or a forest.

I imagined how Dad would interpret the phone call from the State Department.

"Mr. Buckley, I'm sorry to report that your son was killed in action. Well, not precisely in action. He disobeyed direct orders by surrendering to the enemy after losing the battle in the Ardennes Forest—the quitter. But you already knew that, didn't you—that he was a quitter. Unfortunately, we haven't a clue as to his current location. Doesn't matter, most likely your son did something with the kikes that got himself killed."

"Where we're going can't be good," said Wigs. "We better scoot like wild dogs when they open the doors."

"No. You'll be shot in the woods," said the German funktionshäftling.

"We're gonna listen to this '*Frankenstein*' fella? Sit here waiting to get blown up when the Allies circle back to drop more eggs?"

"Your chances of surviving are worse if you run," he responded.

There was an authoritative aura to this German, and sorrow, unlike the other soldiers who had captured us. I wanted to build trust with this strange Nazi, so I asked for his name. With moist eyes, he turned to me, then to Wigs, Jacob, Stan, and Avenado.

"My name is Tomas Frantz."

CHAPTER 12

We smelled putrid and were frozen to the bone when the train stopped, having only consumed a cup of water, a bowl of soup, and a piece of black bread after surviving four unmercifully brutal days on the rails. The boxcar door flew open, bringing in the blinding sun. The guards, including Tomas Frantz, demanded we move out, even though we barely could walk. I grabbed Wigs, Jacob, and Avenado to create a link while being pushed forward into one large group.

"*Bring die schwachen Gefangenen an die Wand,*" ordered an SS officer, looking over his new take.

Some fifty men who were too weak to walk were carried and dropped against a brick wall. A Coca-Cola advertisement of a pretty gal in white shorts holding a perspiring Coke bottle was painted on the wall above their heads.

"*Den Wasserwagen mitbringen!*" the SS commander barked. "Water is coming!"

I did all I could to stay upright, not wanting to be separated from Wigs. The guards picked at their teeth and smoked cigarettes while passing around nude playing cards, laughing at the dirty pictures. Soon, we were ordered to move aside, allowing the water truck to back in toward the brick wall. The soldiers rolled to their knees and extended their hands. The rear flap of the truck flew open. Before I knew the horror of what was happening, sparks sprayed off the wall. From inside the cabin of the truck came an unrelenting barrage of bullets boring through the soldiers, their blood spurting into the air. The shooting continued without mercy, tearing through flesh, the bullets ricocheting off the wall. I reached inside my pocket to feel Sandee's photo and was certain I would never see her again.

Wind swirled below a slate, overcast sky when it finally ended in deathly silence. We were then forced to load the lifeless, bullet-filled bodies onto the "water truck." I hadn't read any protocols that made such requirements of prisoners. This wasn't a conventional war adhering to human rights. This was inconceivable evil. My mind vibrated from the madness around me. It was as if a trapdoor under my feet opened and sent me falling into boundless darkness.

I had blood dripping off my fingers. Tomas Frantz, who had now been given a rifle, along with two other Nazi guards, walked our group at gunpoint up a hill.

I hadn't lost track of the date since crashing in Belgium. I was determined to keep count until my freedom came. It was early morning, five days after leaving the airstrip outside Liverpool, Thursday, December 21. We approached a wooden sign on the entrance post that read, "Stalag IX-B," ending the uncertainty of where we were going and what we would find. A barbed wire enclosure wrapped the perimeter of a large encampment. We were lined up along the chain-link fence where, on the other side, prisoners wandered aimlessly in the crisp cold, wearing the very same army uniforms they were captured in. Armed guards with dark rings around their eyes looked diminished in their baggy uniforms, their rifles weighing them down.

My feet were so numb, I lost my balance and fell against the fence, meeting face-to-face with a man on the other side. I could almost feel his breath. His black, lifeless eyes told the story of this place.

"Are they not feeding you?" I whispered.

He stared from a place disconnected from this world. Without looking at me, he offered a sinister smile. His ashen teeth were broken. Lice crawled from his ear. This shattered man lay his left arm across his concave chest, raised his right hand to the sky, opened his sore-infested mouth, and cried, "Heil Hitler," then walked away.

"He's a funktionshäftling," continued Tomas Frantz, who had stayed with our group. "No *KG* painted on his back."

"I'm not following you, partner," said Wigs.

Tomas raised his rifle. "Keep moving!"

We passed three fenced checkpoints before entering a compound the size of a small town. Trucks motored in and out. The sheer number of soldiers was breathtaking; their hot breath glowed from the sunbeams shooting through the clouds. Some of the guards walking the grounds were older than my father. Scaffolds were erected and manned by guards readied with machine guns. There would be no escaping, no self-determination of any kind from this moment forward, other than to try and survive the madness.

Tomas Frantz disappeared from our group as the bright sun rose over the frigid prison camp. We waited hours to be in-processed. To distract myself from the unhabitable cold, I tried to recall my greatest feats in baseball, inning by inning, pitch by pitch. I was always able to recall every at bat, every defensive play. But standing in this numbing cold, with fear pumping through my veins, I could barely remember my name.

We moved slowly, hour by hour, foot by foot, until I stood before a long table of German civilian workers doing the in-processing. One of them ordered me forward to his spot. I felt a panic and wanted to run or to ask the guard where I could find a train, a boat, a plane that would take me home. He stared at me for a full minute and nodded.

"Jew."

"No." I remembered my training: only give them your name and company. "Charlton Buckley, second lieutenant, 101st Army Air Force."

"You lie. How many Germans did you kill before we shot you down, Jew?" He wrote my name on a yellow pad of paper, then touched his nose and made a hook shape with his finger. "I don't need your tags to know you're a Jew."

I stood there shaking, not knowing what was going to happen to me. I quickly offered him a cigarette. He lit it and sucked it down to the nub with his thin lips as he continued to stare at me with hatred in his eyes. He flicked the burning butt at my chest and took out another from the pack.

"What was your last communication with a commanding officer?"

"I don't remember."

"You lie again, Jew."

"I'm not Jewish!"

My words hung heavy in the air, as if I'd committed Apostle Peter's denial.

He lit the second cigarette.

"No more lies. Too cold for bullshit. What's your job at home?"

"Mechanical engineer."

"Fix our trucks." Next to my name he wrote down my work detail. "Do good, you get cheese on Friday."

He assigned me to barrack 44, "barrack for the Jews." I asked if my copilot could join me. I needed Wigs at my side like I needed air. He ignored my request and shoved the pack of cigarettes in his coat pocket and called over an imp of a man dragging his rifle. "No Jewish prayers," he added. "Or we make you wash shit from latrine with your tongue. Heil Hitler!"

The dour civilian guard stuck his rifle into my back and moved me along. I looked back to find Wigs, Avenado, and Jacob at different tables. I wondered about the Nazi guard on our train, Tomas Frantz, but he was nowhere to be seen.

I was walked through the snow-packed yard where the POWs gathered in groups, heads down, helmets tipped forward. I cramped up and asked the guard escorting me if I could use the latrine. He took me to a line of wooden seats where the waste dropped into a long porcelain basin. The seats were occupied by thin soldiers groaning from dysentery. I climbed up on one and had my first shit in six days.

"Make it quick," the guard said.

An American soldier next to me tore out two pages from his book. "Use one, save one for later," he offered. "Find yourself a book. They don't have TP at this hotel."

"I owe you."

The guard kicked my leg. "Hurry your shit."

The lowly guard banged the butt of his rifle into my back and pushed me inside barrack 44. I covered my nose from the foul stench. There were no bunks, no blankets, no windows or ventilation slats to take out the rancid smell coming from the soldiers hacking and crackling with pneumonia. Dried, expelled phlegm covered the walls. Almost every inch of the ground was occupied with shivering POWs lying on top of burlap bags filled with straw, their eyes receding into shadowed sockets. On the far end of the dank barrack sat a potbellied stove failing to fend off the depths of cold in this rickety wooden structure. On the other end sat a faucet, a sink, and a hole cut in the floor that connected to a cesspool behind the barrack. The walls were made of dark wood planks, the ceiling made of metal, the floor packed-down earth. I took space where I could find in the far corner. Barrack 44—a pitiful place to lay one's head.

"Fucking lice!" yelled a POW. The ground was crawling with the transparent bugs. Men snagged them jumping out from their ears and snapped them in half with their fingernails.

"Shut it, Polack!" shouted a large man with bushy eyebrows. He was oddly separated from the others.

"You shut yours, Victor! And pool your rations like the rest of us."

Victor had a face that said, "Stay away."

Jacob, Wigs, and then Avenado entered.

"Guys, over here!" I yelled.

Jacob shook his head. "This place is sinful."

We settled next to one another in the corner and didn't say a word for some time, not even Wigs. I was twitching from exhaustion. My ribs ached, hindering my breathing; I could tolerate the pain, but the excruciating hunger was inescapable. I thought of Mom's fruitcake and clenched my fists. This nightmare of a place was my new home.

"When do they feed us?" I asked, loud enough for anyone to respond. A fella sat up next to us.

"Corporal James Esposito, 106th. 'Sparky' for short." He looked older than most of us, had a beard, and was built like a tank. "Hoping for some soup tonight from these fuckers. Listen, when I'm going mad from hunger and when they give us our measly ration, I think about my mother's Italian meatballs dripping with the best sauce in the world."

In walked two guards: one was Tomas Frantz; the other was tall, with skin stretched tight over his frown, revealing black eyes and rotten teeth. He wielded his rifle like a sword.

"We're your friendly funktionshäftlings, or *kapos*, for all the new Jews who don't speak German. Nazis won't mind we starve you. You're ours now. You listen to us, or we cut your rations." He spit at one of the POWs, then left. Before Tomas followed him out, he came to me.

"His name is Derek. I know him from another camp. He won't treat you well. Do as he says."

I wanted to run, to never look back until I was safe in the forest, run to the front and be handed a box of food, sleep in a warm tent.

"No cots?" Stan Loeb, who had joined us on the floor lamented. "What about the Geneva Convention? Or have the Germans forgotten already?"

"Bloody sinful," added a POW with an Irish accent lying near us. "I didn't mean to eavesdrop on you, boys. Chaplain Joseph Morris, bred from the sweet province of Leinster." He grimaced while violently scratching at different parts of his body. "On the bay, north of Dublin. Ouch! Blimey bugger bugs." Chaplain Morris slapped at his neck. He had a fair face and kind hazel eyes.

"Jacob Goldmann, 106th Infantry, dispatcher." Jacob shook the chaplain's hand. "Here we are, a chaplain and a rising rabbi . . . prisoners of war."

"Good man, Mr. Goldmann. We're both doing God's work in our own way."

"How did you end up in this mess?" Jacob asked.

"I volunteered for the British Royal Army in the summer after the Luftwaffe air squadron brought my lovely town to its bloody knees. I was tired of Dublin takin' the brunt. I enlisted to offer spiritual protection as a man of the cloth." His eyes went to another place and time. Then he shook his head. "This blot of a prison camp is sinful, all right. We pray for their souls who commit them." He made the sign of the cross. "Try to get yourself on the woodcutting detail. Walks in the forest are a welcome relief."

"How'd you get captured?" asked Jacob.

"I'm too ashamed to admit it. Yet I sense you, fine young men, are God-fearing and won't hold it against me."

Tomas and Derek entered the barrack, took a cursory glance, and then left.

The chaplain shook his head and resumed with a hushed voice.

"Don't judge me. I'm a child of God who's ever repentant." He made the sign of the cross again.

I smiled at Sparky, Wigs, and Jacob over this awkward, utterly wholesome man who seemingly needed to get something off his chest. Other guys moved over to listen in.

"Chaplain, you're among sinners in this hellhole," piped in Stan Loeb. "Let it rip."

"Our regiment was violently pushed back in the town of Amnéville, northeast France," the chaplain began. "I enlisted to pay last respects and call the men to prayer, but the commanding officer had forced a rifle under my arm and shoved me into battle. The shelling pushed us backward into the village. We found ourselves in, well, the red-light area of town, if you know what I am referring to, lads."

"What a waste," said Sparky, laughing. "You fucking hit the jackpot."

"It wasn't funny, my good man! I was mortified. So much so I went into . . . a state. Yes, that's it . . . a state. I became separated from the rest of our lads and panicked and ran in circles and threw my rifle and ran to the door of one of those . . . those houses of ill repute to find refuge. When I got to the door, gunshots banged off the building near my head."

"Fucking hell! Get to the juice already," said Sparky.

"Dearest Evelina. She was different, not like someone you'd imagine in a place like that."

"Evelina," cooed Avenado.

We all laughed.

"Mind you, the bullets were deflecting off the building!" The chaplain paused and looked skyward, as if trying to find his way back to his Evelina. I felt that same gut-wrenching yearning for Sandee. "I was in absolute shock," the chaplain continued. "Evelina pulled me inside and into her rose-scented boudoir, a smell similar to the nape of my mother's neck—may she rest in peace. I gave Evelina all the francs I had left—for refuge, of course."

Sparky knocked off the end of his burning cigarette and choked with laughter, then responded using a lousy Irish accent, "Refuge? My good man, your monetary consideration created a contract to stick the lassie." We burst out laughing like a pack of wailing hyenas.

"You are not being kind! I will go no further."

"Okay, okay, sorry, Chaplain," said Sparky. "We're listening. Just get to the juice."

The chaplain had us hanging on every word.

"Evelina lay me on her quilted bed and placed my head on her ample bosom. She was, after all, a child of God—plump, pink, soft skinned, fair haired. She removed my coat and jersey as the building shook from explosions in the plaza, but Evelina remained calm as a daisy in the breeze, smiling while the shelling cracked the walls. She pulled down my drawers and raised her frock. I thrust all my mortal power into her honeypot as if God had ordained my bestial desire at the precipice of death. Through clenched teeth, I shouted, 'Our Father, forgive my immaculate fornication,' just as the bloody Germans broke through the door. I leaped off the bed in pronated attention. My pants dropped like lead weights to my ankles as I waved a white pillow in surrender and yelled, 'I'm just a man!'"

If I hadn't seen the sincere look on his face, I'd have thought he was joking, but damn if he wasn't. We grinned, chuckled, then found ourselves laughing out of our boots. Then my painful hunger jolted me back to reality; I was a prisoner rather than a soldier. It seemed we all felt this way because our laughter turned to smiles, then to tears. A band of brothers was forming, bonded by the horror of war.

"One for the books," said Stan, wiping his eyes.

I thought of Rails. How he would have loved the chaplain's story.

"Quit bellyaching, *man of cloth*!" shouted Victor from his spot in the far corner. "You caught luck of Irish. I fuck many whores on oil rig at Black Sea," he boasted. "The foreman sent for vodka and pussy to keep us happy."

"Yeah, yeah! We know already!" Sparky yelled back. "Something to be proud of. You're a real man, Victor."

From that day, Stan Loeb, Medic Avenado, Sparky, Chaplain Morris, Jacob Goldmann, Wigs, and I slept together, walked together, ate together, and moaned together. Meanwhile, Victor ate alone or with one of the guards outside, always sharing a cigarette after receiving extra soup and black bread. He looked as if he hadn't missed a meal while we kept losing pounds. Sparky made it clear to keep our distance.

◡

My work detail had me on the north end of the compound, where the top of the hillside was graded level to allow transport vehicles and tanks to be serviced. AC Machinery gave me the skills the Nazis needed to fix their broken-down Horch Kfz. 21 staff transport vehicles. I thought of George Underwood every day, especially while working on brake systems. Since the Nazis forbade any contact with the outside world, I wrote letters in my mind to George, reciting each sequence of my repairs, thanking him, letting him know I wouldn't quit on him—or myself. I imagined he was worried for me—after losing *his* son.

I was assigned to work as the right-hand tool of a Russian prisoner who was the lead mechanic on the site. He refused to talk with me, even demanded that I not tell him my name, threatening my ration of cheese if I gave it up. Nor would he tell me his name. We called each other "You," before I resorted to calling him his favorite Russian curse word: *ubl'dak*, a "son of a bitch," after he accused me of working too slow while swapping out a cracked axle. It was okay for a Russian to insult you, but insulting a Russian was like cutting off his balls, leaving him less of a man.

"My name. Are you ready, Ubl'dak?" I taunted.

"I don't want your fucking name! I told you."

"Why the hell not?"

"Then I don't care if you die."

"Ubl'dak, I have to talk with someone, or I'll go crazy." He turned and went into the warming shed for a break. I followed. "You force me to talk out loud to my fiancée, so here I go: 'Sandee, it's so cold. I'm lonely without you. I have to talk to you because this Russian, Ubl'dak, won't talk with me. The food is getting worse. No meat. Sparky keeps everyone dreaming of his mother's recipe for spaghetti and meatballs. I have a friend, Jacob Goldmann. He's going to be a rabbi after the war. He offered some of the prayers that your rabbi recited at Temple. We also have this chaplain fella who lost his virginity to a prostitute while hiding from the Germans.'"

"Shut mouth! Get back to work."

Walking down the hillside at dusk after each shift, I would stop to look over the forest as vast as the sea. Even if I could escape, I'd be swallowed by the trees and starve to death. I would drop to my knees and dig a hole in the snow until I hit ground, then claw up the dirt and smell it to remind me that this German dirt came from the same planet as home and feel hope. Then I would approach the barracks, hungry and shaking with fatigue; my nerves would burn from hearing gunshots fired in the yard, and I would lose the hope I'd gained. This place was medieval mad. I prayed our guys would come get us the hell out of here. Until then I needed to keep going, and as long as mechanical grease stained my hands, I had a chance to survive.

CHAPTER 13

At dusk, along with several mindless drifters, Jacob and I would amble from one end of the camp to the other, like a pack of zombies killing time instead of Germans. One evening, Tomas Frantz, outfitted in a fresh Nazi guard uniform and jacket, was engaged in some kind of meeting with two other guards and a group of POWs. As we approached, he took notice of me and turned his head.

"I see they've dressed you up, Tomas!"

He rushed over, turned Jacob and me around at gunpoint, and took us to an area well out of earshot behind some barracks. I thought he was going to shoot us.

"Don't call my name in front of the others—ever!" Tomas looked gaunt, his eyes were bloodshot, and his rifle was trembling in his hands. I prayed the safety was engaged. He threw down his cigarette and snuffed it out with his boot.

"What is it?" I asked. "You're shaking." He choked back tears and lowered his rifle.

"What ails you?" asked Jacob. "If you need repentance, I can offer that to you."

Tomas looked at us, as if searching our eyes for solace.

"In late spring 1940, my wife and I moved into my father-in-law's home near Amsterdam, a town called Leiden. Ari Markowitz. He was a master painter before the Nazi occupation." Tomas rambled on, stringing his words together. His eyes were blinking. "We lived near the university. Ari was an art teacher." Tomas lit another cigarette.

"On the day the Nazis took us, they stole one of Ari's prize paintings hanging on the living room wall. The painting portrayed a tragic scene of three emaciated goats chained to an olive tree, wailing in grief out to the angry black sea. A fourth goat lay dead next to them. I'm that dead goat . . . dead in a world that will never make sense to me again. There will be no *repenting*, Jacob. Not for savages like me.

"'Tomorrow will be our new day, my Lovina,' I told my wife, continued Tomas. 'Are you ready?' I had it all set for my family to escape. I had studied at the University of Frankfurt with a friend, Max Fried, who worked on a tanker transporting oil from the Port of Rotterdam to Newfoundland. We would be on that tanker, then make our way to Massachusetts from there. My uncle was a tenured professor at Boston College, teaching twentieth-century British literature. He had lined up a job for me at the German Consulate, working as a simultaneous translator. Being that my father was born in Frankfurt and my mother in Boston, I spoke fluent German and English. My parents met when they were young in the Netherlands, working on separate legal teams for their respective countries drafting the terms of the *Hague Regulations of 1907*, concerning, of all things, the treatment of prisoners of war. They married and settled in Frankfurt and gave birth to me. 'Yes, Tomas. I have sausages and dried fruits wrapped and ready to go,' Lovina said. 'I worry about my father. He's limping again from the gout.' Tomas choked back tears. 'Have him eat the cherries I brought home yesterday. That will bring down the inflammation,' I said."

Tomas put down the butt of his rifle and wiped his eyes. "'Save one, save all,' my Lovina would remind me before going to work at the bakery each morning during the occupation. 'Even if it means your life.' Here. Some bread."

He took out a chunk from his pocket and handed us a piece and then recited a poem he said his father-in-law wrote and taped on their front door, which had a yellow Star of David painted on it by the Nazi party, indicating where a Jewish family resided.

"The serpent licks our houses
identified from a list
branding weeping Stars of David
like the numbers on our wrists."

Tomas stared at his boots while the wind howled under the starless, bitter night.

"What is it, Tomas?" I whispered.

"Get back to your barrack. Don't approach me again."

On our way back, we found Wigs and Avenado in the yard. I came behind Wigs and pinched his neck.

"That's not funny." He jumped. "Scared the shit out of me—if I had any shit to shit." He was not amused and tried to tackle me. We had a rare laugh.

"Who's ready to walk out of this shithole?" Wigs wailed like a wolf. "Steal a plane, fly back to South Carolina—or to sunny California. Let's get out of this icebox."

"And swim in the Pacific Ocean," added Avenado.

Wigs looked down and kicked some snow.

"They moved me over to garbage detail today—the a-holes. We headed out to a landfill area in the forest. I wanted to run but knew better. Dumped all the crap into steel buckets on the trucks and used sticks to scrape off the shit from the sides, then went back for more. I threw up all day. Only good thing was the shower from a hose when we finished. It's nice to get out in the forest and see some nature instead of all the gray faces around here."

"I ran a new electrical line in the guard's quarters today," offered Jacob. "I'd like to run a hot wire up their asses." He added, "We ran into that Tomas guy. Gave us some bread."

"Tomas? The Frankenstein fella?" asked Wigs. "What did he want in return?"

"Nothing," I answered. "He said something about how saving one saves all."

"I'll pass," said Wigs. "Can't eat a fucking thing. I feel like I've been kicked by an angry mule." Wigs was flushed; even in this biting cold, he was perspiring.

The next morning Wigs was delirious with fever. I took him outside to cool him down. Icicles a foot long hung from the eaves of our barrack. I busted one off and placed it on his forehead and walked him to the infirmary. At the entrance, three guards drinking steaming black coffee blocked the doorway. One raised his rifle.

"Barrack number?"

"Forty-four. My buddy is sick."

"Your detail?"

"Mechanical engineer. I repair trucks."

"What do you receive from your detail?"

"Cheese," I responded.

"You give half to Victor. He's in barrack 44, yes?"

"Yes." He let Wigs go in.

"Tell him it's from Boris. Remind him he's short on his rations this week."

There was apparently some underground quid pro quo going on that Victor was a part of. Now I was too.

At the end of my shift, a guard in a brown uniform delivered my usual paycheck: a chunk of hard white cheese. I went to see Victor, who was sleeping on his sack of straw. I looked at him closely for the first time. His arms were flabby. Tufts of hair grew from his ears and nose. I imagined hair grew on his tongue. His face was pockmarked, adding to his murderous aura. I gave him a subtle kick to wake him.

"A guard named Boris said to give you this." I dropped the cheese onto his stomach. "Says you're late with your rations."

"Not my rations, idiot." He laughed. "What's he doing for you?" Victor looked at me with opportunistic eyes, wanting to feed upon me like a piranha.

"He let Wigs into the infirmary."

"I keep eye on you," he said.

"I'll do the same for you," I shot back. "We need to look out for each other, don't we, Victor?"

"Of course," he said as he bit the cheese with his tiny, smoke-stained teeth.

Days later, Wigs gingerly walked back into the barrack. He flinched when I put my hand on his shoulder to help him down.

"God almighty, don't ever go in that place, Buck. Not if you can help it. I swore I saw the light." I gave him what was left of my cheese. "I can't make it without you, Charlie. Take me home, will ya?" He quietly cried. "Let's escape."

"You and me are gonna make it back home, Cal. Do you hear me? Now get some sleep before *I* start crying."

It was before dawn when a pair of Doberman pinschers entered our barrack, snapping their jaws. Tomas and Derek held the dogs back on a leash and ordered us out to the yard for roll call. In the freezing wind, four Nazi officers began an onslaught of vitriolic slurs while making two hundred of us stand on one leg. Hour after hour they continued to sling dehumanizing insults. One of the Nazis put his nose to mine and spit in my face.

"I have news. You're never going home, Jew. Keep jumping!" he yelled. "Jump, jump, Jew, jump, jump, jump," as if reciting a nursery rhyme.

I had read about this type of war crime tactic in my World War I pilot journals. I also remembered that no matter the abuse, one shouldn't engage in any way that would give them license to escalate further. I wanted to scream and strangle the guard yelling in my face. The constant heckling was more damaging than the corporeal abuse; my morale was being smothered from an avalanche of debasement. The Nazi's goal was to turn us into "filthy swine," making it easier to absolve their guilt for denying us showers and toilet runs, weakening our will to defend our own personal dignity. I couldn't bear my own stench. Then they cut our rations to one thousand calories per day, consisting of turnip and potato soup cooked by Russian prisoners—which made us shit for days.

The faces of my fellow POWs developed blotches of pink-and-white spots. Noses had turned black with frostbite. It was so cold that my jaw shook to the point I thought it would break.

On the sixth day of this abuse, as the sun sank behind the pines, I smelled something so glorious, so delicious it made me cry: baked bread. The guards were crazed from hunger themselves and began poking and prodding us like rabid dogs. I took a jab to my injured rib and dropped to a knee. When I looked up, an SS officer was walking toward us. His caramel clothes looked poured over his athletic body, his boots wet with polish; a piece of a clay-colored hose hung from his right hand like a riding crop. His elbows pointed away from his body. He stumbled along the icy path, then stood tall in front of us, snapping his head into place. Steam rose from a chunk of warm bread in his hands. He slowly took a bite and spoke with his mouth full.

"Excuse me . . . this bread is to *die* for." He smiled, then chewed slowly and swallowed. "I apologize for the unseasonably cold weather, especially to all the Jews from the desert." His beady eyes pressed his pug nose like a rodent. His thin lips smacked when he talked, and his fine blond hair seemed immune to the wind. "I'm your new commandant, Walter Von Hanzel," he said with his mouth full. "Know this, my good prisoners: the German army is winning." He took another bite from the warm bread and continued. "Look what countries are now under our rule: Poland, Denmark, France, Sweden, Norway, Belgium, the Netherlands, Yugoslavia—twenty. Twenty lovely countries! You lost the battle and will soon lose the war." The commandant took his last bite. "I'm cold. And I want more of this delicious bread." He did an about-face and retreated to his warm quarters.

Unfortunately, we weren't at liberty to be relieved from the brutal weather. The guards held us deep into the night until one of the POWs broke the line and ran for the fence. The guards caught him from behind and slammed his head several times against the icy ground, then took his unconscious body away in a truck.

After finally being allowed back in our barrack, Avenado, Jacob, Wigs, Sparky, Stan, the chaplain, and I huddled near the warming stove.

"Utter barbarism," said Jacob. "Did anyone know his name?"

"Shut the fuck up, pussy!" yelled Victor from the far end of the barrack. "Lucky it wasn't you, little Jew."

"What a piece of work that fucker is," whispered Sparky. "Reminds me of all the bullies I used to crack the shit out of on the Jersey shore. They'd pick a fight, and I'd tear them apart." Sparky shook his head. "I'd better not get into it with Victor. He's got friends in high places."

"I need a writing pad," said Jacob. "To account for what's happening here. If I die, it needs to be carried on by one of you. Understand?"

"I'll make a deal with you." I jumped in. "I'll steal a notepad from work if you stop talking about dying."

"You understand, though, don't you, Charlie?" Jacob's eyes were welling up.

"I'm starving, dear God," piped in the chaplain. "I can't afford the temptation to dream of food, lest I go insane."

"We know what happens when you're tempted, my good chaplain," said Sparky. "You might eat one of us." He laughed. "I have a better idea. When one of us loses our mind from hunger, someone has to recite their mother's recipe to their favorite meal."

"I've lost my fucking mind," said a voice I knew as well as my own. It was coming from the far end of the barrack tucked in the corner. I stepped over bodies in the dark to move closer to the prisoner. "My mother cooks a mean pork loin."

From the dark space, I saw his eyes open and close. I moved in to see it was John "Rails" McNamara, curled up like a wounded animal with fear on this gaunt face—until he saw who was looking down on him. He smiled. "Of all the places to meet up. Jesus, mother of God," Rails gasped. "Charlie." He sat up and hacked from his putrid lungs. Out of breath, he added, "We're true Americans now, buddy boy. Baseball, apple pie—and war."

"What happened to you, Rails?" His once bulked-up body now looked ghoulish.

"The guards said I deserved to be with you *swine*, so they moved me in with the 'barrack of the Jews.' No bunks for us blots on society, huh?" Rails kept coughing. "Not you, though, Chuck-a-Duck. How'd a nice Catholic choir boy get thrown into this mash-up? Trying to be a fucking hero again?"

"Let me help you lie back down," I said. He felt like a bony cat ready to die.

"All the way from Wauwatosa, and here we meet. That's the land of the fireflies for all you fresh-off-the-boat foreign fuckers."

"What happened with the Cubs?"

"Miss the chance to have a go at those French hookers?" His laugh triggered a coughing fit. "They're worth dying for."

"Why'd you go and do a stupid thing like that?"

"Cubs folded up their tent, Charlie. Everyone went to war. My fucking father got his wish the day I enlisted. Little did he know. Be careful what you wish for, Pops." He coughed and put his hand on his chest. "How's your skinny girlfriend?"

"I proposed to her the day I shipped out."

"Sentimental sap." His lungs crackled as he struggled to breathe.

"I don't like the sound of that, Rails."

"Always such a worrying snatch. I'll give you a tip, buddy boy: don't trust these doctors with their meds. They shot me up . . . and now. . . I'm an open sore . . ."

Rails rolled over.

Sparky, Jacob, and the chaplain gathered next to me, like elephants surrounding their young to keep them from falling. They could see I was gutted.

"I've known this guy my whole life," I cried.

"Avenado, can you barter with the Nazi medical officer for some antibiotics from the supply cabinet at the infirmary in exchange for rations?" asked Jacob.

"I'll trade him for my cheese on Friday," I added.

"I'll do it," responded Avenado. "Hope it's not too late."

I stayed with Rails throughout the night, worrying he was giving up, imploring him to keep fighting. But Rails had no gal back home to live for, so it was like asking a dog that could no longer walk to rise up and run.

～

At my detail, two guards were smoking and milling about outside the small shed at the mechanic station where I hoped to nab a writing pad for Jacob. I went inside and found spiral notebooks for logging inventory sitting on the left side of Ubl'dak's desk where he was working away.

"It's fucking cold. My hands are frozen, Ubl'dak. I need to get them warm so I can work."

"Five minutes. And shut door, idiot."

I sat on a crate near his desk. "Did I ever tell you the story about when I fell into an icy creek as a kid?"

"I know how it end. You lived. Now shut mouth."

"I was chasing my sister, Ginger. We call her Gingersnap. Anyway, she was on the other side of the creek. I bet her I could jump over it without landing in the water. It was so cold, Ubl'dak . . . like today. My poor sister. She saw me preparing to jump and was screaming, 'Don't do it, Charlie!' She was terrified I was gonna fall short and drown under the ice."

"I don't care about this story."

I was losing energy to keep this up. Our barrack hadn't received rations in two days, and I felt dizzy. I caught my breath and continued.

"I kept yelling, 'Gingersnap, I'm coming to get you! I'm coming to get you!'"

"Five minutes over. Go back to work."

"It's been one minute, Ubl'dak. We're just getting started. I slipped on a wet branch and skidded into the creek on my ass. Broke right through the ice." I moved up close to him and garnered all the force I had and yelled in his ear, "*It was fucking cold!*"

"Fuck you! Get out."

"If you give me one of those empty booklets and a pencil so I can write down my childhood stories."

"You write them, I don't hear them."

"Deal."

I had Jacob's journal and shoved it inside my jacket and went to work on a transmission.

That night Jacob wrote down the names of everyone he could identify who had died, along with the cause of death: *starvation, disease, blunt force trauma, gastrointestinal infection, pneumonia, fever . . .*

As he wrote, and while I was cleaning my ears with a stick, the door flew open—not by the gusting wind but by the commandant, Walter Von Hanzel. He was followed by Tomas Frantz lugging in a food cart, carrying a large vat of hot soup, bowls, and spoons. Tomas slammed the door, leaving the howling wind behind.

"I never step foot inside Jew synagogue. *Nie!*" said the commandant. He was sloshing his words like Dad when he was drunk. "Hot soup for cold night. Cooked potatoes, corn." He stopped to catch his breath. "And you . . . you Jews will love me now . . . kosher meat."

Those who were strong enough to rise made a circle around Tomas and waited for their portion. I tried to wake Rails, but he was too weak. I was losing strength in my legs but would have stood all night; I welcomed the hot soup.

Avenado finished and handed me his bowl. Tomas, looking ashen, unable to stop blinking, poured me the soup from his shaking hand, spilling some on the floor. I wanted to save him from this Nazi bastard.

"Thank you," I whispered to him.

"Drink up," Tomas said, feigning a smile to the commandant.

Strands of stiff hair floated on the surface. The muddy-colored broth smelled wrong, yet I couldn't resist and slurped up the foul soup. When the vat was empty, the commandant ordered us to gather in a circle to relish the "quality of the meat" sitting at the bottom. There lay three maggot-infested rats. He squealed with delight while we ran outside to puke up the soup. Most of us spent the night behind our barrack cramping and throwing up onto a snowbank against the fence.

～

Two nights later Rails woke in a fever dream.

"Blood, ice. Ice, blood," he whimpered. "Can blood freeze?"

I placed my jacket over him and put a small piece of cheese in his mouth. Rails grabbed my shoulder. He could barely talk. "Our championship game . . . that play . . . that play at home plate, Upchuck . . . the ump missed the call. You were safe. I missed you, buddy boy."

I slept by his side into the night until Sparky tugged my arm. Rails wasn't breathing. I rolled him over like a collection of brittle sticks in a sack and tried to shake the life back into his limp body. Jacob and Sparky pulled me away. Victor was chewing something a few feet away.

"What's that in your mouth, Victor? Spit it out!" I shouted.

"He was a thud anyway," Victor grumbled. A *thud* was a term used when someone died during the night.

"You pried the cheese from his mouth with your dirty fingers, you sick bastard? Who's the enemy now? The Nazis or you? Maybe we should be fighting you!"

Heaving tears, I ran at him, but Sparky and Wigs held me back.

Rails had no essentials. No family photos. Sparky asked for his boots. I nodded, then took the tags from around his neck in hopes of bringing them back to his family. Sparky put on his new boots and went with Jacob and Wigs outside in the snowstorm to fetch a wooden plank stored behind the barrack. Under guard, we placed Rails on top of the plank and walked him to the pit located at the base of the hillside at the far end of the camp. Bags of lime bordering the square grave stood erect like family members paying their last respects. We brought more boards to lay on top of the dead bodies and walked Rails to an open spot where he could rest in peace. When Sparky threw lime over Rails, I thought I'd suffocate. My heart pounded through my chest. Jacob rested his hand on my shoulder.

The chaplain arrived and offered a few words.

"Father, lift up John 'Rails' McNamara to the highest order. May he find peace and harmony in the ever after, for we know, as did Jesus Christ our Lord, he will rise again in all his glory."

I beat my chest with Rails's dog tags squeezed inside my fist and wondered which one of us would be next to receive the chaplain's benediction in this ungodly cemetery. I couldn't take another moment in the pit and ran out.

Halfway to the barrack, my intestines cramped, and I had to let it go in my pants. I pulled them off and cleaned my legs with snow. A guard nearby was kind enough to look the other way. I felt no shame under such conditions; I was unraveling into the Nazis' desired creation: a *filthy swine*. I cleaned my pants with cold water from a puddle and placed them near the stove inside the barrack. Jacob, Stan, Sparky, and Wigs came over for a prayer while I continued to cry.

"We mustn't let Rails's soul die," said Jacob. "Therefore, we remember him. The ink in this pen, gifted from my father, will be used to scribe Rails's name inside my journal and the names of all who die from Nazi war crimes. Each soul will be remembered for eternity with their name herein. One day they'll be accounted for in the proper way." Jacob glanced at the door, then called out as he wrote the name: "*Prisoner #23 John "Rails" McNamara—land of the fireflies—died from consumption and lethal experimental serum injections.*

"We recite this Jewish prayer when someone we love departs: *Hamakom y'nachem.*"

"Hamakom y'nachem," Sparky and I repeated.

I bowed my head.

"*Etchem b'toch sh'ar,*" continued Jacob.

"Etchem b'toch sh'ar," we repeated.

"*Availai tziyon.*"

"Availai tziyon."

"*V'Yerushalayim.* May God comfort you among all the mourners of Zion and Jerusalem."

"V'Yerushalayim."

I held on to the hope of holding Sandee's hand in prayer one day soon.

"I lost another one, my brothers." Jacob spat out a tooth. "If we don't get liberated soon, I'll be number twenty-four, and you'll have to add me to my own journal."

Jacob hid the bound journal inside the lining of his threadbare jacket as we lay down and waited for another sunrise, hoping our liberation would come.

༄

The image of Sandee's face was fading from my memory. While working under a truck, I attempted to conjure up all her features. *Her pale blue eyes . . . or are they hazel? How long was her hair . . . to her shoulders, her elbows? Is her birthmark on the right or left cheek?*

"You! What fuck is problem?" shouted Ubl'dak. "Get moving. Too slow today. Finish and get to next truck—or no cheese!"

I was losing my way, confused as to where I was, not recognizing how to fix a clutch system that normally I could do in my sleep. I swirled with dizziness and vomited on the way to the infirmary, terrified they might poke me with injections.

The nurse with glossy eyes handed me a jar of white pills and sent me back to my barrack without consulting the doctor. But when I woke that night, I was in a dire sweat. The evil bug advanced like the German army plowing through the Ardennes. My heart was pounding as timpani drums thundered in my ears. I tried to lift my head and whimpered like a wounded animal. I became delirious. Jacob and Sparky, along with a much older prisoner, brought packed snow from the outside to place on my forehead.

"Jacob! I received a letter from Sandee today."

"There are no letters, Charlie. I want you to meet Rabbi Benjamin Levy. He's here to pray with you."

"'My baseball man,' she wrote, "'did you die . . . or are you playing hide-and-seek? Are you in the forest . . . or are you already dead?'"

"Charlie, open your eyes." Rabbi Benjamin Levy had a patchy salt-and-pepper beard with kind brown eyes.

"George?"

"No, Charlie, I'm Rabbi Levy."

"*Baruch Hashem*, Rabbi Levy . . . Sandee . . . Sandee . . ."

"*Baruch Hashem*, Charlie." He smiled. As I fell back asleep, I heard him whisper in my ear, "My brother, it will not end with you calling out for Sandee from this wretched place. You will leave this earthly world holding her tender, wrinkled hand."

⌒

It might have been hours or days when I finally woke from a turbulent fever dream where I was clawing my way through spiderwebs toward my father. I couldn't get to him, unable to rip myself free from the sticky silk strands wrapped around my limbs. It was my own cry that woke me.

As the bitter wind battered the barrack, my morality was torched by the tongue of the serpent; the devil had returned in the form of hunger, and I would eat—no matter the cost. *I'll steal from a thief.* I slithered like a snake along the floor toward Victor; he had to have a potato stashed somewhere, undoubtedly one he'd stolen from someone else. As I drew closer, I was divinely saved by a horn blaring in the yard. The headlights splintered through the siding, halting me from entering further into Victor's web. He would have strangled me to death.

A rush of hope came from those trucks. I scurried away from Victor and peered through a crack on the west wall and saw the Red Cross pull into a makeshift overhang. A metal floodlight swinging on a rafter washed over the dirty deeds of the Nazi guards. The scavengers began opening *our* rations, gorging themselves. I pressed my eyes against the siding and watched their mouths being stuffed with food. I pounded the wall, then returned to my spot on the floor next to Wigs. I almost didn't recognize him; his flesh was drawn in from the lack of food—and hope.

"What day is it today?" I asked him.

"February something," Wigs answered while scratching lice scabs off his forehead.

"Kapos are eating our rations in the yard. What's your favorite dish your mammy makes you, Wigs?"

"Brisket in the steamer. It'll bring tears to your eyes, Buck. You're hungry. That's a good sign. You must be feeling better."

"Wigs, did we really drop three-thousand-pound bags of flour on those poor boys climbing out from underneath that bridge in South Carolina? That was only weeks ago."

"Where the fuck are our guys, Buck? Where?"

An SS officer entered and delivered a message, along with what was left of the Red Cross packages.

"All Stalag IX-B POWs will report to the yard for roll call tomorrow at 0600 hours!" he yelled. "All the Jewish prisoners will be promoted to a new work detail at another POW camp. Three hundred fifty are needed. There will be more food, fresh water for bathing, and recreation in the yard. Anyone protecting a Jew or Jews hiding in the barracks will be shot. At roll call, the Jews will take one step forward from the line when the commandant gives the order."

The guard left us with ten packages from the Red Cross for over two hundred of us to share. Rabbi Benjamin Levy divided the packages into two groups: those having trouble swallowing were given the mashed peaches, and the rest would share cans of tuna, powdered milk, chocolate, raisins, and vitamin C tablets.

"I'm not stepping foot to my death," said Jacob. "Better conditions at the next camp? My God, they're going to kill us Jews tomorrow."

"No, Jacob," said Rabbi Levy. "Not if *all* the prisoners take the one step forward. Our survival will depend on uniting as one."

"How in the heck we gonna do that?" asked Wigs. "Jews are scattered all over this dang camp, not just in our barrack."

"There are many throughout the camp, this is true," responded the rabbi. "We must send out a message through the night. We will take turns going to the latrine until we meet at least one POW from each barrack and tell them to *all* take a step forward tomorrow morning—or we will *all* die."

War training, no matter from what country you served, made it clear to its soldiers: find your allies, and stick together.

⌒

The sun had not risen, yet the rifles were out. Tomas and Derek came in for us and emptied the "barrack of the Jews" into the yard, joining thousands of prisoners shaking from the cold. Army jackets were no match for the unrelenting northerly blast that swept through the camp with the power of Boreas. The yard was frozen underfoot. In the weeks since our heads were shaved, our beards had grown. Icicles dangled from the hair on the rabbi's chin. The collective steam coming from four thousand mouths made the encampment look like it was burning down.

"Are you ready for this, Cal?"

"Never felt more ready in my life," he said, shaking from the wind. "Fuck these guys."

Puffing steam from his nose, wearing no overcoat, looking crisp and crazed, Walter Von Hanzel, the Rat, entered the frozen yard.

"Stay close if things get crazy, Wigs," I whispered.

The Rat marched in front and took his position atop a crate and stared at us with the grin of a schoolyard bully during recess. "To all the Jewish soldiers, this is your day," he yelled through a bullhorn. "You will be honoring your country with bravery by serving ours. And when you are let free after the war, you will be remembered. Jewish soldiers, please take one step forward."

All went quiet; only strong winds could be heard whipping through the trees until together, every soul from Stalag IX-B shuffled one step forward. My knee shook while taking that step with my brothers, Cal Wiggins, Jacob Goldmann, James "Sparky" Esposito, Chaplain Morris, Medic Avenado, Stan Loeb, and Rabbi Benjamin Levy.

"No, you idiots!" yelled the Rat. "We only need the Jews!"

Only a handful of prisoners stayed back from the thousands who took their second step forward. Victor was among the defectors. Jacob waved him forward, but he gave him the finger.

The wind snapped an immense tree branch, sending it crashing to the ground, echoing through the gray dawn. The commandant stood in silence, his head violently twitching. One minute passed. Two minutes. Three. Then the Rat bit. He pointed to a terribly thin soldier standing in front of him. A guard pulled him from the line.

"That's Yannick," Wigs whispered to me. "He's on my garbage detail—talking poems he makes up in his head."

"Take off your clothes," the Rat demanded.

Yannick shook his head.

"*Schießen ihn in den Kopf*," he called to the guard, who then pointed his rifle at Yannick.

I couldn't hear the shot among the snapping tree branches but saw Yannick crumple to the ground.

"Those who refuse to remove their clothing will be executed where they stand!" screamed the Rat through his bullhorn. At gunpoint, the commandant watched us strip down, then headed back to his heated quarters.

The hurling subzero wind and snow chafed my body. I tried to stay warm by jumping up and down, hoping not to shit my guts out. Soon, men began to fall. No one dared move to help. Farther down the line, the good chaplain collapsed and exhaled his last gurgling breath.

#24 Chaplain Adam Morris, Leinster, Ireland. His only love, Edwina. Cause of death: Hypothermia—frozen to death in a lineup commanded by SS commandant, Walter Von Hanzel, the Rat.

Thousands of teeth chattered like sewing machines. I fought the cold by mentally replaying every kiss with Sandee. Where, when, how long, what it led to. I disassembled and reassembled the R44 tractor over and over in my mind. I fantasized a new version that could have a bin for catching the cuttings. I conjured up the smell of Mom's chicken soup filled with carrots, onions, celery, salt, pepper, and a touch of garlic, the delicious aroma steaming above the pot.

"One more time!" The Rat returned to the yard and yelled through his bullhorn, "Jews step forward—or the shooting begins!"

This time Stan, Jacob, Avenado, and Rabbi Levy, along with one hundred or so, took a step forward. I stayed put. The Rat had had enough; he and the guards began making their own selections. Prisoners went scurrying. The guards shot two of them running for their lives. I grabbed Wigs before he took off running himself and told him not to move if we wanted to live. The Jews and those who were perceived to be undesirable to the Nazis were being separated and corralled at the gate. The Rat grabbed Victor and added him to the group. I stepped back and pushed Wigs behind me as the Rat grabbed *my* arm and swung me around. I wanted to yell that this was a mistake, that I wasn't Jewish.

It was all happening so fast.

"You. And you!" he yelled at Sparky as he yanked us over to the chosen ones.

"I'll go," yelped Wigs. I raised my arm up to stop him.

"See you on the other side of this," I cried out as I was being taken away. "Promise me you'll live."

"I promise!" Wigs yelled back. "If you promise!"

CHAPTER 14

There would be no chance debating with the authority that this was all wrong, a terrible mix-up, that I was a Catholic-baptized choir boy misidentified as an American Jewish soldier. I would not be heard. There would be no distinction, no special treatment—whether I'd beg otherwise. And why should there be? I was squeezed against quaking bodies pumping with blood no different than my own.

Rabbi Levy, Jacob Goldmann, Sparky, Stan Loeb, Medic Avenado, and I were once again stuffed into another wooden coffin on the rails, heading to God knows where, wondering why our America and our Allies had forsaken us. Victor stood in the far corner, pushing others away so he could have more space.

The intolerable uncertainty of not knowing where we were going, or when we would arrive, or how we would survive infected my thoughts. I needed Wigs; I was lost without my copilot navigating our way. I dug into my pocket to pull out Sandee's photo. A smudge on the surface ran through the middle of her face. I lost my breath and became untethered, terrified that her features had faded from memory. Or was I fading from the relentless hunger that had stripped away, layer by layer, my connectedness to the world—to my past, my future? I pressed the photo to my dry, cold lips and prayed I would see her again.

Lights flashed through the wooden slats onto tight faces wincing from every wobble; our bones banged together as we roared past German towns through the frightfully cold night. *Were people in those homes not aware of how their Nazi party treated its prisoners? If they knew, would they not bleed compassion? Or are these people living behind poorly insulated walls, too cold to care?*

I pressed my nose against the wood siding, desperately trying to smell the sweet scent of freedom on the other side.

"There is great irony today, my brothers," said Rabbi Levy, his shoulder bouncing against mine. "I believe today might be the Fast of Esther before Purim. Who will fast with me?" His gentle laugh turned into irrepressible hacking.

"I will, my rabbi," said Medic Avenado, breaking into a smile.

"Me too," I said and thought of when I fasted for Sandee.

The rabbi raised his chin and took in a labored breath.

"Let this cold boxcar be our synagogue. Recite a prayer with me. You, too, Charlie—for Sandee and your child one day. The moon wanes, symbolizing our sins along with the erosion of a divine presence."

Jacob joined the prayer and grabbed my hand as the rabbi continued.

"Even a new moon shines through these walls of darkness, and as such, we are grateful."

With his coughing, the rabbi could not continue the prayer, so Jacob carried on.

"We Jews will fast and pray. Let us raise our heads toward holy Jerusalem."

Jacob placed his hand on my shoulder. My body was shivering to the bone, my mouth parched, my mind locked in a permanent fantasy depicting a heroic liberation: a bomb would drop, and Allied troops would burst through the singed earth, halt the train, and take over the Krauts. Freedom! I'd pick up where I'd left off—with Sandee—and leave this horror behind.

Jacob took my hand. "May it be Your will, Hashem, my God and God of my ancestors, to lead us home in peace."

Rabbi Levy responded, "May You rescue us from every foe, every impossible tyrant, every stolen hour . . ."

Rabbi Levy, Medic Avenado, Jacob, Stan, and all the other Jews locked in this moving prison found solace in their faith—and they included me as if I were a member of their tribe. I felt abandoned by my faith, my country, my father. I banged my head against the siding. Rabbi Levy asked me, "What will you eat as your first meal when you return home, my brother?"

Before answering, I whimpered from a sensation in my heart all too familiar. For honoring my country, for stepping up, for becoming a gentleman, I still couldn't escape abuse. *Where was my protection at home? Where was it now?*

"Charlie, Charlie, my boy, tell me, what will you eat?" the rabbi asked again.

"Bratwurst," I cried as the rabbi held my hand. "From Usinger's. The best ever. They serve it on a kaiser roll."

He chuckled, then coughed. "You're a Catholic, yes? From a town filled with German immigrants. But now you're being taken by Germans for being a Jew—Germans who also produce your favorite nonkosher sandwich on a kaiser roll. Do you know what *kaiser* means?"

I shook my head.

"German emperor." Rabbi Levy laughed through his awful wheezing. "Pray for a world gone mad."

～

Stan Loeb yelled to be let out. I hadn't realized the train had stopped. I had no sense of time—three days, perhaps four, were spent on the rails in agony. The guards could be heard laughing from outside our boxcar. One of them let out a squeal so familiar, it was as if my chest was hit with shrapnel. The latch released, and the door slid open to a blinding, colorless sky. Below were salivating shepherd dogs ready to break from their leashes, baring their fangs, choking themselves for the chance to tear us apart. Jacob and Rabbi Levy moved to the edge of the open door. It was a good six feet to the ground. I peered over Jacob's shoulder. And there he was, boots gleaming, freshly shaven.

"You thought you'd seen the last of me?" yelled the Rat through his bullhorn. "All Jews step forward!"

Any sliver of hope in appealing my fate had vanished.

Rabbi Levy raised his hand. "We've been standing for many days," he barely could utter from his raw throat. "We'll need help getting down. And we must have food."

"You must *work*!" he spat.

Rabbi Levy offered a forgiving smile and put his palms together. Then as if in slow motion, he bowed and fell headfirst to the concrete platform below, his neck snapping like a brittle branch. Jacob lost all sense and jumped down after him. A guard grabbed Jacob and tossed him aside like waste.

"*Bring sie zu Berga!*" the Rat shouted. Two guards dragged Rabbi Levy's limp body away. "*Wirf diesen Juden in den Wald.*"

Rabbi Benjamin Levy was tragically gone, a brilliant light snuffed out.

Hundreds of POWs helped one another down, holding hands for balance, gathering on the landing. Then at gunpoint we were moved out of the station on weak legs, falling like fawns.

The snow-covered hills looked like white silk among the shadows nestled within the undulating topography. I inhaled gusts of crisp air reminiscent of Meyer Creek in the dead of winter. I yearned for home and feared I would not be ice-skating with Sandee in the park anytime soon.

It was maddening to be in such a place of beauty with rifles pointed at our backs. Shades of dark orange and pink illuminated the sky, signaling night was imminent. We plodded through quaint villages dotted with dollhouses puffing smoke from their chimneys. I wanted to be home sitting by the fireplace, even if it meant being next to Dad in his recliner, passed out from drinking.

I thought of Rabbi Levy's unyielding faith, then grabbed my stomach. Gestating anger, perhaps for a lifetime, uncontrollably rose in my chest. Was it the total loss of my free will or the death of Rabbi Levy that suddenly caused my thoughts to turn dark? I fantasized about the commandant dying in a most horrific way. *When he sleeps, I'll shove a maggot-infested rat in his mouth, then slam his face with my fist, causing the jagged bone in his nose to pierce his brain and bleed out from his eyes.* I gasped for air, not from slogging through the heavy snow but from the demonic transformation taking hold in my consciousness. I shook the violent images from my mind and carried on.

As the sky dimmed and more snow fell, we encountered three women swaddled in clothing, pushing wooden carts filled with radishes. The stout women looked away in disgust, as if they were in the presence of lepers. The guard with a scar on his chin approached them and pointed at their radishes. The women raised their arms and shook their jowls, yelling, "No, no!"

Weren't they perhaps mothers themselves imagining this could be their sons starving to death if the tables were turned? The guard plunged his hands into the radishes and pulled out fistfuls, tipping over the cart, leaving the women gobbling like turkeys. He threw them a glance while munching on the radishes. We moved on from the women along the winding slope that overlooked the majestic vistas.

After trudging one foot in front of the other well into night, we came upon a camp that was not for POWs but civilians, many of whom had drawn figures of the Star of David in the snow. Fingers popping through mitten holes clutched the frozen chain-link fence. A sign was lit up and hung above the entrance that led into the yard of the camp: *Berga 1.* Armed guards inside the fence flanked hundreds of withered men, women, and children dressed in pajamalike, striped clothing. With hollowed faces void of expression, they huddled together in the bitter wind. Near me was a little girl drawing stick figures in the snow, perhaps of her family members whom she'd been separated from. *How many of these wretched camps were dotted across Europe? Why weren't our planes tearing through those clouds and dropping paratroopers? For the love of God, where are our saviors?*

As we traveled alongside a frozen river, I looked to the darkening sky, praying for a divine liberation while thinking about those deathly, gray faces behind the fence at Berga 1, juxtaposed against this divine landscape, trying to reconcile the madness of man.

We turned from the riverbank and made our way uphill to another encampment perched on a plateau. Thick pines taller than any building

I'd seen in Wisconsin banked the far end of two small barracks. The snow-filled yard was empty of prisoners. A rusty metal sign was illuminated from a lightbulb swinging above the gate entrance: Berga 2.

As mothers were polishing silver flatware in Wauwatosa, with children playing near the creek, or Sandee and her parents readying to light the candles for Shabbat, I had slipped through the cracks into the abyss, having no idea whether the world knew if I still existed or not. I wanted to turn left, run down that barren hillside, and keep going. Our guard wouldn't shoot me in the back. To the front I'd run. All I had to do was simply turn left.

My delusion of escaping ended with a rifle jabbed in my back like a cattle prod used to move me through the gate and into the dark yard. The moonlight poured onto a small cinder block building, prompting whispers of a word wafting through the POWs like echoes from beyond the grave: crematorium. I held back a few strides to meet up with our guard with the scar on his chin.

"If you murder us, when this war is over, they'll put you away for life," I said.

"Be quiet!" someone shouted from behind. I turned to see it was Tomas Frantz. His eyes were sullen. No longer in uniform, he was dressed in civilian clothes, wearing a tattered wool coat that could have been plucked from the lost and found. "We're not going to be murdered," he blurted out. He moved up beside us.

"What are you doing here?" asked Jacob.

"I've been demoted—or promoted, depending on how you view it. I'm just a prisoner like you, now. Best be quiet."

A half-track drove in with the commandant in the back seat, gripping his brown hose. Without leaving the vehicle, the Rat shouted in German and drove off. Jacob, Sparky, Stan, and Avenado all turned to Tomas for the translation.

"*Gib ihnen ihre letzte Dusche.* Give them their last shower."

We were ordered to remove our clothing and line up in front of the tall steel doors that led into the cinder block building. *Would it be fast or slow? How much pain would rip through my throat?* Jacob held my arm, while Avenado, Sparky, and Stan linked arms as we entered. The door banged the steel jamb and locked into place. The moonlight streamed through open slats at the top of the tiled walls that were much too high and narrow to escape through. The soft light spilled onto our emaciated bodies. My rib cage extended outward from my body. Purple veins snaked under my translucent skin. Jacob caught me trembling from my own ghostlike vision.

"We're beyond what we see and what the mind comprehends, Charlie. Don't be mesmerized or amazed by the illusion." Jacob lifted my chin, taking my eyes away from my corpselike body. "Rabbi Levy would tell us that the body returns to the earth, dust to dust, but the soul returns to God who gave it. Repeat it: the soul returns to God."

"The soul returns to God."

I shook so violently, weakened from the paralyzing fear of being gassed, I could barely stand. I rested my hands on the cool tiled wall to steady myself. The pipe that hung above our heads creaked as if it would burst. A minute later, exhilarating water shot from tiny holes dotting the pipe. It didn't matter that it sprayed wildly and felt like shards of ice tearing at my skin. For my parched body, it was life itself. We opened our mouths and lapped up the water like thirsty hound dogs. Weeks-old dirt pooled at our feet before streaming down the drains. The water shut off after a minute or two. The steel doors slid open as I dribbled out the last of my brown urine.

The cold air felt like a thousand needles pricking my skin. We dressed back into our filthy fatigues and were moved to the open yard. Two small clapboard barracks were set a few feet from the fence; only yards beyond, the forest beckoned. Another wooden building sat on the south end, where three SS officers convened out front. I had a sick feeling about the large depression in the ground on the north end. Empty—for now.

A giant tree was in the center of the camp, its barren branches burdened by the weight of the snow. The guards started a head count. One of them turned, and it was Derek from Stalag IX-B. He caught the eye of Tomas and went to him. As Derek was pretending to count, he and Tomas had words. When they finished, Derek and the guards kept counting, slower the second time around. Then again and again until dawn, when we were placed in one long line and were demanded to give our name and rank, which was then documented on a yellow legal pad.

Stan, Sparky, Medic Avenado, Jacob Goldmann, Tomas Frantz, and I were assigned to barrack A. Victor took his spot on the far end of the lower rack, shoving some of the other prisoners aside. We were given a thin sack of straw for bedding and slept on triple-decker wooden planks that extended the length of the rickety building. Beetle holes the size of quarters riddled the siding. The roof had been chewed through by varmints, and most of the wood plank flooring had been damaged by termites. No heating. No waste hole. The shitting would happen over a porcelain tub outside connecting to a cesspool.

"Let's grab space together," Jacob suggested. "You'll be with us, too, Tomas."

We took space on the upper row, leaving the lower ones for many who were too sick to climb up. Avenado, Stan, and Sparky piled in next to Jacob, Tomas, and me. Engraved into the wood post just an arm's length from my head were two names: Max Straus / Alex Levine. I wondered where they'd gone and why this camp was empty upon our arrival. I dared not engrave my name for fear of tempting fate.

"Tomas, how long were you a Nazi?" Sparky asked.

"I was *never* a Nazi," Tomas responded. "I was an architect, then a baker. On June 26, 1941, three years, seven months, seventeen days ago I was forced to begin guarding political prisoners . . . Jews . . . locked away in holding rooms." Tomas took a breath. "The poor, confused faces of those children peering out into the forest, hoping they would be saved by magic animals who would take them home. I had no choice but to put those children and their parents and grandparents on trains to Auschwitz." He paused. "I looked forward to every sunrise when I would read from my favorite philosopher, Immanuel Kant on the principle of *the categorical imperative,* which dealt with the theory that the rightness and wrongness of our actions does not depend on their consequences, but on whether they fulfill their duty. I had no time to read the morning we were taken by the Nazis. My little boy was crying from a rash on his bum. I gently applied some ointment on the red bumps and kissed his toes and spun a dreidel toy we used during Hanukkah to fascinate him. As the dreidel whirled, I heard the front door crash open. Ivan jumped. I picked up the dreidel and put it in my pocket and carried Ivan quietly into our bedroom, where my Lovina stood erect in abject fear.

"'Get your father to the top floor right away,' I demanded. Like mice, we scattered upstairs and hid inside the wall where I cut a hole and used one of Ari's paintings to cover us up. Lovina gave Ivan crackers to distract him from crying. The old home shook from items being tossed against the walls. The banging on the wooden steps gave clues to the Nazis' proximity—they were close, perhaps only a few feet away. I was doing everything to keep Ivan from crying, but he screamed and bit my finger to remove my hand from covering his sweet lips. Can you imagine? Muzzling your boy who only wants to be free?

"The Nazis found us behind the painting and pulled us from the hole. Lovina's father raised his arms. 'You foul Nazis will be cursed by your demonic deeds and suffer interminable guilt!' he cried. 'Your children's children will languish in the black ether of your eternal sin! This will never go away!' he yelled. 'We will never forget!'

"With that, one of the guards slapped this beautiful old man across his face. I grabbed Ari to steady him, pleading with the guards to let us go, only to be met with a rifle whip across my back. I held Ivan while being pushed down the narrow stairway at gunpoint into the bright, empty street. Lovina took Ivan from me to calm his hysteria—and hers."

He paused and caught his breath and wiped the tears from his eyes.

"I asked the Nazi guards where we were going. 'To live with "other Jews,"' he said, smiling through his teeth that looked like they had settled badly from an earthquake. I wanted to choke the life from him. The Nazis collected other families and dragged us to a field behind the Leiden Cemetery. I recognized many of my neighbors who came to me for bread at the bakery. And now they were digging their graves.

"Not me. I was dragged away from the cemetery by a Nazi guard."

Tomas could no longer hold in his suffering. He heaved out tears as we held him. "I tried to resist," he said. "The guard pounded on my back with his rifle and tossed me into the backseat of a truck. Little Ivan, who'd finally fallen asleep in Lovina's arms, was startled awake by her desperate scream. 'No, don't take my Tomas!'

"This grubby SS officer with a greasy mouth from eating a buttered sandwich held a pistol to my head. I thought it was over. 'We could have made you dig your own grave,' he said, 'for marrying a dirty Jewess. Welcome to the Nazi party.'"

After a long pause, Tomas shook his head. "They're going to work us hard tomorrow," he added. "Derek said something about caves."

I yearned for home and the knotty pine ceiling in my bedroom. *What if I die on this wooden board?* I broke into a sweat. "Jacob, I . . . I need one of your prayers."

"*Mi Shebeirach avoteinu, M'kor hab'racha l'moteinu.* May the source of strength who blessed the ones before us help us find the courage to make our life a blessing, and let us say, amen."

I repeated, "Find the courage to make our life a blessing."

"You're going be okay, Charlie." He reached over Tomas to hold my hand.

My sweat turned cold as I shivered my way into some version of sleep.

⌣

Derek yelled for us to move out before sunrise. About one hundred of us in barrack A proceeded to walk along the river for a few kilometers and then turned uphill past an abandoned farmhouse. We stopped in front of a series of cave entrances blown into the hillside, where sepulchral figures holding pickaxes emerged from the darkness, waddling nearly on all fours, bobbing their heads on limp necks, tongues wagging from their gaping mouths—Berga 1 prisoners. One of them tentatively touched the air force patch on my shoulder with his dusty finger. He struggled to speak from his dry, ravaged throat.

"American soldier?"

"Yes."

"What hope is left if you are here with us?" His head dropped as he handed me his pickax.

Derek shoved our group into the cave entrance that had the number 14 chiseled into the rock. The air tasted of iron. Jacob, Stan, Sparky, Avenado, Tomas, and I were loaded onto an open metal tram with other Berga 1 prisoners. The dim sunlight receded behind us as we fell deep into the dark abyss. I closed my eyes. The rhythm of the tram made me sleepy. I was being pulled away from my painful reality by the gift of Hypnos, setting me free of my conscious state and into delicious delirium, before the tram slammed to a halt at the bottom of the shaft.

Every time I woke from sleep, the primary sensation wasn't discouragement, sadness, or fear, although I constantly felt them all. It was hunger. Intense, unyielding hunger. Even interned in this dusty, acrid-smelling hellhole, the devil had control over my malnourished brain, controlling my senses. Inexplicably, I smelled ham sizzling on the skillet.

A Berga 1 prisoner refused to leave the tram. He struggled to breathe; saliva bubbled from his mouth. He pointed up the chute, begging to go back to the surface. It took two guards pulling his fingers off the railing to move him out. He fell, and they beat him while he was curled in a ball. I wanted to jump the guards and help this poor man who was suffocating from claustrophobia.

We left him fetal and crying as we were pushed through a narrow tunnel that opened up into a voluminous cavern the size of the factory at AC Machinery. The cave teemed with Berga 1 prisoners banging pickaxes against a black wall, loading the chiseled rocks into wheelbarrows, then dumping them into large buckets on the tram. Engineers supervising the construction of a hydrogenation plant were wearing work shirts branded with a patch from a German company. Their army was wanting for fuel. Being hidden underground would protect their asset from bombardment. I couldn't bear knowing that my labor might help them win the war.

A squeaky voice came from a nub of an SS officer hardly taller than my chest.

"*Willkommen* to our caves, Jew prisoners. We have been waiting for you." He swayed side to side while burnishing his pistol with a cloth. "First, you will work until we win the war—or you die. So don't die! Second, you will use pickax to make holes for the powder sausage. Then some will attach wire to ignitor. Once we have twenty-four holes, you blow the fucking wall. Boom! Dig, blow, dig, blow. Boom! Then carry rocks to tram then to river and dump. Then start again. Your life now."

I tried to assess the safety of the operation through the darkness and dust but realized I was kidding myself. There would be nothing safe about this operation. I dropped to a knee and realized we weren't going to be rescued down here.

I grabbed the oak handle of my pickax, the grain stained with blood. I raised it above my shoulder and slung it against the black stone. Without an ounce of fat to absorb the blow, the impact rattled my bones. I took in a deep breath to keep on living and banged the wall again and again. We all did, hour after hour.

"*Schlug ihen auf den Rücken!*" an SS officer shouted through a bullhorn. Without provocation, like some masochistic ritual, the guards began to beat on our backs with the butts of their rifles. After the beatings, we were oddly given a water break—as if the guards felt guilty for their abuse. A lump grew on my back from a blow Derek delivered.

"This is criminal," cried Sparky. "I want to jam my pickax up their asses."

"One day there will be a reckoning," said Jacob.

"Don't plan on that," said Tomas. "There'll be no redemption for those who have committed crimes beyond description."

"There will be," Jacob responded, "for those who repent."

"Not for beasts like me." Tomas hung his head. "I pointed my rifle and shoved families taken from their homes through the wet, dense fog that had swept in off the Black Sea, hovering a few hundred yards inland. I was ordered to tell them lies, give them hope to keep them moving along the road. 'We are on our way to a new town where you'll live in harmony with your other Jews,' I told them. 'First, we have to stop at a silo for potatoes.' Some older men carried their Torahs, while women carried their young. There would be no potatoes taken from a silo. Instead, we lined them up and placed their heels on the edge of a dug-out ditch along a dirt road splitting the potato farm in two. Some of the guards doused the families with petroleum, including the children."

Tomas took a sip of water, his hands shaking. "The SS taught us to look away at the moment of death. 'If you don't see it, you won't remember it,' they promised. I wanted to believe my own lies. Right before the first bullet landed, this Jewish community, taken from their small village, shifted their gaze southeast toward Jerusalem—and prayed: *The Lord is our guardian. The Lord is our protective shade at our right hand. The Lord will guard us from all evil. He will guard our soul for all time* . . . Lovina's father often recited that prayer.

"I did what I was told, Jacob. I shut my eyes . . ." Tomas paused. "Yet I heard their cries and smelled their burning skin. I smell it now." Tomas began to cry.

"They took my family and murdered them, and I've been a ghost of a man ever since. They knew I was destroyed and turned me into the devil's making." I put my arm around him as he shook.

A horn signaled the first blast of the day. We huddled on the far side of the wall and readied ourselves. The explosion sent shock waves through my body. The cloud of dust came roaring like a desert storm. I used my shirttail to cover my mouth, but there was no way to escape the pernicious particles crawling like a colony of red ants on the attack over my hands and face, stinging my eyes, burning the valley of my throat.

I felt someone grab my hand in the dark, dusty storm. Tomas was giving me a piece of bread.

"Save one, save all," he uttered.

I took a bite and placed the bread in my jacket before the dust had settled and was ordered back to the wall. Fifty political prisoners and fifty American soldiers choking and blinking from a blanket of dust resumed the brutal work because our lives depended on it. The heavy tool dulled by countless collisions made the job interminably slow. Twelve hours later I was back at the barrack, lying on my rack, vibrating in pain. Raising my arm to scratch at the lice was nearly impossible. My muscles had stopped firing. I lay lifeless while my stomach growled with anger, demanding food.

Tomorrow would be the same and the next: torturous labor, a bit of turnip soup, black bread crawling with bugs, two water breaks, and then back to the rack for rest.

⌒

Night after night the unceasing wind kept flinging the barrack door open; the frame securing the latch had been destroyed by termites. Although I had warm bodies pressed against me, I remained cold and alone—and abandoned. The skies went silent. No one was coming. We were on our own; just wrapped up stray dogs that had been kicked to the curb, huddling to keep warm.

"We'll die soon if we don't come up with a plan for more rations, blankets, and showers!" said Jacob. He sat up and continued. "Listen, everyone. We must strike until they comply with the Geneva Convention."

"Good speech," Victor responded. Victor hadn't said a word since we arrived at Berga. He'd lost his network of cronies back at Stalag IX-B. He slammed his hand against the rack and laughed.

"Are you in or out, Victor?" Tomas snapped.

"Shut mouth, kapo."

"They'll need us to work if they hope to win the war," I added. "And I sure as hell don't want to help them win. I'll strike."

"We stop working. You think they bring us steak and wine?" asked Victor, turning away from us on his rack. "Idiots. I go back to sleep."

"I'm in," said Stan, lying below us. "They need those refineries up and running. The game is over if they can't refuel their panzers."

"If you're with us," I yelled to everyone in our barrack, "knock on your rack!"

A unity of thumping indicated the strike was on.

The door swung open before sunrise. Derek entered the barrack with another gangly guard holding three sharp-toothed canines chomping their jaws. Derek gave the order to get moving to the caves. My hands trembled. Sparky came off his rack and stepped forward.

"Not until you double our rations and give us more breaks during our shift."

Derek glanced over at the guard who was holding one of the dogs.

"*Lass deinen hund los.*" The canine leaped forward and latched its teeth into Sparky's arm, shaking its head, ripping Sparky's flesh.

"*Halte den Hund an, Derek!*" yelled Tomas. "*Wir warden Kommen!*"

"*Ruckzug,*" Derek called out.

The dog unhinged its jaw, leaving Sparky bloodied.

"I need medical supplies to close his wound," Avenado pleaded.

"Stay with him. The rest go to cave," Derek ordered. "Now!"

We left Sparky and Avenado and walked into the cold white air, utterly defeated.

"Nice plan!" Victor yelled to the sky and laughed. "You got your meatball friend torn up."

"How'd the guards know to bring the dogs in today, Victor?" Jacob shot back. "Trading secrets again?"

"Fuck you, Jew."

I wanted to bust him up good. But neither I nor anyone else had the strength to take on Victor.

We carried on with the dogs on our tail until we entered the blackness of cave 14. Derek, no doubt, had been instructed to work us beyond our limits as punishment for our plan to strike; he cracked us harder than ever.

"Keep banging, keep going, no stop . . . keep going!" he shouted.

I hit the rock as hard as I could, causing sparks to fly in the black air like dancing fireflies at dusk. After many blows, my shoulder seized up. Derek belted me again, but this time with little force. His eyes were moist. He stopped pounding on the backs of the prisoners, resorting instead to verbal abuse. There was something human in him after all.

I returned the pickax to my right hand, bit my lip from the pain, and kept striking the black wall while only thinking of food and freedom. No matter the physical pain, my thoughts conjured images of hamburgers and shakes at the Jip-Joint or the Allied liberators storming the cave with guns blazing, taking out the Krauts. Whether in the cave, walking back to the barrack, or lying on my rack, my ears stayed tuned for planes in the air while thinking of food. And in my fleeting moments of sleep, my arms flailed about, hammering at the rock.

Every shift Derek yelled for us to keep going. The prisoners lining the wall could barely lift their pickaxes. The flicker in their eyes were burning out; some had fallen unconscious and were dragged away.

"*Mord nicht durch Vergasung, sondern durch harte Arbeit,*" Tomas groaned. "Mord nicht durch Verbrennung, sondern durch harte Arbeit."

"What does that mean?" I asked.

"Death by labor—not by gas," Tomas answered.

CHAPTER 15

The Nazis continued to force water from the rock, sending us to the cave for our fourteen-hour shifts when we had no strength left. Arms broke, and legs gave way. Jacob had written down six more deaths in his journal. As the days went on, conditions worsened, if that were possible. Less food. More dysentery. Fewer medical supplies, more pneumonia. Dried blood was caked on all the racks from choking up dust. I could see an impending death in the eyes of those whose minds had been eaten away from pain and hunger. The twitching would stop; their scratching would cease. It was only hours, not days—the end would come, another thud in the night.

If the outside world could've witnessed this unyielding torture, there would've been enough tears to transform the Sahara into a wetland.

Sparky, unusually quiet of late, was unable to wake one morning. Stan shook him, begging him to eat, forcing scraps of cabbage into his mouth. That all-too-familiar dead look in his eyes had emerged. He couldn't manage a smile when I asked him to leave out the oregano in the meatballs.

"I'm going to heaven when I die, fellas," he finally whispered. "Do you know why? Because I've already been to hell."

Derek came in pointing his rifle, yelling for us to move out to the caves. I explained Sparky wasn't unable to make his shift.

"Get him up and move out, or no rations today for anyone."

Victor jabbed at Sparky with his stubby finger.

"I will not be deprived ration because of you, stupid wop."

Victor left the barrack and came back with a bucket of snow and dumped it on Sparky, sending him into a seizure. Medic Avenado put a stick in his mouth to prevent him from swallowing his tongue. After a minute or so, Derek ran from the barrack after seeing Sparky jettisoned off the rack and convulsing on the ground, as if possessed by the devil. Sparky's face turned into a tawny bronze, his lips became supple, his cheeks flushed. He even appeared to smile before sinking into his clothes, his face falling into his skull.

Sparky was gone.

As I looked down on him, I understood what was happening to us. The acrid truth about war burned the roof of my mouth: we were being used by men of seemingly great wisdom and intelligence to instigate war by using men with seemingly less intelligence. Sparky was used in such a way. We all were.

What would be provided for those of us who made it out of this death camp when the world would never understand what it was like to be used by such men, men who cowardly sent us to do their murdering? Would they one day suffer from the sins of the serpent? Would I one day walk down Main Street in Wauwatosa and wave hello to ignorant men of culture and education who would inevitably use their power again in this way? If I made it home, in what state would God leave me to untangle death from life?

On our way to the cave, Tomas, Stan, Jacob, and I stopped at the pit to lay Sparky to rest. Jacob was too weak and distraught to offer a prayer.

Tomas sprinkled lime over Sparky's stiffening body, which was also being covered by a thin veil of snow. We held hands and cried. Tomas and Jacob were more than motherliness, more than my sadness. Their cries of shared grief seeped into my heart and pumped my blood, infusing me with the strength to live another day.

"They put hydrated lime on their bodies so their bones will never be discovered," cried Tomas. "No one will ever know. Governments will bury the truth of what happened here. It will be as if it never existed."

"Humanity must never forget," said Jacob. "My journal will make their souls everlasting. One name represents a thousand."

James "Sparky" Esposito. Murdered by shock, physical labor, and malnutrition. March 1945.

⌒

The suffering was the living; the living was the suffering. We were all half of ourselves now; our thoughts, our bodies were like clay molded together by the same misery. Clawing my way to sleep the night Sparky died, sepia-toned images clicked through my mind like slides spinning in a projector, flashing the devilish memories of my grim existence: bodies shredded in the Ardennes, Sparky choking for his last breath, Rabbi Levy's fall, Rails all skin and bones. I limped outside on weak legs and grabbed a handful of icy slush to wash my oily face and went behind our barrack to piss. Tomas was leaning against the siding, having a smoke given to him by Derek. He looked gray and deeply sad. One of the guards walked across the yard, so we strolled a bit farther behind the barrack.

"She was a beautiful woman, my Lovina, so devoted to her faith and family."

"My fiancée is Jewish, Tomas," I revealed.

"When you make it home, don't wait to convert. But if you're fortunate to have a child, as I was with Lovina, you'll be able to join your family in prayer regardless. That I didn't convert is my greatest regret."

We trembled from the sharp wind. Tomas took a drag on his cigarette.

"Derek is sure there'll be no more rations by the end of the week. Only for the SS and guards. He'll try to find a way to smuggle us some beans or potatoes." He paused and took another drag. "Starvation may come for us before the liberators do." Tomas threw his cigarette in a puddle, and returned to our barrack.

The luminous moon sliced through the planks, catching Stan Loeb's tortured, milky eyes pinched above the bridge of his nose, disappearing into dark sockets. He was pacing, babbling unintelligible instructions.

"Shut it, Stan!" yelled Victor.

Stan tried to stifle himself, but he kept on groaning. "It's time to go home."

"Shut it, or I shut your face," Victor pressed.

"Bug off, Victor!" I shouted.

Victor rose from his rack. The moonlight caught his grisly face, a werewolf on the prowl. He put his grimy hands on Stan's head.

"I crush skull if you don't shut mouth."

Stan went quiet. Victor released his grip and retreated to his rack.

But later that evening, Stan was up again, standing over me.

"We have to escape, Charlie," Stan whispered. "Otherwise, we'll end in the pit. I'm almost there. Come with me, guys," he pleaded.

"We're all too weak to make it through the forest," Jacob whispered back.

"The guards themselves are too weak and sick to catch us," responded Stan. "Most of them are worthless at night."

"Don't be stupid," Tomas whispered.

"You understand more than any of us, Tomas. The Allies aren't coming for us Jews."

We're going to die. A plane flies over every few days . . . but not for us.

"We have to save ourselves!" Stan shouted. He leaned in and brought his words to a whisper. "The fence is seventeen feet from behind our barrack. About forty feet to the trees. We hock a set of wire cutters from the cave, cut the bottom of the fence out back, and we're gone. We can reconnoiter the area to find our way to the front using a map I stole from under the seat of one of the trucks."

"I'll grab a set of wire cutters from the munitions area," I offered.

"We go tomorrow night!" Stan demanded. "When there will be no moon in the sky."

Tomas, Jacob, Avenado, and I agreed to go. I was half dead. If I didn't use the last bit of strength to save myself, the other half would follow. I touched the edges of Sandee's photo in my pocket. Stealing the wire cutters was the first step to being in her arms again.

During the next shift, I made my way toward the munitions engineer and offered to engage the final blast of the day. Adrenaline raced through my withering veins, causing my hands to shake. The engineer looked up and handed over the ignitor. In a wooden crate next to him were two spools of wire and three cutters. I grabbed one and carried the spool thirty feet to the cold black wall, stripped the end of the wire, placed the sausage of powder into the hole, and connected the line to the ignitor. During the dusty explosion, the engineer was busy making the next round of explosives as I slid the wire cutters into my pocket.

As the dust cleared, I headed to the tram to get my ass out of the cave. Derek shoved a prisoner out of his seat and sat down next to me for the ride up.

"Beans and potatoes for you tonight," he grumbled. "Officers have chicken."

It was the first time Derek had taken a seat next to me. My knee shook.

"I take scraps and bones off plates before I give to washer. Have to be careful, though. Never know who's watching."

I held the wire cutters in my pocket as we continued up the chute in silence and exited the cave into the dark, moonless night. As we made our way into Berga 2, the SS officers could be heard singing with full voices inside their quarters, perhaps drunk on their whiskey.

I took to my rack, anticipating our escape, imagining kissing Sandee again. We waited far into the night for the guards to fall asleep, hanging on hope, counting the seconds until we were free.

Derek entered the barrack for his final walk-through, making his perfunctory searches along the rack. As he came to Tomas, he stopped and whispered to him, then went over to Victor and gave him something. Afterward, he turned and walked out without finishing his round.

"We're not going anywhere tonight," Tomas said.

"What do you mean?" shouted Stan.

"Derek warned not to do anything stupid. They know."

Victor laughed. "You guys so *stupid* . . . always talking, talking . . . making plans. Good luck."

"It was him," Jacob said. "It was Victor who spilled it."

"I spill nothing."

"I'm going anyway!" Stan shouted. He grabbed my chest with both his hands and pulled me in to his face. "Charlie, give me the fucking wire cutters. Now!"

I took the cutters from my jacket and handed them to him.

Victor laughed while tearing into a chicken leg with his tiny teeth and tossed the empty bone at Tomas. Tomas's eyes went bloodred. He went to Victor and grabbed him by the neck, but Victor was too strong and smacked Tomas's arm away and shoved him back to the ground. Victor laughed and wiped the grease off his chin.

A few hours later, Stan removed three planks of wood siding on the back of the barrack—and was gone.

"You smart boys—not go with stupid Stan," said Victor.

⌒

Although we had gone without rations for two days, my mood was buoyed by the possibility that Stan had made it to the front. It had been quiet; every hour he was gone felt like victory. Tomas and I walked back from our shift in the footprints of men who might never walk in them again. I wobbled on legs with no meat on them. Jacob had sores on his lips. While tromping through a light snow under a crescent moon, full-throated howls echoed across the silvery fields. The dogs were out.

My heart raced as we stumbled along, making it to the entrance of Berga 2. And there, swinging naked from the lamppost, was Stan Loeb, covered with puncture wounds. Blood stained his gray corpse. The dogs got to him, then the Nazis hung him. I collapsed to my knees and screamed from my ravaged throat, but was unable to produce any sound beyond a raspy gasp. Tomas put my arm around his neck, picked me up, and walked me back to our rack.

Staring up at the planks above my head, I transposed each pine knot from my bedroom ceiling on to the ceiling above. I traveled the planets all night long until I was jolted awake in the middle of the night by the vision of Victor's face in my dream. I thought about how Stan had been set up by Victor, the canine teeth tearing into him. And Sparky's cold death by Victor's hand. On his last breath, Rails saw Victor's stubbled face eating the cheese that had been taken from his mouth. I needed to imagine this. It would motivate the madness required to do what must be done.

"Guys, Victor knew about our plan to escape. He's been stealing, threatening, cutting deals, trading secrets and lives for his own." I leaned in close to Tomas. "I'm not going to die from his hand. No one will again. Victor has to go."

The door suddenly flew open. Hanzel the Rat made a surprise visit, stumbling into our barrack, looking shockingly disheveled, his hair a mess, his eyes tearful. He wandered about, appearing untethered from reality.

"There is no escaping Berga," he barely uttered. He tripped over himself, sending his rifle tumbling to the ground. He stood up and grabbed a few guys off the rack and dragged them outside, leaving his rifle behind. I picked up his rifle, pulled out the magazine, smashed it against the ground, shoved the dented magazine back in the rifle, and dropped it on the ground where it lay, just before the Rat returned to reclaim it.

The Rat ordered the rest of us who could walk to move outside into a lineup as a mix of snow and rain pelted our bodies. The skin on the Rat's face was flushed. His bloodshot eyes were wide with shock. He yelled at us like a tragic drunk screaming in the middle of a crowded town square.

"*Sie haben meine Familie getotet. Sie sind alle tot.* My home is burning. My beautiful city. Dresden is no more . . . gone! I'll shoot you in your dirty Jewish mouths." The Rat tried to point his rifle but fell over to one knee. "Fucking Americans are coming," he whined. "I hung your comrade. Now my home burns." From his knee he sadistically swung his rifle and pointed.

"Foolish rat," said one of the prisoners who was in charge of repairing the wheelbarrows inside the caves but had not made his shift the last week. "They are going to string you up by your balls and let you hang until shit spills from your mouth, you heartless drunk."

The Rat struggled to his feet and put the point of his rifle into the prisoner's chest and pulled the trigger. Only a solitary click was heard. He pulled the trigger again. Nothing. The cartridge was jammed.

"*Halt. Ich werde euch alle erscheissen.* Time to die, Jews." The Rat frantically tried again, pulling the trigger repeatedly. He became undone, then kicked the prisoner to the ground and slobbered like a mindless vagrant and vomited on himself. He turned and zigzagged back to his quarters, leaving us in the cold rain. We helped carry the prisoner back to his rack, but hours later he became a thud and went into Jacob's journal.

~

A violent storm invaded Berga, battering the roof, flooding the beetle holes. Lightning flashed, followed by cracks of thunder. Exhausted and emaciated, the bodies of my brothers slept through the torrential rain. Not Avenado, Jacob, or Tomas. They knew what was coming.

Late into the night, I crept into position at the head of Victor's rack and hoisted a pickax I'd smuggled inside my jacket from the cave. Victor was snoring on his back with his mouth opened wide. It made for the perfect drop point. Thunder smacked the sky. I gripped the handle like the barrel of my Louisville Slugger. *Wigs, call out the coordinates.* I zeroed in on the target right between his rotten teeth. Lightning flashed. *Twenty degrees south, Buck. Altitude three feet . . . two feet . . . one foot . . .*

I raised the pickax high above my head. My arms shook and returned it to my shoulder. "Come on, you coward. Let it drop," I heard my father say. "Victor killed Rails, Sparky, and Stan. He'll kill others." As lightning struck, I raised the pickax once more. Suddenly, I felt the barrel of the pickax ripped from my hands. At the crack of thunder, Tomas had grabbed it and thrust it into Victor's mouth. Victor's eyes shot open. Tomas tried to pull the pickax out, but it stuck in the wood behind Victor's head. Another heave dislodged it. Victor's head still remained on the spike. I kicked it off with the heel of my boot.

Tomas's eyes were clear. He seemed to be smiling.

"For you, Lovina," Tomas uttered. "*Pikuach nefesh.*"

Lightning lit the night sky as we dragged Victor along a sloshy trail. It took every bit of strength for Tomas, Jacob, Avenado, and me to carry Victor to the pit. We carried him through the mud, dropping him several times in puddles. The guard on duty gave us no mind. Just another dead Jew in the night on its way to the pit.

Before rolling him in, I pressed my fingers into his full arms as if examining a nice piece of meat at the butcher.

"You guys head back," I said. "I'll cover him with the lime."

Overwhelmed by hunger, a wave of madness set in, distorting all methods of survival at any cost. I climbed out of the pit to search for a sharp object and found an empty can with a serrated lid still half attached. I went back to Victor and stood over him in the punishing rain.

The serpent arrived blowing winds and cracking thunderbolts—singeing my soul.

Raindrops poured off my nose, dripping down onto the gray underbelly of Victor's bicep. I stood transfixed, holding his arm; the more I thought to eat from it, the less human I became. Flashes of lightning lit the sky. The wind blew the rain sideways. I turned white with madness. I had to eat or would soon die. I sliced a chunk from Victor's arm and tore off a piece with my teeth and chewed on his sinewy flesh. Suddenly, my body shuddered, as if Victor's soul had passed through mine, transfusing the devil's blood into my veins. In horror, I spit out Victor's flesh and ran from the pit, trembling in the downpour, praying to be cleansed, fearing Victor and I would soon meet in the underworld, two soldiers turned into the Sleeping Souls.

Jacob's journal entry: *#31 Victor Stanovich, traitor, murderer, thug.*

CHAPTER 16

The arc of my days had been bent by the devil, leaning me closer to the end. I could feel the varied crevices on my bones, the odd bumps, plucking my tendons like guitar strings; I was utterly confounded on how I was able to walk another hopeless day into the blackness of cave 14, having consumed only a scrap of black bread filled with roaches and sips of turnip soup. Inside the cave, Tomas and I fortified ourselves by reciting prayers with Jacob, making us feel closer to the Jewish women we loved. I knew Sandee was begging for me not to give up. Yet to imagine what I'd be when she saw me was terrifying. A man or beast? A sinner or saint? *Would she have me as I am?*

Jacob showed he'd lost nearly all his teeth, and his skin had yellowed. I gave him the last of my bread I'd rationed from two days prior. I had no hunger. Not since that stormy night in the pit with Victor. I also lost hope. Until Tomas came in from outside during an April thunderstorm.

"We're getting out of here," Derek said. "They're planning to take the prisoners south to hide from the Allied advance. Hang on a couple more days . . ."

"They're not coming for us Jews," Jacob cut in. "They'd have been here by now." He removed his glasses to wipe his goopy eyes. "They're going to take us out and march us to our death, shoot us on the road, call it an escape killing. One of you must survive. If I don't, the last of us must protect the journal. Charlie, it will be in your care if I go first.

179

Do you understand?"

"We're all going to survive," I said. "And we're gonna meet in Wauwatosa for my wedding. That's an order."

I loaded the rocky holes with explosive material just as I had done for the last forty torturous days. But now I was having trouble seeing and kept falling. I worried I might be shot before the chance to be shot by a firing squad on the road. I pried my thoughts away from the bullets and imagined flying again; my mind battled between living and dying. A firing squad execution on a dirt path, in the chest, the face. My hands shook while holding the spool of wire. Derek hit me from behind and told me to cut the wire and connect it to the explosive. After struggling to make the connection, I walked the ignitor to a safe location but lost my footing when the world ruptured and went black.

Through a red veil of blood, I saw Avenado pressing his hand on someone's leg. We were on the tram while racing up the shaft. Three prisoners in striped clothing from Berga 1 were writhing in pain, their arms bloody.

"What happened?"

I screamed but couldn't hear my own voice through the strident ringing in my ears. Then I felt a piercing pain so great I dry heaved. It was *my* leg Avenado was holding. I clenched Jacob's arm, and then realized . . . I triggered the explosive when I fell.

Blood-colored raindrops sprinkled my face as I was being carried out of the cave on a wood board. I didn't recognize who was carrying me. I looked closer. It was him. All this time, he was there. "Help me, Dad. Take me home."

"Easy, Charlie," said Tomas. "We're almost there."

⌒

What woke me from being unconscious was the stench of death from inside the cinder block building where I'd taken my last shower. My eyes were nearly swollen shut. I stretched them open to find a dead soldier on the ground to my left. I heard another moaning for his mother. I lifted the blood-soaked fabric that was wrapped around my pulsating leg. The skin was splayed open, exposing the bone.

Nothing will ever hurt me again. And when I die, they'll throw my Purple Heart into my coffin.

Avenado came in and tipped water from a metal canister into my mouth.

"They're gone, Charlie. All of them. The lily-livered Rat escaped with the SS officers in the middle of the night. The guards were left behind and are now taking all the prisoners who can walk out of the camp. The rest are being shot. Allies are advancing, Charlie. Hang on."

On angels' wings, Avenado rolled me out in a wheelbarrow to meet up with Tomas, Jacob, and the last of the guards wielding their rifles at the gate. They moved us out of the camp as Allied bombers roared overhead. Avenado applied a bandage he'd absconded from the infirmary and stopped the bleeding, but the pulsating pain persisted as we rattled along the pockmarked road.

"The guards are shooting prisoners behind us and in front of us," said Avenado.

Will it end this way—with a bullet landing in my heart after a quick journey through the spring air? Or will I slowly bleed to death?

I tried to hold steadfast to the words of Rabbi Benjamin Levy: "You will be holding Sandee's wrinkled hand in the end . . ."

The sunlight broke through the fast-moving clouds as Avenado and Tomas transferred me onto a large horse-drawn wagon with piles of other sick and wounded soldiers. I was lucky to be placed on the edge, where I wasn't too burdened by the weight of skin and bones. But not soon after, two prisoners had to be taken off the cart, dying of suffocation, and were buried in a shallow grave. I closed my eyes and heard Judy Garland singing "Over the Rainbow," accompanying a mass funeral procession. Rails was waving his catcher's mitt, Mom and Gingersnap were passing out fruitcake, and Sandee was crying under a barren willow tree under a summer sky. I was slipping away. My breath was shallow. I knew where I was heading from watching so many others closing down.

"Joey Berger, 106th," said a soldier next to me, bringing me back from death's abyss.

"Charlie Buckley, 101st," I barely responded.

"Horseshit smells good," he groaned.

"Better than ours," said Jacob, limping by the side of the wagon. "You're going to have one hell of a scar, Charlie."

Rattling machine guns pierced the air as we trundled to the base of a steep hill and stopped. Derek and the other guards scurried the prisoners out into a field to hide, leaving us in the wagon. Rounds of gunshots snapped across the open landscape, the sound much like the ones played on the cowboy shows I listened to on the Victor radio at night with Dad. The audio effect of the popping bullets was true to life. Yet this was real.

Not a single tank came our way. The low-lying clouds moved across the sky as reverberations of gunfire faded, along with my hope for being saved.

The guards lined up the prisoners, and we continued uphill.

"It must have rained. The road is wet," said Jacob.

"Irrigation runoff," added Tomas.

But the pooling at their feet wasn't water.

"*Lieber Gott!*" yelled Derek.

I thought I'd seen the worst. We moved up hill following a stream of blood and found the prisoners from Berga 1. Hundreds of men, women, and children were left with the last expressions on their faces. Some had been dragged over barbed wire, flesh torn off their cheeks, their striped clothing no longer striped but soaked solid in blood. A boy on his knees, leaning against a fence post on the edge of the road, with big brown eyes like mine, was left with a look of confusion on his sweet face.

There would be no way of accounting all the dead for Jacob's journal. Simply:

Scores of Jews murdered in cold blood by the Nazi army
on a road in the middle of nowhere. April, 1945

"We have to . . . keep, keep . . . keep moving," Derek said, weeping while giving orders. "We go on. We . . . we go on."

↶

The infinite stars sparkled like diamonds in the night sky as our wagon rolled over the bumpy road. I fell into hot sweats and had to shake my arm every few minutes to confirm I was still alive. Joey Berger stopped breathing and was taken off the cart and buried in a nameless grave where he might never be discovered.

> *#32 Joey Berger, 106th Army Infantry. Cause of death: Slave labor, starvation. April, 1945.*

Boeing engines sporadically roared overhead, renewing hope that at any moment paratroopers or Allied tanks would stop our death march and save us. But we kept on, passing town after town, losing more prisoners, some disappearing into the villages, some into the forest, others into their graves.

On day four, a northerly blast of cool air changed the sky from a blinding cobalt blue to a muddy gray. The horse carrying us pathetically bobbed her head as we pulled up in front of a farm. Derek and the guards gathered, yelling among themselves, probably coming up with an escape plan or wondering what to do with the last of us who were still alive. The air was laden with the bloody scent of my impending execution.

An old woman and young girl, who might have been her granddaughter, were sitting on the front porch, cringing at our repellent state. A farmhand approached the guards with a large brown sack over his shoulder. Derek yelled for him to stop. The farmhand raised the sack above his head. "*Spargelzeit!*" he yelled and walked toward Derek, offering his sack. Derek was losing his mind and kept yelling and yelling for him to put the sack down. He pointed his rifle that was trembling in his hands. The farmhand's eyes shot open as he dropped his sack, a bullet blowing open a hole in his shoulder. Derek froze, then grabbed

183

the fallen sack.

The woman and the young girl ran to the farmhand as he collapsed.

Derek handed out stems of white asparagus until the sack was empty. The vegetable glistened in my palm. It seemed impossible to reconcile the perfection of this vegetable and the imperfection of man, bound together by a farmhand who was bleeding to death—while we ate his crop to stay alive.

"Eat, you two," said Tomas, who was walking along the wagon that now carried Jacob. I stared at the asparagus as if in a trance, not knowing what to do with it. The echo of Tomas's command for me to eat arrived inside my washed-out brain minutes later. I bit off a piece and chewed it for the longest time, then let the slimy vegetable slide down my burned-out throat. Jacob didn't eat his.

Dying was so lonely. I didn't want to let go. Not then. Not without Sandee at my side. I had no prayers that would bring me comfort, not even the Lord's Prayer; I couldn't remember a single phrase. We pulled off the road under a star-filled night as the nightingales sang their standards. I could no longer feel my leg. More seconds were passing between each of my breaths. The cart, once filled with twenty prisoners, was down to three. *It was then, or never.* As I lay on that wagon next to Jacob, I made the decision to die as a Jew, as Sandee would one day; bound together if not in body, then in faith.

I called Tomas over to join me.

"Jacob, I want you to convert us to the Jewish faith," I pleaded. Tomas nodded.

Although Jacob fell in and out of consciousness throughout the night, we managed a call-and-response from parts of the Torah he was able to recall. I held my Star of David, while Tomas held the dreidel toy Ivan had played with. We held these treasures to our chest and prayed.

In the still hour, before the soft glow of the new dawn, Jacob kissed his hand and touched our faces.

"Like newborn children, *K'tinok she'nolad*, I will give you a Jewish name. You, Charlie, are now, Charles Benjamin Levy Buckley, named after our fallen brother, Rabbi Benjamin Levy. Benjamin means 'the son of my right hand.' Tomas, you will be named Tomas Ivan Frantz, after your child. Let us pray. O God of forgiveness, forgive us, pardon us, grant us atonement. Avinu Malkeinu, our Father, our King, we have sinned before You. Avinu Malkeinu, in Your abundant mercy, cleanse us of our guilt before You. Avinu Malkeinu, bring us back to You in perfect repentance." Jacob reached for our hands. "Though short as this life may be, you have given me life as a rabbi. I am fulfilled," he said as tears streamed down his cheeks.

I woke underneath a canopy of pine branches dusted with fresh snow. Winter had not died. Nor had I. The dull air indicated we weren't moving. Tomas came from the road.

"All the guards sprung loose," he said. "The Allies must be close. We're on our own . . ."

Tomas paused. He put his hand on Jacob's neck, then closed Jacob's eyelids. I was barely of this world, yet I could feel my heart break inside my concaved chest. Was Jacob dead, or was I, or was this all a dream? A glimmer of divine consciousness intervened just before Tomas slid Jacob off the cart. *Jacob's journal.* I removed it from the lining of his jacket and carefully placed it inside mine as if it were a plate of crystal.

I listened to the wind, the birds, and my rattling breath. I reached into my pocket for Sandee's photo and held it to my heart. I was going to die, not because I was giving up but because I could no longer live. I closed my eyes.

I woke, lying in a cornfield thick with fog. The ground rumbled from the vibration of a panzer. My leg was bleeding again, perhaps the last half pint left. I called out to Tomas, but I was alone. Frantically, I reached inside my jacket for Jacob's journal. It was gone.

"No!" I let out.

The panzer shut off its engine not twenty feet from me. I prayed the Germans didn't see me hiding in the brush. The cornstalks shuddered from a gust of wind, prompting a pheasant to flee. As I watched its wings soar into the overcast sky, I heard murmurs floating underneath the murky surface of my fading consciousness. I squinted through the opaque mist and saw an almighty, multicolored prism of sunlight beam onto what I thought was the panzer. But on the back end of the tank, fluttering in the wind, was the star-spangled banner—yet waving.

It must have been difficult for my liberators to differentiate the brittle cornstalks tremoring in the wind from the ghostlike, gray skeletal figure crawling through them. I tried to scream, "I'm an American POW," but was unable to make a sound from my ravaged throat. Bullets snapped the stalks, yet with tears streaming down my face, I rose up tall and walked on. Feeling the warmth of the splintered sunlight shining on my face, shaking on one leg, I saw an American soldier run to me before I collapsed into the arms of freedom.

～

Lying on the back of their truck, the liberators were muted, as if paying last respects. A full-faced medic tried to give me water, but I couldn't open my mouth. He stuck me with morphine and placed his hand on my thigh, then retracted it, perhaps shaken by the utter ghoulishness of touching a leg with so little flesh on the bone. His face was so alive. I touched mine and screamed inside my mind, "*What took you so long?*"

As the morphine set in, I took out Sandee's photo and noticed a brownish-yellow smear had gone across her crooked smile. I yearned to have Sandee breathe life back into my charred lungs. I closed my eyes and felt the medic take the photo out of my hands and place it tenderly back inside my pocket.

Inside a school gymnasium much like the one where I'd enlisted a lifetime ago, the nurses gingerly removed my clothing. I snatched back my threadbare jacket and rocked it in my arms as if it were my child. I was unwilling to let it go. *What would I be without it?* Sadly, I let it go before being weighed and before DDT was dusted over my body. The medic called out my weight: 87 pounds, and then placed Sandee's Star of David, her photo, and Rails's tags in a small paper bag and set it beside me, then injected two more shots of morphine in my ass; the only place he could find some meat.

CHAPTER 17

The sweet aroma of lavender was so strong I sneezed, the brilliant purple-and-orange blossoms dancing on the windowsill so bright I closed my eyes, the sheets caressing my body so soft I cried. It was as if I'd woken from a nightmare and landed in Oz.

A woman holding my hand was wearing a bright white dress with a Red Cross emblem on her cap. I'd never felt something so smooth, so soft and gentle. *Where is Sandee?*

"*Sois beni!* Hello, young man. "I'm Nurse Benoit. I will be attending to you. What's your name?"

Her voice was languid, not head-splitting like the Nazis. Her cheerful smile burst from her flushed cherubic cheeks, revealing brilliant white teeth that sparkled. Everything about her was so alive.

"Ch . . . Charlton Buckley . . . I was a pris . . ." The words churned in my throat like gravel. Two other soldiers wrapped in bandages were lying on beds next to mine. Other nurses were attending to their wounds, speaking different languages, mostly French.

"Here, *un peu*. A little sip, Charlton. What a lovely name." She put a straw between my lips. The water dribbled from my mouth. It hurt too much to swallow.

"Where . . . am I?"

"Lyon, France. We're going to take beautiful care of you until you fly home, *oui*?" She put her hand gently on my shoulder and looked into my wet eyes.

"What's the date?" I asked.

"April 25, 1945—springtime in France. *C'est magnifique!*"

A tall doctor holding a tray came up from behind her.

"Hello, soldier." He took my hand. "We have a conversation. Not an easy one, I'm afraid. The trauma to your tibia, the big bone in your shin, was catastrophic . . ." I barely heard a word after hearing he would try to save my leg above the knee. "We have to go into surgery right away. I'm sorry."

"No!"

Nurse Benoit held my arm. There wasn't time to negotiate as the anesthesia he injected took hold, no time to process, or call Mom, or let Sandee know she was going be marrying a cripple.

I woke up from surgery in the middle of the night, my bedsheets sodden with sweat. What I would have given to return to oblivion, to sleep forever, to never have had to look under the sheets to find out. *Maybe the doctor had saved it. Maybe my leg was still there.* I barely had the strength to lift the crisp linen and saw white space below my knee. I threw up bile. Nurse Benoit rushed over and sponged my face with warm water and held me.

"It's a miracle you're alive, Charlton," she said in a calm voice.

"What did they do with it?" I cried. "I want it back."

"You are going to put this all behind you and live a long, happy life."

A long, happy life . . .

I moved what was left of my leg and groaned from a spike of pain shooting in my knee.

I'll never be able to jump across Meyer Creek again.

"*D'accord*, Charlton. Let's go easy. I have a nice egg for you to eat. Breakfast in the evening. Why not, no?" She sat at my bedside and placed a tray on my lap. She also brought over a telephone connected to a long cord that went out the door.

"After we eat, you may use this phone to call home, *oui?*"

The sumptuous smell of the egg brought on crushing cramps. Nurse Benoit mashed it into pieces and fed me my first bite of food in more days than I could remember. The salt, the texture, the rich taste were too much. I wanted to eat, yet a single swallow ignited shock waves through my gut. I became dizzy and put the fork down. One stinking bite was all I could handle before humiliating myself in a cloth diaper.

"Take it away, please."

After she finished cleaning my bottom and redressing the bed, Nurse Benoit handed me the telephone.

"Call your family, Charlton."

What could I possibly say? Everything about who I was had changed. There wasn't any life left in the life I'd left. *Not for savages like me.*

"I'll put you through now, soldier," said the hospital operator.

The ringing of the telephone brought back the musty odor in the back hallway where the phone stand stood on a crochet throw rug near the back door, where the hinges squealed on the swinging door that opened out to the backyard, the basketball hoop towering over the blacktop. Chicken soup on the stove. Gingersnap giggling at something stupid. Dad obtrusively snoring on the couch while WI 40 radio played Thelonious Monk.

"Buckleys . . . hello? Is anyone there?"

"Mom," I whispered.

"Hello? . . . Charlton?"

From the deepest part of her soul came a primordial cry only a mother makes when her child has risen from the dead. Then the phone went silent as we tried to catch our breath and slow the earth spinning wildly off its axis—or returning to it.

"Charlie, my dear son?" She yelped. "You're alive?"

"Tell Sandee . . . please tell her . . . I'm . . ."

"A war hero, Charlie. She never lost hope. No, no. Not for a minute, Charlie . . . Charles? Are you there?"

The tenor of her voice had changed, altered by months of worry and grief.

"I'm here."

"Your father. Charlie . . ."

I cut the call short. I didn't have it in me to continue. Nor mention the body part I wouldn't be bringing home. "I'll see you as soon as I can, Mom."

With that, I hung up the receiver and tried to remember Dad's face before his stroke, but all I could conjure up were the features of a grotesque monster breathing his last breaths.

⌣

Soon, I graduated from an egg to ham and eggs and from my bed to wheeling myself around in a chair. I learned basic French from the radio and finally joined in on group talk with other soldiers who had lost limbs. During one of our sessions, a tall, muscled military officer interceded and tapped me on the shoulder with authority and asked to speak with me privately. I wheeled myself away from the group into a small office off the common room.

"Charlton Buckley of the 101st Army Air Force, I'm Lieutenant Aims, from MIS, Military Intelligence Service." He was flashing me the Purple Heart of Valor in the palm of his hand. "Ever held one of these, soldier?"

"No, sir."

"How are you feeling?"

Alive . . . deadly alive.

"Okay, sir," I answered with clenched fists.

Lieutenant Aims shuffled some papers. "Well . . . you, you keep your chin up and heal well, soldier, and leave the rest to Uncle Sam."

"Second Lieutenant, sir," I said.

"I'm sorry?"

"I'm a second lieutenant—even on one leg."

"Yes, Lieutenant. Of course." He kept hold of the Purple Heart while a letter trembled in his other hand as he read, "On behalf of the United States of America . . . Lieutenant Charlton Antonio Buckley." He cleared his throat and continued. "For your extraordinary service and sacrifice, you'll be receiving the Purple Heart of Valor in conjunction with signing the Berga 2 Security Certificate for Surviving Prisoners of

War." He paused before continuing. "It states the following:

"I, Charlton Antonio Buckley, Second Lieutenant, US Army Air Force, will not discuss, publish, or otherwise disclose to unauthorized persons the existence of the Berga 2 prison camp. The activities of American prisoners of war within the Berga 2 prison camp must not be revealed, not only for the duration of the war against the present enemies of the United States but in peacetime as well. The authorship of articles or stories on these subjects is forbidden, and military personnel are warned that they will be held strictly accountable for the communication of such information to other persons who may subsequently publish or disclose such material. I, Charlton A. Buckley, understand that any information suggested above is confidential and must not be communicated to anyone other than the agency designed by AG of S, G-2, War Department, or the corresponding organization in overseas theaters of operations."

I prayed Tomas had taken Jacob's journal when he left me in that cornfield thinking I was going to die, and found his way home.

Lieutenant Aims placed the certificate in front of me. "You're a war hero, Lieutenant. Sign here."

I threw the pen back at him. "Why do I have to keep what happened to me a secret? The Nazis tortured us. Do you understand? They worked us to death in the caves—"

"That's none of our concern, Lieutenant. Your obligation under this certificate comes from an order executed by the US State Department. That's all you need to know."

"What do I tell my mother when she asks how I lost my leg?"

He took out another document. "On December 16, 1944, Second Lieutenant Charlton Antonio Buckley was shot down by German ground fire and was subsequently taken to Stalag IX-B, where his leg became infected from the crash. He was transported to a classified medical facility, where his leg was removed to save his life, and remained there to recover until his return home."

Lieutenant Aims moved to my side and leaned over me. "I'm terribly sorry for what happened to you, Lieutenant Buckley. But let me give you some advice—for your own good:

"The sooner you forget, the better."

By what measure could I possibly forget? Booze? Barbiturates? Wail on the streets of Milwaukee like a madman into my old age?

I put pen to paper and lost my freedom once again.

PART II

CHICAGO, 2001

CHAPTER 18

A fter attending Wisconsin University, Gingersnap followed her college sweetheart, Paul Sussman, a prolific journalist, *so they say*, to New York City. Paul wrote a number of World War II articles for the *New Yorker*—exploiting veterans for a good byline. He pressed without success for my story to be included in his feature commemorating the fiftieth anniversary of the end of the war, accusing me of being an unpatriotic ass.

"Your incessant hubris is your tragic flaw, Charlie. I'll write your story one of these days. You'll see, old man."

That was seven years ago. Gingersnap and I speak a few times a year on the phone, but I held to my guns, not seeing Paul, even after his many attempts to engage. Gingersnap refused to visit me without dear Paul, so that was that. Until today.

"The two of you look like a portrait from *On Golden Pond*," she says quietly. "I'll join you for our chat after I freshen up."

The redheaded spitfire, still fair, now wrinkled, enters the living room, perspiring from her walk along Lake Michigan after having arrived unannounced for a one-day visit to have *a talk* with me. She leaves Sandee and me sitting by the large encasement windows in the living room, taking in the view of the harbor.

"I put the towels on your bed, Ginger," Sandee calls out.

The Chicago weather is warming after a long winter. Sandee slings open the encasement windows to welcome in the early spring air. The back door in the kitchen is left ajar to catch the cross breeze. I haven't been able to fully enjoy the fresh air since my lungs were a mess. The chemo hasn't done shit other than lying me flat.

I peer out through the windows toward the blurred horizon. The small sailboats are soaring over the dark water, looking like the white napkins that Mom used to fold into tepees for Sunday dinners. Dad flashes through my mind and gives me a jolt. I haven't thought of him in years yet suddenly feel him on my skin. I touch my face, and it's his. I breathe in; he breathes out. Two sets of heartbeats pound inside my sternum. I feel a panic coming. A groan rises from my throat.

"Sandee," I utter.

"Yes, dear."

She's reading the *Tribune*, unaware of my distress until she turns to see me clutching at my chest. She recognizes what's happening—but not why. Every once in a blue moon, I would have a series of these panics, but not in years.

"Ten slow, deep breaths, Charlton." She brings over a vase filled with tuberoses. "Smell these."

The tranquil, sweet scent of flowers is her special antidote to my unrest. After a few moments, I calm and doze off until Gingersnap returns with tears running. She leans down and gently wraps her pale arms around my shoulders. I try to move away, but she refuses to let go. Her body shakes.

"It's time, Charlie. I'm so sorry," she says, becoming undone.

Thank God, Sandee is there to wrench her hands away and set her on the couch.

"What is it, Ginger?" Sandee asks.

"My dear brother. Your iron pride was there from the beginning. Remember the time I stole the dime off Dad's nightstand? He threatened that whoever did it would get a lashing? You said it was you. He beat you, yelling at you to stop covering up for me, to admit *I* did it. He said awful things to you, Charlie. For weeks, Mom washed your infected welts. I was only six years old."

"I don't have any recollection of that. But I'm sure you didn't come all this way to reminisce over childhood calamities."

"You do remember missing Mom's funeral. Too busy on your business trips acquiring farming equipment companies to raise the value of AC before selling it—leaving your son without a job."

"What the hell is this all about?"

"You do remember not visiting me in the hospital after I lost my chance at motherhood, saying I was foolish trying to bring a child into this world. How dark and hurtful you've been."

"I think I'll go for my nap."

I try to move my wheelchair, but Sandee places her foot in the way.

"Please hear me out, Charlie. Then I'll return to the airport." She waits for me to respond. I nod. "I caught the first plane here after talking with Paul."

"Here we go." I sigh.

"He's doing a story on death camps throughout Europe. Camps that were never disclosed—kept classified. Paul is certain you were in one of them and were ordered to keep quiet, Charlie. He doesn't know which one, but he heard from other POWs who are finally coming forward as they reach the end of their lives. Paul says many prisoners were taken from their POW camps and worked to death by the Nazi army. He looked for your medical records on your leg, Charlie. He was unable to find any at the POW camp you said you were at, Stalag nine something . . . what really happened to your leg, my dear brother?"

I want to cover her mouth, wheel myself back to my bedroom, or jump from the window.

"I'm heartbroken for you, for us, for your own son, and dear Sandee. The government had no right forcing you to keep crimes against humanity their ugly secret, Charlie. You kept it to yourself, didn't you! The great Charlton Buckley and his iron pride."

"It's my life. My fucking life!"

"Oh, Charlie." Ginger heaves tears, ending the inquisition as a gust of wind catches the drapes and lifts them in the air.

"I forgive you, my brother, and pray you will soon find peace—because you deserve it."

Sandee lifts her foot, freeing me to wheel myself out.

⌒

I wait for Ben in my favorite booth at the Shoreman's Room on Oak Street. I haven't stopped stewing since Gingersnap went back home to her derelict husband. I'm sure the other guys who signed the certificate to keep quiet didn't simply let it out; no, they were backed into a corner by journalists like Paul looking to make a name for themselves.

I finish my whiskey and flag down the waiter for another. I notice a woman sitting alone in the next booth. She looks familiar—wrinkled skin, white, wispy hair, and jade green eyes. *It's sinful, sinful,* the woman said back in December 1944, rolling by me the night I saw my father dying in the hospital. She raises her glass, dips her chin, and smiles.

When my drink arrives, I turn to toast the woman, but her booth is empty.

"Hello, Dad."

"Oh! Ben."

"Didn't mean to startle you."

"No, no. Sit."

Ben has gained weight, his pale blue eyes are puffy, and his jet-black hair is receding. He slides his wide girth into the opposite side of the booth, banging the table. He places the napkin in his lap, at the same time reaching with his other hand for his water glass, which slips through his fingers, crashing on the table, breaking into pieces, sending the water splashing across the table. The busboy quickly changes out the tablecloth and settings while we sit on our hands. Ben is perspiring.

"Not the smoothest way to start," Ben says.

I did this to my son.

"Let's try again. Hello, Ben."

"Hi."

"The three pounders arrived today, from Boothbay Harbor, Maine." I smile. "I remember how you begged for lobster as a little tyke right here in this very booth. I told you that you were born with a red shell on your back, which—"

"I know the story . . . I went crazy until you finally said they removed it after birth."

"A cruel bit, I admit." I laugh.

"Traumatized for life."

Ben orders a beer from our waiter, and we sit quietly until it arrives. I finally break the compressed air between us.

"Thank you for coming, son."

"You can thank Mom."

"I'll do that." I sip my whiskey, then begin. "Listen carefully to what I'm going to tell you, Ben. Your aunt flew into town last week. Says your uncle Paul wants to write some bullshit puffer piece about unknown POW camps during the war. If he or Aunt Ginger mentions any of this to you, just know it's all crap."

I take another swig of my drink. "He should leave us soldiers alone. It's not his business or the *New Yorker*'s. Got it? He knows nothing about sacrifice."

My body is vibrating. I feel another damn panic coming. And then, as if water bursts out from a rusted-out fire hydrant after being closed off for half a century, I spray my disjointed words in all directions. "Crashed in a field . . . Wigs pulled me out of the burning cargo plane . . . brain matter covered the icy trench . . . the Nazi SS blew the back of his skull . . . turnip soup . . . Rails was thrown in the pit . . ."

Ben looks at me as if he's wandered into the wrong restaurant and met a stranger. After a long moment to allow me to catch my breath, I down the rest of my whiskey and continue to share fragments of Stalag IX-B plucked from memories embedded in my tortured mind, holding Berga off, keeping it locked in its cage. Yet the key to free the beast is dangling in my hand.

"Whatever your uncle writes, he manipulated information out of some poor soldiers, creating complete fabrications, all in pursuit of a fucking Pulitzer, goddamn it! Not me. I'm not spilling. Not this guy."

The foam on Ben's beer has gone flat below the rim, not a sip taken.

I cough, and the room goes spinning. I place my hand on the table to steady myself. Ben puts his hand on mine.

"Dad, stop. No more. Let's order some food, and I'll fill you in on your grandson."

Like a punch-drunk boxer ready to fall, my body goes limp. Berga . . . saved by the bell.

With wet eyes, I raise my hand, indicating to the waiter we're ready to order.

"How old is Lewis now?" I ask.

"Twelve," Ben answers, looking down into his beer.

CHAPTER 19

A *potato falls from Victor's grimy pocket and rolls toward the end of the boxcar, where it disappears into the shithole. Venom pulses through my withered veins. He'd stolen it! If he had one potato, there had to be another. My chin scrapes along the floorboards covered in dried phlegm as I crawl toward him. The prisoners piled up dead on either side of the boxcar stare at me in judgment through their dark eye sockets—all because I'm still alive. I jump Victor and rip off each arm and reach inside his pocket. Empty! I flip him over and choke his neck—Dad! He spits Four Roses bourbon into my mouth as red-hot fireflies attack my eyes. I run to the door and start banging. "Let me out ... let me out ..."*

Sandee is standing over me with her hand on my chest, squinting, searching for clues that might offer insight to my continued nightmares. I'm breathless.

"I soaked the sheets again."

"I'll throw them in the wash while you're bathing."

She moves to open the windows.

"No! Keep them closed, please." Undeterred, Sandee unlatches the floor-to-ceiling encasements that bring in a warm breeze.

"The large boats should be arriving in the harbor soon." She turns and gives me that crooked smile, the same she flashed in 1944 that tilted my world before it shattered into a thousand pieces. "Do you remember how we used to lie beside the creek under the willow tree when the weather turned warm, staring through the branches whispering in the winds?" Sandee begins to sing.

"Willow, weep for me, bend your branches down along the ground and cover me."

"Help me into my chair, will you?"

"Your dream. You were shouting for someone to let you out."

"I don't remember."

"It's been years. Why do you think they've returned?" Sandee waits patiently in her blue silk robe for a response.

"I don't know," I lie.

"Let's move you into the shower and get you dressed for Temple. Ben is saving us a seat."

"I'm not up for it today, Dee."

"It's been weeks, Charlie. The doctor said it's important for you—"

"I heard him." I move away from the cold, wet sheets and sit on the edge of the bed.

"You can rest before the game tonight."

"What game?"

"Ben. He's taking you to the basketball game. Did you forget?"

I stand down off the bed on one leg and drop into my chair, holding Sandee's arm.

"No."

"You haven't been with him since your dinner last month."

"I'm tired, Dee."

"Don't do that, damn it!" She rolls me into the bathroom. "You can watch the rest of the games on television. But tonight, you're going to the game with your son."

Inside the glass shower stall, the hot water pelts my back. I violently rub the bristles on my crusty stump, then squirt cream over the pink scales and massage the useless nub. I miss my leg every damn minute of every day.

～

As I drift off between passages from the *derasha*, Ben nudges my arm to wake me.

"You're wheezing, Dad. Are you okay?"

"No. I'm dying. Or did you forget?"

"Shh. Your grandson is behaving better than the both of you," whispers Sandee.

The rabbi continues, "Remember, my chosen people. On Earth we experience great anguish and confusion. We may be shaken to our core by the sins of man and faint from evil. At such a time, we stand back up and lift our heads and call on redemption to salve our wounds."

With challah still swirling on the roof of my mouth, we make our way outside the synagogue. I hold Lewis's hand until we reach the courtyard.

"Before you run off, my grandson, tell me how your Hebrew lessons are coming along."

"I won't be ready." He looks down at his shoes.

"He'll be ready," Caroline interjects and lifts his chin, then puts her arms around Lewis like he's a six-year-old, not twelve and about to have his bar mitzvah. The coddling is unbecoming. I never treated Ben with such kid gloves. Lewis will be in shock one day when his sweet eyes see the world turn inside out, and there'll be *no sow to suck on*.

"You didn't have a bar mitzvah, did you, Bapa?"

It's Ben who is now looking down at his shoes.

"Not all Jews do, Lewis," I respond.

Sandee abruptly diverts our attention and points.

"Here comes the rabbi, Charles."

I can't get home fast enough. My leg is killing me.

"*Baruch Hashem*," bellows Rabbi Abulafia. "Good morning to the Charlton Buckley family. Sandra, you look as effervescent as ever. Finally, we are graced with a glorious day in Chicago."

"A glorious day indeed, Rabbi," says Sandee. "I adore the cherry blossoms that run along Lake Shore Drive this time of year. It's a shame the bloom dies off so fast."

The rabbi's cheeks puff like bellows as he speaks. "God of God and our ancestors, may it be your will to renew your blessing of the world in our day, as you have done from the beginning of time. The prayer for the moment, Sandra. Our bloom will return in the spring through our redemption."

My cane drops as I shift off my prosthetic. The rabbi catches my elbow and picks up my cane.

"Charles, stay for a few minutes and join me in my office for a visit. It's been too long." The rabbi seizes on what Sandee undoubtedly has orchestrated behind my back. My chest burns. Sandee smiles and places her delicate hand on the small of my back.

This better not be about formally converting again. I'd left that honor for Jacob.

I nod, acquiescing to the rabbi's request. He smiles at Sandee triumphantly and moves on to others to further engage in post service drivel.

I wave to Lewis as he runs off with one of his pals into the sun-splashed courtyard.

"Perhaps I'll talk with the rabbi about officiating the youth basketball game coming up." I smile in jest. "I think I still have my old whistle."

Sandee takes my hand and kisses it. "Talk with the rabbi, darling . . . about the nightmares. For me. Time is precious—now more than ever. I'll see you back at home."

With her silk skirt swaying side to side, Sandee saunters down the granite steps, still skipping my heart after all these years.

I wait ten minutes for Rabbi Abulafia outside his door as if I'm about to enter the confessional. Yet I'm the true victim of sin. My hands are clammy. The walls close in. My stomach lurches while the past grabs at my throat like a thug in a back alley. I can't take it any longer and clutch my cane and escape through the side exit out into the bright sunlight and wobble down the handicapped ramp. I hang onto the railing and wait for a spell of vertigo to pass before proceeding down the sidewalk—the death camp nipping at my heels.

I arrive at the small neighborhood park where Sandee and I took Ben after Temple when he was a toddler. We'd pack a lunch and feed the pigeons the crusts from our sandwiches. Then I was on to my noon poker game, where I gambled and drank good whiskey and arrived home numbed out and hungry.

As I catch my breath from the walk, I see the old woman again with the white wispy hair leaving the park while whispering under her breath, "It's sinful."

I squeeze my cane—as if it were the man's neck who'd sent me the damn claim letter—drudging up the past like a barnacle-encrusted shipwreck being raised from the ocean floor, a past I was told never to let resurface.

I perch myself on a bench underneath a large maple tree and remove an old package of crackers from my pocket and offer them up to the pigeons, then pull out the letter from my breast pocket, the same I was going to read to the rabbi. I read it to the pigeons instead.

CJMC / April 11, 2001

Survivor, Charlton A. Buckley
101st US Army Air Force Division, WWII

The Conference on Jewish Material Claims Against Germany is pleased to present you with an award under the Claims Conference Program for Former Slave and Forced Laborers. See attached check for $250,000. The US State Department's WWII Prisoner of War Certificate, dated April 25, 1945, remains classified and thus has legal effect under military law. The certificate continues to prohibit you from disclosing the Berga 2 prison camp. If you are in possession of any documentation or are aware of any personal recordings of events perpetrated against the prisoners at Berga 2, please contact our office immediately. The CJMC continues our work with the governments of the United States and Germany to declassify what occurred from February 9, 1945, to April 25, 1945, regarding Jewish soldiers taken from Stalag IX-B and sent to the Berga 2 Nazi slave labor death camp. In some small measure, we hope this award offers you closure.

Sincerely,

Rubin Stern, Treasurer, CJMC

A pigeon hops up on the bench, eager to be my confidant. "They hope that I have something to help pressure the government to declassify Berga. Well, I don't, goddamn it!" I'm yelling at a pigeon, indicating it was time to hail a cab and return home for my nap.

⌒

The bedroom door opens as I snap awake, coughing up the dust from cave 14, escaping the clutches of yet another nightmare. I roll over and cover my head to avoid existing.

"That was a long rest," Sandee says while opening the blinds. "Are you okay, darling?"

"I'm fine."

I'm not. My torso aches from hacking in my sleep, probably warranting another visit to the damn oncologist.

"Ben's here."

"What?" I pull the sheet off my head.

"You don't look ready to go, Dad."

"Damn it! I'm sorry, Ben. I'm not up for the game tonight." I try to repress my cough.

"I've bought premium seats, Dad."

"You're not listening."

Sandee pours me a glass of water. "Let's get you up and moving. You'll feel much better—"

"Don't, Dee."

"Mom, stop. If he's not feeling well—"

"Quiet, Ben." Sandee places a pitcher of water at my bedside table and circles the room. "Charlie, why didn't you meet with the rabbi today? He called while you were resting and said you never showed up after the service, yet I left you at the synagogue. You couldn't talk with him—for me, Charlie? For me?"

Ben looks to his mother for an explanation. "What's this with the rabbi?"

"You better get going," I say. "You'll miss the start of the game." Sandee puts up her hand, indicating Ben isn't to go anywhere.

"There is a rather large check in the top drawer of your father's desk from the Conference on Jewish Material Claims Against Germany, an organization that pays out claims to prisoners of war who are Jewish."

"Jewish? Claims against Germany? What the hell is going on, Dad? You weren't Jewish!"

"It-it was a mistake. I'm sending it back. And what is it of your business snooping around my desk, damn it!"

Sandee grabs the glass of water out of my hand.

"I've never pushed this, Charlie." She starts to shake. Her soft blue eyes fill with tears. "Is it true what Ginger said? About Paul finding soldiers who were in secret camps?"

I remain quiet.

"You've been a damn mystery my whole life, Dad. I'm going to the game."

"Wait, Ben." Sandee takes my hands. "Charlie, before your son leaves, burdened with disappointment yet again, let me ask you this: What will you leave us with when you die?"

Tears fall from her eyes. My Sandee, the girl who'd kept me alive with hope when I thought I'd die at Berga ten times over and has kept me alive ever since.

"I'd hoped to leave you both with everything I was—before I was taken."

Sandee and Ben hold still as the sun sets behind the buildings on East Lake Shore Drive, shadowing the gray walls. I stare into Sandee's red, tired eyes. They wait for me to utter the words I've kept hidden from them for decades. And finally, I break the oath with my government.

"Paul was right."

The words slowly rise from the depths of my burdened soul: *the Rat, slave laborer, Rabbi Benjamin Levy, death camp, cave 14, the death march, Victor, Jacob Goldmann's journal and the promise I made to keep it safe, and the Nazi kapo, Tomas Frantz, my friend who may have taken the journal from me before he hid me in a cornfield and escaped. And all about Cal Wiggins, how his letters went unanswered and how I miss him so.*

Lastly, as the moon rises over Lake Michigan, I finally walk them through the night Tomas and I converted to Judaism on a death wagon before losing our rabbi-in-training, Jacob Goldmann.

I weep from the pain I suffered, from the years of my withholding, from the explanation for not officially converting after the war, my manic episodes, the drinking, the betrayals. Perhaps the most painful realization is that Ben would remember himself as a little boy begging for my attention, knowing now how damaged and incapable I was of giving it. Sandee knew my father's influence caused irreparable harm, but here was the explanation she'd been waiting for to give her the full insight to my psychological decimation.

I slide my knee out from the sleeve and roll into a fetal position and groan into my pillow. When I turn back moments later, Ben and Sandee are gone.

They return before dawn, their faces flush and swollen. Sandee covers me with a blanket and strokes my thin hair singed white from the devil's breath.

I feign sleep.

"Tell me, Charles," Dee whispers. "How are we to forgive this broken man?"

I open my eyes, sit up, attach my leg, and grab my cane. I lean to kiss Sandee's soft, weathered cheek and lead them into the study and drop into my chair, wheezing from my sick lungs. I take out my copy of the Berga Security Certificate for Surviving Prisoners of War I'd hidden below my old baseball glove that will explain why I'm still a captive at Berga—and of the US government.

After Ben finishes reading it aloud, I reach for his hand. I can't get the words out fast enough.

"I need to fulfill my promise to Jacob. I have to go back to Germany and find Tomas Frantz—if he's alive. I need to get Jacob's journal back. The Jewish Material Claims Department wants to know if I have any underlying documents that will help to declassify Berga 2. Their families deserve to know the truth about what happened. Cal Wiggins. I need him. I don't even know if he is alive. I have his phone number on one of his old letters. He'll come, too, if he's able. I know he will."

We sit in silence until Sandee lifts her chin and offers a soft smile.

"Passover is next week. Ginger and Paul will come. You invite Mr. Wiggins to join us for the seder. Once your treatments are finished in April, Ben and I will go with you to Germany and search for the Berga 2 camp—and Tomas Frantz."

"And find that journal," Ben adds.

CHAPTER 20

The blinding afternoon sun flashes through the window, causing me to bang my chair against the corner of the bed. I frantically search the bedroom—for what, I can't remember, another bother that only adds to my frayed nerves before Wigs is to arrive at any moment. I troll my valet hutch, the closet, the bathroom, hoping to jog my memory. I get off my chair and crawl the floor and notice I'm only wearing one shoe. My breath shortens. I look at my brown, spotted, trembling hands and think of Poppi. His old hands were always calm and warm. Mine are cold and restless. I've been edgy all week and now feel a panic building. I take off my shoe and throw it against the wall. Sandee rushes in, carrying a porcelain vase filled with flowers she sets by the bed.

"What on earth, Charlton!" Sandee helps me back into my chair.

"I can't seem to find my . . . brown shoe from last night."

"You wore the black ones, remember? I sent your brown shoe out last week to have the heel replaced."

"I'm all out of sorts, damn it."

"Here, smell one." She picks a tuberose from the bedside vase. I take in the scent, which slows my racing heart.

"How do I look?" I ask.

"Your pants are baggy, but that's the style these days." She straightens my collar.

"Did you put beer in the minifridge?"

"Yes, yes, now calm down."

"I might join him for one. Has Gingersnap and Paul's flight arrived?"

"Yes, dear."

"Ben, Caroline, and Lewis know when to arrive?"

"Yes, Charlie." She puts her hand on my cheek.

"I hope Wigs doesn't feel uncomfortable walking into all this. I don't know about his financial circumstances."

"There's nothing to be ashamed of. You worked hard—"

"Christ, Dee, be grateful you know nothing of shame." Sandee turns to avoid the radioactive material in my dark soul that has been leaking for decades. *I'd have run from me ages ago.*

"Hold still." She helps me put the other shoe on my prosthetic just as the doorbell chimes.

"Let me get it, Dee." I put my hand on my wheelchair and pause for a moment. "Where will I begin?"

"I suppose where the two of you left off."

I move my chair aside and grab my cane. "I'm going to walk."

Wigs steps out from the elevator onto our checkered marble foyer. I wait for my fly mate's features to coalesce like a Gestalt test—first his eyes, then his mouth echoing the demand: *"Promise to live."* His disheveled curly hair has turned white. His raincoat, too large for his once-broad shoulders, is covered with droplets from an April shower. I can't tell if his hound dog eyes are sopping with tears or raindrops.

"I should punch you in the nose," Wigs says, choking back tears.

That wonderful, awful Southern drawl. It's truly Wigs. I embrace him and hold on until the sounds of war dissipate, then hold tighter as we're thrown forward in time.

"Look at you, Wigs, you old goat!"

"You, too, son of a bitch. You gonna invite me into your fancy digs, or do I have to bulldoze right through ya?"

We settle on the couch in the living room as Sandee enters.

"It's so nice to meet you, Mr. Wiggins."

Wigs rises and extends his hand. "And you, Mrs. Buckley. Call me

Cal." Cal turns to me. "Glad to finally meet the filly in your photo, Buck."

"He wasn't supposed to show that to anyone. And please, call me Sandee. By the way, I'm wearing the same dress I wore the night before Charlie and I were married. August 4, 1946—in your honor, Cal. I'm sure you would have been by his side had circumstances . . ." She stops herself.

"Better late than never, Buck."

"I'm eternally grateful to you, Cal. May I offer you a beer? Charlie?" We both nod. Sandee grabs two bottles from the minifridge at the bar and announces she has to make a fundraising call for the Spina Bifida Foundation. "Charlie was wonderful with my sister, who unfortunately succumbed to the disease. Eloise. She loved playing all kinds of tricks on Charlie."

"You should make that call then." My knee is bouncing. Sandee smiles and retreats to the study.

After Wigs sits beside me, I raise the hem of my pant leg. His eyes well up as he puts his hand on my knee.

"Shall we dance?" He laughs, which makes us cry.

"Thank you for coming, Wigs."

"I'm as angry as an alley cat, Second Lieutenant Charlton Buckley," he says, wiping his cheek. "What fuckin' trench have you been hiding in?"

"You have no idea." I stand and walk over to the window with cane in hand. "Come look at this view."

Wigs joins me at the window to look out over Lake Michigan from seventeen stories up.

"Looks like you've made a nice life for yourself, Buck. Glad you kept my letters from the ones I sent to your old address."

I cough into my handkerchief and then point to the outer drive snaking along the shoreline.

"Take that Highway 97 miles north to Wauwatosa, Wisconsin. Only a couple hours north."

We stop talking for a piece, disoriented from the time missed and the questions left unanswered. I know I can count on Wigs for cutting through the cover and getting right down to it, so I wait until he starts in.

"I don't know what the hell happened to you after they took you out of Stalag, but the shit got worse for us, Buck. Our rations were cut to nothing. A lot of guys were thrown in the pit. I was sent back to the infirmary again with the shits. No injections that time. Then on Easter fucking Sunday, April Fools' Day, the joke fell on the Krauts." Wigs took a long swig of his beer. "The Second Battalion, the 114th Regiment, the 44th Infantry Division, the 106th Calvary Group, and the 776th Tank Destroyer Battalion plowed through the front line with machine-gun fire and artillery shells blasting all night. It was more terrifying than on the train when them bombs hit, remember? When the American forces found us, many had died from starvation. But I fuckin' made it, Buckster. Had to. I promised you I would."

Wigs takes me through the postwar years—his first job selling cars while getting his degree in farming at Auburn University. His true love, Misty, wife of twenty-six years, before she died of breast cancer ten years ago. The Ford dealership he owned with his two boys, Joseph and Michael, his love of golf—and his terrifying nightmares.

"I like going into work to look at the numbers. After, I head over to my watering hole to meet the usual suspects, drink a few beers, head home, pass out on the couch watching replays of the games. Then the sons of bitches come a-calling, Buck. The dreams—fuckin' worse than what really happened. Bayonets. Always bayonets. No helmets. Guys getting gored through the backs of their necks like what them Spaniard fellas do to them bulls. Drop dead with their tongues hanging out. One after another. GIs getting gored, dropping dead all fuckin' night. The sun rises, I'm still running, wake up drenched. My lovely cleaning lady never says a word. Noeme, from the Philippines. She knows what happened to me. I tell her everything."

Wigs looks around to make sure Sandee is out of earshot. "Sometimes we have relations. I take good care of her, give her money and all. It's nice having her companionship. Hey, I got a couple sweet-as-can-be grandkids! I call 'em Twinkle and Blinker, cutest twin boys ya ever laid your peepers on. It all works out just as it should."

Wigs stares out over the harbor. How I have missed my old friend.

Wigs puts his arm around me as the luminous Chicago skyline flickers along the golden coast while boats drift back into their slips for the night.

"I've come a long way in two hours, Wigs. Let's sit. Damn leg barks at me all the time." We settle back down on the couch. "I'm the largest shareholder of a tractor- and military-manufacturing company in the Midwest: AC Machinery. I took the company public in the '70s. But I was tangled up inside. Still am. Sometimes I drop out for days, waiting for the cloud to lift. The dreams, the drinking. My son, Ben . . . we've had our troubles. Not his fault. Sandee and I are lovebirds, but I fly with one wing. She doesn't know what happened to me after Stalag." I pause and take a sip of my beer and suck in a couple of deep breaths and start coughing. Wigs waits for me to continue. "That cough is another little problem I have, my copilot. Cancer of the lungs, thanks to our friends, the Nazis. Let me grab you another beer. Hey, you're gonna meet my grandson, Lewis, tonight. Smart boy."

"How long have you got? No BS, Buck."

"They don't really tell you other than to get your affairs in order. Months maybe. Perhaps longer."

"Why didn't you answer my cards? I tried to find where the Nazis had taken ya. I came up empty year after year. I mailed you Christmas card after Christmas card to the only address the army had on record—in Wisconsin. I thought you were long dead."

"Do you remember how the wind was howling the day they separated the Jews and took us away, Cal?" I swallow a lifetime helping of remorse. My shoulders tremble. "Remember how cold it was? Snowing cotton balls in the yard. We all took a step forward, didn't we, Wigs?"

"I remember like it was yesterday. Proudest damn day of my life." Wigs eyes me patiently, then asks, "Where the fuck they take you, and what the hell happened? Whatever you need to spill, you spill it to your ol' fly mate. Been goddamn long enough."

"During all the years apart, all the military honor events or war reunions you may have attended, did you ever hear anyone mention Berga?"

"Nope, never."

"You're going to hear about it tonight. That's why you're here. And to ask you to come back to Germany with me."

"Germany? Why in hoots would you want to go back there?"

"Please, Wigs. I won't go back without you."

"Not if you're flying the bird, I'm not. I remember those landings." We laugh for a good while.

"Have you ever attended a seder before, Wigs?"

"Hell no. Know nothing of it."

"You're going to learn about that too."

Ben, Caroline, and Lewis pile out of the elevator, bringing in bags of supplies.

"Lewis, come in here and give Bapa a birdie and meet my old friend."

Lewis runs over and plants a kiss on my cheek. Ben follows and approaches Wigs with his hand extended.

"Thank you for coming all this way to see my dad, Mr. Wiggins."

"My honor, young man. And call me Cal." Cal shakes Ben's hand with vigor. "You look more like your mother, thank the Lordie Lord."

"I'll take that as a compliment," says Sandee, entering and shooting me a wink. "This is Ben's wife, Caroline. And our grandson, Lewis."

Lewis nods while holding his mother's hand.

"I made the charoset with Mom," Lewis says under his breath, as if he'd been prompted.

"Tell Mr. Wiggins what that is," Caroline says, then turns to Wigs. "Are you Jewish, Mr. Wiggins?"

"Heck, if I was, I would've gone with Buck and the Jews when they separated us."

The room falls silent. "Lewis," Sandee instructs. "Tell us about the charoset."

"It's a mix of chopped apples, cinnamon, and wine made by the Israelites when they were slaves." He rattles off as if he'd rehearsed it on the way over. "I'm in Hebrew school for my bar mitzvah."

The elevator opens, and in walk Gingersnap and Paul.

"Ginger!" says Caroline. "And dear Paul. It's been too long."

Gingersnap is wearing a pantsuit and carrying flowers with Paul on her other arm. He is sporting a navy blue blazer, white shirt, and jeans but didn't bother to shave.

"Look at you, Lewis," Paul says. "You've grown a foot!"

"Swing me around," Lewis pleads.

"Those days are long gone, sad to say. I don't think I have the strength to swing such a big boy."

Paul throws me a glance. I wonder if he suspects what's coming.

"I picked up some challah on the corner," Gingersnap says. "Lewis, put it on the table for me." She turns to me. "Hello, Chuck. You look tired."

"Just old." I offer a hug and feel my body relax. "You and Paul stay after the seder. Family chat."

"So mysterious, my brother." She smiles and places her hand on my cheek. "I'm all ears."

We take our places at the dining room table for the seder.

"Before I bless this wine, a bottle I've been saving since the war ended, I'd like to ask a young man who will soon have his bar mitzvah to light two candles as we turn our eyes east toward Jerusalem. Lewis?"

Wigs catches on and turns his head while Lewis lights the candles.

"Blessed are you, Lord our God, King of the universe, who has sanctified us with His commandments and commended us to kindle the yom tov light. Blessed are You who has granted us life, sustained us, enabled us to reach this occasion."

My hand shakes while holding the bottle.

"Now the kiddush, your father's favorite part, Lewis. As I said, it's a special wine. Dr. Fourget gifted it to me the day I checked out of the hospital in France. It's a 1945 Nuits-Saint-Georges."

Ben holds Lewis's hand. My eyes sting with tears; the truth will soon be set free.

"Blessed are you, Creator of the fruit of the vine. Blessed King of the universe, who has chosen us from among all nations, raised us above all tongues, and sanctified us by His commandments. And You, God, have given us lovingly." I use my handkerchief to wipe my eyes. "Please, raise your glass. You, too, Lewis, but only a taste." I place my hand on Wigs's shoulder to steady myself. "Thank you to my friend, 101st Army Air Force Second Lieutenant Calvin Wiggins, for coming to see his old fly mate. Thank you for pulling me out of that burning cargo plane during a nasty storm, December 16, 1944. You saved my life."

I tip my glass to Wigs and take a sip of the wine that was bottled the same year we liberated France.

"I have to acknowledge Rabbi Jacob Goldmann, 106th Infantry dispatcher. I thought I was about dead when I asked him to convert me to the Jewish faith, Lewis." I pause and look at Sandee, who is tearing up. "Just before he died." Wigs looks into his glass and slowly shakes his head. "He gave me a new name: Benjamin." I smile at Ben. "Here's to Jacob Goldmann—and to you, Cal, and to the war heroes who made the ultimate sacrifice."

"Hear, hear, Buck!" says Wigs. "Now pour some of that French grape."

"Wait!" Gingersnap intervenes. "Before we begin the seder, Charlie, I have something to show you." She removes a drawing from a sketch pad. "I found this going through some old boxes."

"Let me see . . . " says Lewis.

The sketch is of a horse running through the woods during a lightning storm.

"You drew it the night before I left for war."

"I did."

Lewis, ever the student, raises his hand.

"You lost your leg when your plane crashed?"

"Lewis!" Caroline snaps. "That's not appropriate!"

"I think it's a perfectly understandable question, Caroline," responds Gingersnap.

Caroline's face reddens as she glares at Gingersnap.

A half century of my silence is seeping dark sediment over the seder. I look to Wigs, hoping he'll save me again, but I'm on my own for this flight. I take a long sip of wine and continue.

"It didn't happen—my leg—from the plane crash, Lewis. I was a prisoner in a horrible place after Wigs and I were separated. I was taken away from the prison camp to a place no one knows about."

Paul slams his hand on the table.

"I knew it! Good God, Charlie."

"So how did your leg get that way, Bapa?" begs Lewis.

"Lewis, enough," Caroline scolds.

"I'm old enough," Lewis demands.

"I believe we both are, Lewis," I say. "And it's long overdue."

After an abridged retelling of how the Jewish slaves made their exodus from Egypt, we eat, drink the wine, and laugh at bad jokes that Wigs tells, then send Lewis to hide in the "desert," where he is found in the front hall closet.

I feel a rush of heat on my forehead while walking everyone into the living room. It is getting late, yet the night has only begun. Sandee brings in chocolate-covered matzo and sets it on the coffee table next to the letter from the Berga 2 Security Certificate for Surviving Prisoners of War. I pick it up and look at Gingersnap.

"What I am about to reveal breaks my oath of secrecy I've upheld for over fifty years with the US government. The Nazis profiled me as a Jew and took me and other Jewish soldiers from our prison camp in early February 1945, to a horrific place called Berga 2, a slave labor death camp for Jewish soldiers." I glance over at Paul. "Looks like you'll write my story after all."

"With honor, Lieutenant Buckley."

CHAPTER 21

After a much more successful landing than my first flight in Europe, Ben, Sandee, Wigs, and I exit our gate in Frankfurt, fetch our bags, and head to the train that will take us to Berga. Sandee had no luck in her search for Tomas Frantz after calling US government agencies and military record houses in Washington. She tried the US consulate in Frankfurt and asked for help, where they referred her to the German Military War Records Department's central database in Nuremberg. That department conveyed to Sandee that if any archival information existed on local Nazi SS guards or kapos who'd worked for the Nazi Party at Berga, it would be found at the Berga City Hall of Records. Unfortunately, the clerks in Berga were prohibited from giving out information over the phone. The files will have to be searched on site in Berga with an archival monitor.

It smells familiar; a soft rain brings back an oily scent from a half century ago—wet German dirt. I stop several times to catch my breath while climbing up to the platform before finding a bench to rest and wait for the announcement to board the waiting train. I feel pangs of panic from the echoes of the past—bombs exploding near our boxcar, Benjamin Levy falling on the concrete landing. I put my hands over my ears and smell the spring wildflowers, but only the acrid scent sealed away for a lifetime makes its way through. I close my eyes. When I open them to check on Wigs, I see that his eyes are closed too.

Boarding begins. A child runs onto the train carrying her Raggedy Ann doll. An older couple carries sacks of food, while teenagers loaded down with backpacks smoke their cigarettes and shove their way in. I struggle to get to my seat, coughing away the pain in my lungs, but to no avail—not with all the damn cigarette smoke filling the train car. I slide over to the window and take a blast from my inhaler. A pushcart rolls down the aisle with the *International Herald Tribune*. I half expect to see news from the front displayed on the cover.

I catch the sun dipping below the vast green fields of Bavaria as we leave the station. As each mile marker flashes by, the fist of fear grips tighter—Berga is within reach. My mind races along with the rumbling train.

Will the barracks be standing? Will the pit be but a depression in the earth covered with weeds? Will the caves be accessible? Will there be a memorial for the lives lost while the world covered its eyes? Will we find Tomas, and did he take Jacob's journal from me when I lay dying in that cornfield?

Wigs taps me on the shoulder, putting an end to my mental inquisition.

"Buckster, let's wet our whistle and hit the dining car. I'm as dry as the Virgin Mary. Excuse my language, Sandee." Sandee smiles and nods.

Wigs takes off with his tail between his legs. After a few moments, I wink at Sandee and gather myself; my cane leads the way. With all my strength, I heave the steel door open and step in between the train cars. My entire body freezes up. The noise is deafening. The gray metal floor vibrates underfoot—like the tram heading deep into cave 14. The pungent smell singes my nostrils. The black wave of 1945 is crashing over 2002.

I could pass on all this, lean over the chain linking the train cars, and roll off into the pines. I'll soon die on a morphine drip anyway.

The steel door opens in front of me.

"What in sheep's turds are you doing out here, crazy old man?"

"Come in here, Wigs!" I yell. "I'm stuck in my shoes." We hold onto each other between the gyrating train cars. "I don't know where

I am. I'm flipping back the pages, and there's nothing there but Berga. The cold, the hunger clawing at my gut. I can't get ahold of myself."

"Remember how we walked out of the Ardennes Forest, Buck? We're survivors, you and me. Now let's get the hell to the bar car and pour some whiskey down our gullet. My treat!"

Nearly fifty-eight years from the day I limped out of that foggy corn-field, I'm back, perhaps only a few kilometers from the death camp. Our cabbie pulls up to the Landhotel am Fuchsbach under an enormous spruce tree, its branches covering a lamppost that casts its flickering light through the needles onto the driveway. The evening dew smells like sweet perfume, different than I remember. Of course, I never made it to the month of May with its seasonal flora.

I grab Sandee's arm, while Ben and Wigs carry the bags along the pebbled pathway leading up to the landing at the front door, where a petite woman who looks to be in her sixties is there to greet us.

"Welcome to Berga!" My heart jumps from my chest from the ease in which she delivers that welcome. "I'm Herta, the patron of Fuchsbach. You must be the Charlton Buckley party from Chicago. Come, come. I hope you're hungry."

"Starving!" Wigs shouts. "I could eat the north end of a southbound polecat. And one of them cows munching on your field."

"Don't you dare. I send you back where you came!"

Herta's movements are clipped like a flapper in a silent movie as she flutters about, touring us through the dining room, parlor, and library before she escorts us to our pine-paneled bedrooms straight out of a Grimm fairy tale. Thick lace throw rugs cover the plank flooring. Geraniums adorn the window boxes. Although the bed is smothered in quilted coverlets, I instinctively look for burlap bags filled with straw. Flashes of Berga keep assaulting my mind.

"I have delicious schnitzel ready for you," says Herta. "Get settled, then come to the dining room."

At dinner Ben and Wigs finish off two bottles of Riesling, while I can barely keep my eyes open from the time change and retire when the Jägermeister arrives. After a sponge bath, I tuck myself into the featherbed and feel pins and needles pricking at my stump.

"If we find my leg in the cave, I'll put it back on," I yell through the bathroom door. But Sandee is running a bath and can't hear my morbid humor. I try to drift off, but my thoughts won't let me go. The Rat, Walter Von Hanzel, the cave, and Victor—*They'll be waiting for me.* I pry my thoughts away from Berga 2 and stare at the vaulted pinewood ceiling. But my mind wanders back to 1945. I toss and turn, then give up and reattach my leg.

"Where are you going, darling?" asks Sandee as she comes to bed smelling of lavender soap.

"I'm all turned around with the time. I think I'll go look at some of the books I took notice of. I won't be long."

I kiss her and hold my cane and head to the musty library off the parlor to find a couple of old bound books of Berga with the pages torn at the edges. One photo from the turn of the century shows a booming health resort with guests swimming in the sparkling White Elster River while picnickers lounge by the water's edge. The topography is identical to where the camps had been: the rolling hillsides, the cottages by the river, women carrying bread and fruit in wooden carts.

"You're not sleeping?"

"Oh! Good evening, Herta. I'm restless from the travel, that's all."

"I didn't mean to startle you, Mr. Buckley."

"Not at all. I thought I'd look over some of your books on the city. How long have you lived in Berga?"

She tilts her head. "I'll answer, only if you'll join me for a schnapps. My *secret* libation for everything. We all have secrets, don't we?" From a drawer she takes out two cobalt blue shot glasses and the bottle. She smiles. I gently raise my glass and take a swallow as Herta pulls over a chair and sits. "When your wife made the reservation, she asked about a World War II POW camp here in Berga."

"I'm sorry she brought it up that way."

"No, no. Of course, it's all right. Although I told her I knew of no such camp, it had me thinking, which is why I'm having a midnight schnapps with you. I couldn't sleep either." Herta takes a long sip. "As the war was ending, I would sit on the front porch of our family farm with my mother."

I take another sip. The schnapps slides down easy, warming my throat.

"Where's your farm?" I ask, hoping I might be closing in on the location of Berga 2.

"In Puchsmuhl, about a hundred kilometers outside the city. On one tragic morning, an idiot guard wouldn't allow my grandfather to give out any of his asparagus to the passing soldiers and their prisoners. 'Der Krieg ist vorbei, last sie essen! Let them eat!' The German guard shot him. My grandfather didn't die that day, but in truth, he might as well have. He never forgave the government for their lies about the rifle being stolen and fired from the finger of a Jew, not a German guard. But I saw it. I was there." She finishes off her schnapps. "I'm sorry. I haven't thought of this in years." She wipes the back of her hand across her eyes.

"Herta, I want to show you something." I lift the hem of my pant leg. She clutches her chest. "I was a prisoner of war in a camp for Jewish soldiers—we were starved and beaten, some to death. It was here in Berga. My leg was blown up down in a cave while setting explosives for the Nazis." Herta trembles and tries to pour me another glass. I take it from her and pour us another. "I went by your farm the spring of '45," I add.

"*Lieber Herr.*"

I'd said enough. "Your generous schnapps is kicking in. I'll sleep now. Thank you, Herta." I grab my cane. "If you know of anyone who might be willing to help me find what happened to the camp, any information, I would be most grateful."

Herta shifts in her chair.

"Let me sleep on this. Good night, Mr. Buckley."

We arrive at the Berga City Hall of Records as the doors open at 10:00 a.m. The building looks more like a cottage than a municipal edifice. It's perched between two concrete offices, welcoming us on this bright, beautiful day with its red wooden door and green garden window boxes. Inside, however, it smells musty, the walls are clapboard gray, cobwebs cover the windows, and the ceiling fan dangles from its wires. The worn carpet has a single tear up the middle. The clerk who lets us in strolls back behind the counter. The name *Mr. Becker* is embroidered on the pocket of his wrinkled white shirt, which is appointed with a coffee stain trailing down the front; the spill could have happened this morning or last week. Although the day has just begun, beads of sweat bubble on Mr. Becker's brow.

"Good morning." He grabs his coffee cup. "I searched our military files, letters, and certificates from the time period requested by your wife about a prison camp for Jewish soldiers."

"It wasn't a prison camp," interjects Ben. "It was a slave labor death camp. My father was tortured . . ."

Sandee places her hand on Ben's shoulder and moves him back from the counter.

"Please excuse my son. We're all a bit ragged from the time change. Will you help us, Mr. Becker? We're looking for a Tomas Frantz. He was a kapo-turned-prisoner here at the Berga 2 camp. We hoped to search any local military records that would help us find him."

"As I've said, there is no such record of this . . . prison camp."

"No records at all?" asks Wigs. "With all due respect, Mr. Coffee Stain, he should know if the camp existed. He was there!"

"I don't appreciate this rudeness."

Wigs is about to grab the guy by the throat but instead opts to lift my pant leg, revealing my prosthetic.

"Where do you think this happened, huh, bud? It happened in one of those caves by the Nazis! We got all day, partner. Keep looking."

"We're not here to dig up dirt," I implore. "I just want to find a friend of mine who may have what I need." I'm weary and hold on to Sandee.

Like a meandering river, a bead of sweat runs down Mr. Becker's forehead to his chin.

"You may be confusing it with the Buchenwald subcamp," Mr. Becker finally offers. "There are thin accountings of political prisoners, records of some who died at that camp and the subsequent indictments for war crimes. The name of the Buchenwald subcamp was called Berga 1."

I slam my hand on the counter.

"Mr. Becker, there was a *second* camp not far from Berga 1 for Jewish prisoners of war who were tortured there. I was one of them."

"There wouldn't be a Berga 1 if there wasn't a Berga 2," Sandee adds, with a measured tone.

"Sit. I'll return . . . in a few minutes."

"You have to have *some* proof that war crimes were committed against my father!" Ben yells as Mr. Becker enters the back office and closes the door.

We move from the counter and sit in the waiting area. My head swirls as I look out through the dusty picture window. Townsfolk stroll the sidewalk to begin their mundane chores for the day while I wonder if any of them know about the atrocities committed in their own backyard. No plaque, no memorial to remind them. Why aren't the screams for liberation that echoed from the whispering pines reverberating so loudly in my ears not haunting theirs?

A light rain, like tears crying from the heavens, sprinkles down over their city while we wait nearly an hour for Mr. Becker to return carrying two thick binders. He drops them on the counter and returns to his desk. Sandee and Ben sift through the files while Wigs and I nod off. Just before sunset, Ben shakes my shoulder.

"I think I found him!" The needle-nosed clerk, Mr. Becker, rushes to the counter to listen in. "Dad, it's as if Berga 2 never existed. There's nothing in these files that mentions anything about the death camp. But I may have found your Tomas Frantz." Ben sits next to me. "Let me read this to you, and tell me if you think this is him. Okay, here we go:

Tomas Frantz. Leiden, Netherlands. Conviction: Theft from occupied Bakery, 1942. Served his punishment as a kapo for the Nazi army at Herzogenbusch concentration camp, Offag VI-A Prison Camp, Stalag IX-B Prison Camp.

"Now get this, Dad. On February 9, 1944, Tomas is transferred to a classified location to serve out the remainder of his conviction. He then completes a three-year sentence at the Landsberg Prison for unspecified war crimes."

"My God. He went to prison, Dee."

"If it's him, from reading the census, he's living in Hildesheim Börde," Sandee offers.

I turn to Mr. Becker. "Where is that?"

"Farmland. Seventy kilometers to the north."

"He's a sugar beet farmer," adds Sandee, holding one of the documents. "Looks like he married a second time to Monique Gruber. No children. No death notices for either."

"Dad, it's not good if they found him on the run after he left you . . . Tomas may have had to ditch the journal to protect himself."

My stomach recoils.

"Tomas's telephone number is unlisted," Sandee adds.

"Buckster, the only way to find out if he has that journal is to pay the man a visit, for Pete's sake."

"Ben, just you and I will go after breakfast tomorrow. I don't want to overwhelm him with all of us."

⌐

After renting a car, Ben and I arrive at a stone farmhouse after a two-hour drive north to Hildesheim Börde. As I am mustering up the courage to knock on the front door, it opens. An elderly woman with dark, inset eyes pokes her head out and purses her lips.

"Mrs. Frantz, Good afternoon. My name is Charlie Buckley. I know your husband, Tomas, from the war. We were together at the Berga 2 camp."

Perhaps knowing the echoes of war would reach her doorstep one day, she retreats inside her home and shuts the door. We return to the car and wait. After a few minutes, the front door swings back open. I tap Ben on the shoulder and point. Monique Frantz is waving us in.

She walks on bowed legs into the parlor filled with heavy, dark furniture. There are no pictures of children on the walls. But she is holding a laminated photo frayed at the edges and passes it to me. It's of Tomas in his Nazi kapo uniform, hunched over as if all the air had been sucked from his lungs. His eyes vacant, laying bare the pain of his deeds and the grief of losing his wife and child. I make to give it back, but she insists I keep it.

Then I see an old man in the living room sitting in a rocker by the fireplace. I look at his face to collect the pieces of our ravaged past in hopes of burying them once and for all. We are broken men, together again.

"Tomas." My eyes burn with tears. "It's Charlie."

He looks through me with those once-brilliant blue eyes, no longer clear; Tomas has receded from the here and now.

"I'm sorry, I speak little English. I try," says Monique Frantz. She is squeezing her apron with both fists. Tomas's eyes are searching, as if trying to untangle a world caught in a web of confusion. "His mind is not here," she says.

Tomas spastically bobs his head up and down. Then for a fleeting moment, his body quiets. He leans forward, attempting to take me into his lost world. Then returns to a catatonic rhythm, his head twisting right to left.

I want to learn what happened to Tomas after he'd left me in that cornfield seemingly on my last breath, and if he has Jacob's journal.

I move my chair close to him and point to Ben with my cane.

"My son, Benjamin, named after Rabbi Benjamin Levy. He's going to help me get the word out about what happened to us, Tomas. Berga 2 was classified by our governments. They ordered me to sign an oath of secrecy. No one knows, Tomas. All these years."

I pause, searching his eyes for a glimmer of comprehension.

"Jacob Goldmann. Do you remember him, Tomas? His journal? He was documenting the names of those who died?" Tomas's eyes frantically scan the air, as if searching for fireflies in the dark. "Did you take it from me, Tomas? You left me in that cornfield, remember? You took it from me, didn't you?"

He turns and stares out the window.

"Tomas, can you understand me? Do you have Jacob's journal? Please remember, Tomas. Please!"

Tomas continues staring and bangs his fist on his knee over and over.

Monique goes to a chest of drawers.

"I'm sorry. He never had a journal from the war, never spoke about Berga. But he always had this with him." Monique Frantz pulls out little Ivan's dreidel toy and hands it to me. I try to give it back, but she refuses. I place the dreidel in my pocket as she puts her hand out to shake mine, our signal to leave.

I grab hold of my cane, but before leaving, hoping to evoke a memory, I place my hand on Tomas's shoulder and look into his cloudy eyes.

"Save one, save all."

He lightly bobs his head, then returns to staring out the window.

On our way back to Berga, I think of Jacob Goldmann, his wire-rimmed glasses, his unbridled courage and determination. He gave me the gift of the Jewish faith, and I gave him my confidence that the names written in his journal would forever be remembered—and I'd failed him.

"I waited too long, Ben," I cried, peering out over the farmland. "I'm too late."

CHAPTER 22

erta is waiting for us on the front landing of the inn as Ben and I are dropped off by the rental car company.

"Mr. Buckley," she calls out. "I may have someone who might be of help to you. He's quite persnickety about his time, so we must go now."

Ben, Sandee, Wigs, and I pile into Herta's clunky '97 Volkswagen and zip out of the city along a dirt road that hugs the White Elster River. The windows to the Passat are half-opened, bringing in the moist, muddy smell of the riverbank. The water is high, roaring downriver, pulling me downstream toward my past. The tops of the tall pines seem to lean, as if tipping their hats, welcoming me back. The farther along we travel, the more familiar the rolling terrain becomes. My knee shakes.

"I haven't spoken with Gunther in years," says Herta. "We were young lovers once a lifetime ago, but he was too complicated. Always lost in history books. He lives not far from here by the river. I mentioned I have a guest looking for a Berga prison camp for Jewish soldiers. He said to come right away."

I'm encouraged. Perhaps this Gunther will explain why the city of Berga seems to have no recollection of the death camp.

We ride along a rocky road bordering the river for a few kilometers before pulling up to a Dutch-style box house. Bavarian beer cans are strewn across the property. Old newspapers are piled by a rocker on the porch, where four bony cats huddle under the edge of a raised foundation. A rusted-out VW Beetle rests in peace with dead vegetation climbing through its windows. Limestone boulders rolled from the riverbank are placed in front of the steps that lead to the front door, forming a blockade, perhaps to discourage visitors, including me. I'm ready to pull the plug on this meeting before it begins just as Herta whistles for her historian friend.

Moving spryly from behind the house, Gunther emerges, wearing overalls with no shirt, gripping a beer bottle with rubber gloves. His hair is wild and gray; his bushy rust-colored beard looks like it was attacked by crows.

"*Willkommen* to my piece of paradise on za Elster River, my new friends. Herta, Herta, who is that beautiful woman next to the old man with the cane?"

"Mrs. Buckley, this is our *famous* local historian, Gunther Wilhelm. Gunther, this is Charlton Buckley and his wife, Sandee, and son, Ben. That funny man there is Mr. Wags or Wogs. I'm sorry, I forget."

"Second Lieutenant Cal Wiggins. Excuse me, Mr. Gunther, but what the heck happened to your place here?"

"He *is* a funny man, Herta. Lieutenant Wiggins, some may judge my habitat as . . . out of the ordinary," he responds, waving his arm. "For me, it's as it should be. Come, let's sit inside my fine dwelling and get . . . what do you say in your land of the free, home of za brave . . . ? On the right foot. Yes, yes. I want to know *why* you need *me*, Mr. Buckley. Come, let's go inside."

Gunther sounds like the Rat, sending a cold shiver through me, inducing the urge to strike him with my cane.

We enter an apocalypse. A footpath winds through hordes of old magazines, soiled T-shirts, and encyclopedias. Polaroids spill from many shoeboxes. Crusted food is rotting on white china plates, and half-consumed Coke bottles sit on his large desk next to piles of books and three typewriters, two of them overturned. Crumpled paper encircles his chair. Gunther grabs a can of Lysol and sprays the air as if trying to kill off mosquitoes.

"Please, find a seat. Isn't this fun?"

He clears space on two Victorian couches, both frayed to the batting. Sandee refuses to sit, choosing instead to stand far enough from objects she might accidentally brush against.

"Oh, Sandee, Sandee, why insult me? Do sit."

I take Sandee's hand, and we sit on the couch, not before patting the dust off the cushions. Looking around in disbelief, Wigs and Ben hesitantly take their spots on the couch opposite.

"You're in my home, Mr. Buckley. One of the very few people I have allowed in. I am curious, what can the greatest German historian do for you?"

Finally, he is ready to listen and leans his shoulder against the mantel of the fireplace.

"Thank you for seeing us on such short notice, Mr. Wilhelm," I begin. "I'd like to ask you some questions about a Nazi prisoner-of-war camp for Jewish soldiers in Berga."

"A camp for Jewish soldiers here? In Berga? There was only one camp for political prisoners not far from here toward the end of the war. But I never heard or read about Jewish soldiers imprisoned in Berga."

"That's wrong, Mr. Wilhelm."

"Why? And please, call me Gunther, Mr. Buckley."

"And you call me Lieutenant Charlton Buckley, 101st US Army Air Corps. Because I was tortured there—Gunther. That's why."

He squints and cocks his head.

"Because you were there? That's why? No, no, *that's* a lie. Ha! That's why, that's a lie! I'm a poet!" Gunther starts moving about the room like a professor teaching a class. "The question of the day is whether or not we will find *poetic* justice."

"See for yourself what was taken from me there, and let's talk about justice." I hike up my pant leg.

After a long silence, Gunther taps his forehead, then points in the air, as if to mark some nefarious conclusion.

"Who would like a beer? The weather today is so . . . as the British say, *bloody* hot. I put a few in the icebox out back before you arrived.

235

How about you, my Greta Garbo? I see the resemblance in your stunning blue eyes."

"No, thank you," answers Sandee.

"I'll take one, partner," Wigs demands.

"Only if it's cold," adds Ben. Once Mr. Wilhelm is out of earshot, Ben jumps up.

"This guy is off his rocker, Dad. Let's excuse ourselves before we pick up some disease. I don't think he knows what happened this morning, let alone back in 1945."

Sandee puts up her hand.

"We've come all this way, Ben. Let's hear what Mr. Wilhelm has to say."

"Sandee has a smart noodle too," Gunther says, returning with the beers. "Yes, hear what I have to say, say, say before you go, go, go." He starts singing and dancing in an approximation of a goose-stepping military march. I quiver and clench my teeth. I want to strangle the life out of him.

"Gunther, hear what *I* have to say first," I demand. Gunther ceases his mocking. "There was a maniacal Nazi commandant, Walter Von Hanzel. He selected 350 of us, mostly Jewish soldiers, from Stalag IX-B and stuffed us in a boxcar and transported us to a death camp called Berga 2. My leg was blown up working in a cave to help them build an oil refinery for fuel. After I was found in a cornfield, I was hospitalized in France. It was there I signed an oath of secrecy with *my* government never to mention Berga 2. I kept my word."

Gunther sits, looking at me from his desk chair, and takes a long slug of his warm beer before responding.

"As I told you, Lieutenant Buckley, Berga 2 *was a lie*. What you are looking for didn't exist. And *that*—is the lie."

"I want to speak, if I may, Charles," says Sandee. "We're not here to play word games a minute longer, Mr. Wilhelm. Nor are we here to place blame on your government, or ours, for abandoning those poor young men. We're here to heal from it! My husband needs evidence to help declassify the horror of what happened to those boys at Berga 2."

"What do you know, Gunther?" asks Herta. "For God's sake, where is the Berga 2 location?"

"You were there, Lieutenant Buckley, yet there is no official record of it—not here, nor from your country's industrial military complex that has betrayed you flat—flat as your American beer."

"Okay, I've heard enough." I move to the end of the couch and reach for my cane. But Gunther snatches it and uses it like a king's scepter as he prances among his chaotic debris.

"Do you honestly think if the Berga 2 camp was filled with Catholics and Anglo-Saxon Protestants, they would have been left for dirt? Your government would have turned those who survived into war heroes and exploited them. They abandoned all of you proud Jewish American soldiers because, like the German Nazi party, the international governing bodies of both of our countries were *anti-Semites* themselves!" Gunther moves toward the fireplace.

"But moreover, there was much too much money flowing in trade between the stakeholders to let your story out. US of A's capitalistic addiction and Germany's thirst for engineering dominance was much more important than a group of twenty-year-old Jews. The United States Commerce Department was desperate to protect trade with Germany. Coca-Cola sells. *It's the real thing!* And the next time you drive a German car, remember your government's silence helped pay for it.

"After the war, your government allied itself politically *with* Germany," he continues. "And against who? Can you believe it? The Soviets! Revelations of the atrocities committed at Berga 2 . . . knowledge of Jewish US soldiers being tortured to death would have been a disaster for the alliance. Mercedes-Benz must be sold. Are you getting *my drift*, as they say? You were collateral damage. Nothing more. Now you know why Berga 2 never happened, Lieutenant."

He continues, "Imagine, right after the war, what the grave consequences would have been had the front page of the *New York Times* read, '*State Department Fails to Rescue American Jewish Soldiers Tortured and Murdered in a Nazi Slave Labor Death Camp. Investigation Begins!*'"

"Then where does this all leave me, Gunther?"

"Here in this mess with me." He laughs and hands me back my cane. "So many mysteries in our universe."

I get up off the couch and ready myself to leave. But not before the mad historian takes the last swig of his beer and heads back to the fireplace. He lifts a cardboard box off the mantel, as if it were waiting for the right moment to take center stage.

"I was an impetuous high school student in 1949. The war was my investigative playground. I wrote many articles on the Nazis: Where are they now? That sort of thing. My stories circulated in local publications, which prompted an ex-kapo guard to find me after his incarceration." He takes a brown paper notebook out from the box.

"This might be of importance to you, Lieutenant Buckley. The ex-kapo lifted it off a POW who died at the end of the war. He hands it to me and says, 'Save one, save all,' and nothing more."

Gunther places the tattered notebook in my open palms. My entire body vibrates in disbelief as I open the pages. "This is it. Jacob's journal."

Ben reaches for my arm to steady me before I nearly collapse.

"Why in hell didn't you publish this?" asks Ben.

"I'm a great historian but a greater coward. The Gestapo disbanded after the war but continued to hunt down traitors who ended up never seeing the light of day again. It wasn't my battle to win, young man. Only to lose. I feared for my life. Still do."

Gunther puts the empty box back on the mantel and walks us out.

"You never saw me, Lieutenant Buckley. Do you understand? Do what you must, but never mention my name."

"You have my word."

Ben takes the journal from my trembling hands.

Gunther puts back on his rubber gloves.

"I'll leave you with this last quandary, Lieutenant Buckley: Was Berga 2 and the loss of those poor souls a catastrophic failure of intelligence, anti-Semitism, or a multilateral monetary strategy? We may never know the full answer, but in my long years of analyzing history, when you search for the truth, *follow the money!*

"Travel along the White Elster River another four kilometers, come to a rocky road that forks, and proceed up the hill. You'll find what you're looking for. If you want to go to the caves, continue along the river another three kilometers. When you pass a collapsed farmhouse, veer to your right."

~

Herta stays put in the car, clutching both hands on the wheel, and drops us off. Two squawking black hawks soar overhead as we walk to the top of the hill. With each labored step I take, the sense memories come flooding back. A wave of terror runs through me. I'm chilled to the bone. The barren trees drop icicles. Human waste contaminates the air. My skin itches from the ceaseless lice. I keep on—walking in the footsteps of the dead.

"Buck, are you okay?"

The Sleeping Souls are back.

"Orders are to keep moving!" I yell from my raspy throat while the SS shouts its commands.

Line them up. Get that one. Hang him. Throw him in the pit. Take his rations. Give them to Victor.

I'm starving . . .

Itching . . .

Burning . . .

Freezing . . .

"Charles dear!"

"Sandee? I'm coming home."

Yearning . . .

Missing . . .

Crying . . .

Murdering . . .

A deep contraction in my gut charts a course north, rising to my chest, rattling my injured ribs. There it grows, ending in my throat. Like a horror movie, I feel my face morph into those faces I saw at war.

"No! Not the children." They lie on the road in front of me.

The guards are crying in grief to the heavens—like that goat wailing out to the black sea in the painting Tomas had described. I look at Wigs, but it isn't him; it is Victor with his arm eaten off.

The obstruction in my throat bursts like a broken dam, expelling a primitive cry. I drop to my knees.

"The army said they would never betray us. They left us to be buried, then buried the truth."

Sandee takes me in her arms. And with that, another full round of guttural cries.

"I love you, Charlton," she repeats over and over as I cry out the tears I've been holding since Nurse Benoit rocked me in her arms after they took my leg.

Sweet sparrows sing. I smell the sap seeping from the spruce trees and blink the tears away.

"Wigs!"

"I'm here, Buck."

"Help me up and let's keep going."

We reach an area where the ground levels off. I'm back at the entrance to Berga 2. Only one post remains in the ground, the same that held Stan Loeb hanging from a rope. And there it is—or isn't. The death camp is gone, as if it had never existed.

Sandee and I walk hand in hand across a field of wild alyssum, thick as snow. We come to a corroded pipe poking from the ground where the latrine once stood. Fifty paces beyond, Stan and Sparky lay in the pit, now filled with concrete ravaged with weeds splitting through cracks.

"Over there. Do you see it, Dee?" A piece of dark wood is exposed on the edge of the tree line. I walk over to where my barrack once stood. Part of a rotten wall is still standing. I trace my fingers over the termite-riddled post to find a stretch of thick moss. Under my fingertips I feel the names engraved in the wood: Max Straus / Alex Levine.

As the wind roars through the same trees that witnessed the horror during the winter of 1945, their green-needled branches now whistling a dirge, I drop to one knee and dig a hole with a stick. I reach inside my pocket and take little Ivan's dreidel toy and place it in the ground and cover it with dirt.

Sandee holds my hand and recites a prayer.

"O God of forgiveness, forgive us, pardon us, grant us atonement. Avinu Malkeinu, our Father, our King, we have sinned before You. Avinu Malkeinu, in Your abundant mercy, cleanse us of our guilt before You. Avinu Malkeinu, bring us back to You in perfect repentance."

The entrances to the caves that once receded into the black dust are now boarded up. Ventilation slats are open at the top. Sandee translates what is inscribed on a metal sign: "The International Conservancy for the Protection of Endangered Big-Eared Townsend Bats."

"International protection for bats? Buck, those flying rats are gettin' more international protection than you ever got."

"Pray for a world gone mad." I point to the number *14* chiseled into the one of the cave entrances. "That's the one. Hand me that rock over there, Wigs. I want to engrave my mark."

> *US Second Lieutenant, Charlton Benjamin Levy*
> *Buckley. "Buck."*
> *WWII POW Jewish American Survivor / Berga 2*
> *Nazi Slave Labor Death Camp*

The wind whips across the hills as Ben, Sandee, and I cling together.

"I'm so sorry for my *iron will*. So deeply sorry . . ."

Wigs wraps his long arms around us.

"You forget all of that, Buck. That's an order. We won the damn war and survived to tell the tale, and tell it you will. Now let's get the hell out of this miserable country and back to drinking some real beer."

With a brisk wind at our back, Wigs leads us from the caves and back to Herta, who has the car running.

"I hope you found what you were looking for, Mr. Buckley."

"I did, Herta. I'm ready to fly home."

CHAPTER 23

The captain dims the cabin lights as we level off. He announces there'll be turbulence ahead, but the air will soon clear.

I did what I had to, what God had planned, as it was written on the first page of Jacob's journal.

> We Jews are the ones who were born to die, then brought to life to be judged by God our witness, the complainant, and that God will summon to judgment. Blessed is the One before Whom there is no forgetting. It's all here in this journal. All is according to the reckoning. And let not your impulse assure thee that the grave was a place of refuge for us; no, no . . . for against our will we were formed, against your will we were born, against our will we live, against your will we die, and against our will we will give an account of what happened at Berga 2 and be reckoned with before the supreme ruler of all rulers, the Holy Blessed One.

Wigs is snoring and had been since we lifted off, Ben is deep into *The Battle of the Bulge*, and Sandee is resting her head on my shoulder. I hold her wrinkled hand in mine and stare at her diamond ring twinkling like shooting stars, then take a deep breath and drift off into a long sleep.

◟

I lie near the creek holding my glass jar while staring at Sirius, the brightest star in the galaxy. Summer evening breezes pulse off Lake Michigan. Clouds thundering in the distance send vibrations up my spine. Two beams of light flash up the driveway. Dad's home. I jump up and run to him. His large hand swoops me off the grass and into his arms. He swings me around in circles, tickling my tummy as I watch the willow tree whizzing by and by. He then carries me into the house and kisses me good night. I run to my bedroom and unscrew the top of the jar, hoping there'll be at least one firefly trapped inside that I can save. But there are none. I turn off the light and climb into bed.

Moments later, a flicker, then a flash. Light explodes into the darkness. I look to the jar! It wasn't empty after all. A firefly had gone free.

ABOUT THE AUTHOR

CHRISTOPHER BENSINGER is a James Kirkwood Fiction Award nominee. He earned a UCLA Certificate in Fiction with distinction and has a BA in psychology from Bowdoin College. *The Sooner You Forget* is his bucket list debut novel. Chris retired from his real estate executive position and became a Tony Award–winning theatrical producer of *The Book of Mormon, American Idiot, La Cage aux Folles,* and others. He is an avid sportsman, husband, and proud father of two wonderful children.